The Boy in the Well

Dan Clark

www.darkstroke.com

Discover us online:
www.darkstroke.com

Join us on instagram:
www.instagram.com/darkstrokebooks/

Include **#darkstroke** in a photo of yourself
holding this book on Instagram and
something nice will happen.

For Rachel.
Thank you for the constant support, guidance and love, and most importantly, for believing in me and shutting down any self-doubt I had.
I love you.

About the Author

Dan was born in the northwest of England. He started reading Stephen King from an early age and is still a committed fan today, believing this is what inspired him to start writing.

After leaving school, he studied Accounting before realising working with numbers wasn't for him. He has done numerous jobs which include, working in retail, in busy restaurants as a Chef, driving a taxi and moving on to driving lorries.

Dan lives with his fiancé, Rachel, and easily annoyed cat, Burt. In his free time he loves to find a comfortable chair with a large cup of tea and read thriller and horror novels. He enjoys walking and being out in the countryside and devotes most of his time to his passion: writing his own stories.

The
Boy in the
Well

Chapter One

October 2nd 2019

Carolyn hits the button on her phone's screen suddenly, to silence the alarm before it can wake her sleeping husband. It's useless, though – he's already awake. The vibration, rattling on the wooden bedside table, was enough.

Simon groans and turns to face her with eyes still mostly shut. He fixes the pillow underneath his head. "Hey, how come you're getting up so early?" he asks, yawning. "Isn't it your day off?"

"Yeah, well, no… it was supposed to be," she says, giving him an apologetic smile. "Remember, I took that order for the birthday party. I didn't have time yesterday afternoon to finish it, so I'll have to get it done today." She pulls the duvet off and slides her legs out of the bed. "It's supposed to be delivered this afternoon."

Simon rolls over again and stretches. "Oh yeah. I forgot. Well, I'll tell Mum and Dad you said hi." He mumbles the *Hi,* and his breathing changes, informing Carolyn that he's gone back to sleep.

She finishes washing and dressing, kisses Simon on the cheek, then creeps past her six-year-old son Ryan's room, before heading out of the house. They live in a three-bed semi-detached new-build, although it's hard to call the six-by-four third room a bedroom rather than a storage cupboard. They'd moved onto the new housing estate just before Ryan was born. The houses were built on the old Brennan's Industrial Estate. It's a short drive from Leeds city centre, fifteen minutes exactly. And that's fine by Carolyn and Simon Hill. They enjoy the peace that the new estate offers.

The shop, Happy Bakes, would usually be closed today, but as it barely makes enough to pay the rent and give Carolyn a liveable wage, she has to take whatever orders she's asked for. Besides, today she doesn't mind. She, Simon and Ryan won't be doing anything outdoors, not in this rain.

***

In Manchester, Simon is strapping Ryan into the child's seat in the back of the car. They've just finished visiting his parents.

"BYE!" Ryan shouts to his grandparents before they head back inside, escaping the wet.

On their way home, Simon pulls into the M62 service station. The rain has increased tremendously, and the car park is overcrowded. The majority of people don't like to drive in bad weather.

Simon makes a call to Carolyn at the shop.

"Hello?" Carolyn answers.

"Hey, we're finished. How's it going? You nearly done?" Simon asks.

"You're finished already?"

"Yeah, we didn't stay long. Ryan had Dad running around like mad."

Carolyn doesn't answer, causing Simon to laugh.

"What's so funny?"

"I asked how it was going, and you ignored me. I bet you've got your tongue bit between your teeth as you concentrate, haven't you?"

He's seen this so many times before, like when Carolyn is reading the instructional manual from the IKEA furniture, or painting in the finer, harder-to-reach places. She has the steadiest hand out of the two of them.

"I'm sorry. I'm not far off finishing."

"HI MUMMY!" Ryan shouts from the back seat.

"Hey sweetheart. Having fun?" she asks.

Ryan doesn't reply. He's gone back to steering his fire engine along the seat next to him, followed by a police car.

"Anyway… we're on our way home. What do you feel like for dinner?" Simon asks.

Carolyn grunts. "Something that doesn't involve prepping, or a lot of tidying up!" she states. "Oh, and a bottle or two of red."

They say their goodbyes and end the call. Simon picks up dinner – a family-sized throw-in-the-oven pasta-bake, a ready-prepared bag of salad, and the wine – and they re-join the motorway.

They head on towards Leeds, playing I-Spy in the rear-view mirror in an attempt to keep Ryan awake so he'll sleep properly that night. Ryan's head springs up as the loud hum of a passing car's exhaust disturbs him. He jolts up, lifting himself closer to the window, watching the passing car with excitement. Simon turns the wipers to a faster setting, as the rain he'd waited to die off at the service station increases again. He acknowledges the car to his right, a Honda Civic fitted with a huge spoiler and rear tinted windows, and driven by a man in his mid-twenties. As the car passes, the CDs in Simon's door pocket rattle from the loud music and huge exhaust.

"WOW!" Ryan calls out, staring at the uncommon car. "Daddy… Look."

"Ah, feeling more awake are we, son?" Simon asks, flicking the indicator to overtake a lorry that is transporting farming tractors, before moving back over. The car in front is spraying Simon's windscreen from the wet road surface. A second car speeds past so quickly that Ryan doesn't have the chance to see it, but he spins his head anyway. It carelessly swerves in front of a camper van up ahead, barely making the motorway exit in time. The driver of the camper van stomps on his brakes sharply, and the driver in front of Simon reacts in just enough time to swerve to the next lane.

Simon, his vision still marred by the spray on his windscreen, doesn't respond quickly enough. By the time the brake is pressed, his car is already skidding straight for the back of the camper van. His mind instantly falls to Carolyn at the day of Ryan's birth. He pictures his wife in the hospital, cradling their new-born son. He tries to call out her name, but his voice is silent. He looks up to the rear-view mirror for the last split second he has left, and his eyes meet Ryan's.

Simon's car ploughs into the back of the braking camper van. The lorry behind, carrying the farming tractors, slides on the wet road surface, and over forty tons of weight crash straight into the back of Simon's Vauxhall. Simon and Ryan are both killed instantly.

***

The cake is finished and loaded into the back of the van. For the first couple of months after the bakery first opened Carolyn had tried to deliver things herself, but she soon realised she wasn't gentle enough on the brakes. The cakes would often arrive sloped, squashed or even on the floor of the van. Then she'd have to refund the upset customer, hurting not only her finances, but her business's reputation too. So, after a good few costly incidents, she'd hired a delivery driver who was happy to work on an as-and-when-needed basis.

After seeing off her delivery driver with the instructions, she locks up and changes out of her buttercream-stained baker's uniform into jeans, Converse and a t-shirt. She sighs as she releases the clasp which has been holding up her long brunette hair all day.

Outside, she turns the key to operate the shutters then pulls her phone out to message Simon, telling him she won't be much longer. As the shutters reach the floor, a police car pulls into the lay-by and parks in front of hers. Two men step out with serious faces. The officer who was driving is short and stumpy, and they both have plump stomachs.

A sense of utter dread rushes through Carolyn. She looks down to her phone, hoping Simon has replied and this will demolish any disconcerting thoughts.

Unfortunately, the phone screen offers no reassurance.

"Mrs Hill?" the taller officer asks.

Carolyn tries to stay professional. She smiles and nods,

hoping that the visit will be about nothing more than the kids playing in the abandoned shop next door. But she already knows it isn't going to be about that.

The expressions of the two men are filled with sadness, compassion and dread. Carolyn looks down to her phone again.

Come on, please! she thinks, before looking the tall officer in the eye.

"Mrs Hill, is it possible to go inside?" the officer asks.

Carolyn freezes, the smile starting to escape her face.

"What is this about?" Carolyn asks, her voice sounding wavy and nervous.

"I think it'll be best if we go inside."

Carolyn shakes her head. Awful images start to occupy her mind. "Simon and R-Ryan…?" she asks, tailing off. The two officers clench their jaws simultaneously and look to the ground.

"Tell me… please." Carolyn watches the two men and waits for their response, though she already knows she doesn't want to hear it. Later in life she will wonder whether, if she hadn't taken that cake order, any of this would have happened. She, Simon and Ryan would all be together. They'd probably take a different route home, perhaps after taking Ryan to the cinema. What if she wasn't busy decorating the cake and had kept Simon on the phone for just a minute longer? Would he had been in that spot on the motorway when the accident happened?

The officer looks up from his boots. "We have some terrible news," he says, and steps a little closer. "Your husband and son have been in a serious accident. I'm afraid to say they're both…"

Carolyn doesn't hear much else after that awful word, the word she was begging not to be spoken. Her knees buckle, sending her backwards. Her shoulder hits the shutters, causing them to rattle as she slides down to the floor, every muscle in her body limp and useless.

No, no! It's been a mistake. They're not dead!

Carolyn lifts the mobile to her face with jelly-like arms,

praying that Simon has messaged and she can show the officers how wrong they are.

Of course, Simon hasn't replied.

They're not dead. They can't be dead.

She unlocks the phone with trembling fingers and opens the recent calls list, presses Simon's name and holds the phone to her ear.

It rings, then goes to voicemail. She tries again and again and again. The smaller of the two officers stoops and takes her hand, lifting her back to her feet.

"A-are you s-sure?" Carolyn stutters.

The two men nod and lower their heads again.

Simon had always been a joker. He'd place whoopie cushions under the sofa, and plastic spiders on the kitchen floor. Carolyn begs for this to be one of Simon's jokes – a little too far, but they can argue about that later. Right now, Carolyn just wants to go home and find Simon and Ryan safe.

The crushing realisation hits her, the thought of never again watching Ryan play and laugh, never watching as he becomes excited building sandcastles. The thought of never again being able to hug her loving husband, Simon, after a hard day's work, to cuddle him in bed and speak of their future.

Carolyn leaves her car outside the shop and the two officers drive her home. She's silent as she looks through the window. The world around her becomes blurred and non-existent.

The shorter policeman walks her inside and pours her a glass of water. Her neighbour, Sarah, is alerted, and she makes the call to Carolyn's mother.

Carolyn is deflated. All of her energy has been swept away. She looks around the living room. Ryan's toys are in the corner. Simon's slippers are next to the sofa where he had left them the night before.

This can't be real.

She rests her head in her hands and cries.

Chapter Two

October 18th

The funeral is a blur, a horrendous living nightmare. Carolyn is expecting, at any moment, to jolt and wake up panting next to Simon, who would be sleeping with his wrist resting on his forehead, and Ryan, her snoozing son, wedged in between them both, also snoring loudly.

But it isn't a nightmare. It is very, very real.

Carolyn watches in a daze, from the face of Simon's manager at work, and a few other work colleagues, to the squeaking of the coffins lowering and the thud from handfuls of earth landing on them. She feels a hundred eyes looking from the grave back to her, as if expecting her sorrowful expression to change.

Jeanette, Carolyn's mother, tells her it was a lovely send-off ('lovely' is probably the wrong word choice, but Carolyn ignores it anyway) and that they'll be up there looking down over her with Carolyn's late father. But Carolyn, despite her Catholic upbringing, doesn't believe in that sort of thing. She believes that Simon and Ryan are together, yes, but they're not looking down over her – they're waiting for her to join them.

The idea of speeding up that reunion begins to take over the rational side of her mind, more and more.

***

Jeanette pulls open the curtains, allowing the sun to light the room, before taking a seat at Ryan's desk. The chair is from a *Thomas the Tank Engine* chair and desk set, and is made of strong quality wood. Not that Jeanette weighs much, she's just under five foot and shy of eight stone. She sits and refuses to leave, calling Carolyn's name until she wakes and is out of bed. It's 11 am, and if left alone, Carolyn would spend the day in Ryan's room, leaving only to use the toilet and make a Pot Noodle before heading back.

Today, Carolyn has her first appointment with a grief counsellor. She'd cancelled the previous two, and promised Jeanette she'd keep to this one.

Carolyn had got the number from a friend, Nicola, who'd had sessions herself after losing a child. She admitted she'd felt better after them, and more able to cope with everyday life, but it hadn't stopped Nicola and her husband from divorcing. "Some things can't be saved," she would shyly joke.

"I know you don't want to go to this session," Jeanette says. She's now at the edge of her seat, resting her palms on her knees. "But it'll do you good. Even leaving the house and going to the shop will help."

Her daughter has locked herself in Ryan's room for the last three weeks. It had started with sleeping in his bed and cuddling his favourite tiger teddy for a night or two, then three or four. Now Carolyn practically lives there. Her skin has turned pale and spotty. She refuses to open the curtains, or even the windows to allow some fresh air in. Her weight has dropped alarmingly. She refuses to eat anything, even when Jeanette orders her favourite takeaway. Carolyn just picks at a few chips from the plate and leaves the rest.

"It's not going to help, Mum. Nothing will," she says, running her fingers through greasy hair and pulling it free from the side of her face. She feels dazed and headachy.

The ray of sun coming through the bedroom window annoys her and sends a siren through her ears. Everything annoys her lately.

After a shower, her first in over a week, Carolyn studies herself in the long mirror attached to the back of the bathroom door. The person staring back is unrecognisable. The bones of her rib cage are more exposed, the bags under

10

her eyes are noticeably darker, and her lips are dry, cracked and discoloured. She realises she must look dreadful. Standing in the bathroom, the tiles cold under her bare feet, she opens the medicine cabinet for her toothbrush and spots the box of razor blades. She holds the box in the palm of her hand for a moment, as she's done many nights while Jeanette slept, and contemplates the idea of ending it all, of making the unknown journey to join her husband and son. Like all the times before, after careful consideration, she puts the box back on the shelf. She couldn't do it to her mother. It wouldn't be fair for Jeanette to find her like that.

Do it. You'll feel better, an inner voice insists.

But Carolyn doesn't reply. On a few occasions she's thought about telling her mother about the inner voice. It had started not long after the accident. It always gives her the wrong advice, and tries so hard to persuade her to do something she'd later regret. But Carolyn can't tell Jeanette about the voice. If she does, she knows exactly what will happen next. She'll be sleeping in Ryan's bed, and when the curtains are pulled open to wake her, it won't be her mother, but a couple of stocky men in white coats. They'll pull her out of bed and take her away, away from Ryan's room, away from his teddies, away from his crayon drawings stuck to the wall, and away from the rest of the things that once belonged to him. Away from Simon's things too: his clothes, and his old tatty t-shirts he'd wear only for bed.

No, she can't have that.

"Nearly ready, love?" Jeanette shouts from downstairs.

Carolyn clears her throat. "Yeah, won't be too long."

She dresses in the clothes Jeanette has picked out and ironed: a navy-blue vest top that hangs loosely from her shoulders, feeling as though it no longer belongs to her, grey jeans (her least favourite pair), trainers, and a casual baggy hoodie which had actually belonged to Simon. He'd use the hoodie for the garden, or, on the rare occasion, the gym. Carolyn puts makeup on to try to hide her pale skin and cracked lips. At the dining table she forces what breakfast she can down her throat before it causes her to gag. She fights it

11

down with orange juice. She unscrews the cap on her pill bottle and shakes out two Mirtazapine, then swallows them with the little juice she has left. Her GP had prescribed the tablets a couple of weeks back to help with her depression and anxiety.

They arrive outside the grief counsellor's office ten minutes early.

Carolyn examines the small building from the outside, debating whether to tell her mother to turn back, and she'll come another day. The recurring image of the box of razor blades sitting in the palm of her hand comes to mind. Maybe she'll finally take the inner voice's advice.

If nothing else, this session might help with the suicidal thoughts, she thinks, knowing that if asked she could probably recite the numbers under the barcode on the side of that box of razor blades, and that it weighs approximately thirty grams.

"You'll be fine, love," Jeanette says with glazed eyes. "I'll be out here the whole time. Don't worry. I'm proud of you for doing this."

Carolyn turns the ignition off. She wants to thank her mother, to pull her close and hug her tight, burying her face in the nook of her neck. But she can't. Carolyn's throat has begun to swell up, and she knows she wouldn't be able to let her go. Tears fall down her cheeks, creating a black mascara line down to her mouth. She looks back towards the building and takes a deep breath to prepare herself. She cleans her face before opening the car door and stepping out. The sounds of busy Leeds traffic almost knock her over. The people on the pavement, in business suits and office attire, out for their lunch, are heading right for her and she'd better move out of their way.

She's enjoyed hibernating in Ryan's room these past few weeks, coming to realise how calm it can be, with no responsibility, nobody to comment on her unbrushed hair or snigger about her grey jeans being a little short up her ankles, exposing her socks. Being in Ryan's room was peaceful: just her and her thoughts.

Carolyn stands up straight and breathes in, concentrating on the front entrance of the building and nothing more. Nothing that could take her mind off what she has to do. Jeanette shouts words of encouragement through the car window, but Carolyn doesn't hear clearly enough and she doesn't turn to reply. She just has to keep walking towards the building.

This is the first step. And, finally, she's taking it.

An hour later, she is back in the car.

"Well?" Jeanette asks, sliding her bookmark in place and dropping the book into her bag.

"It went ok," she says, pulling over the seatbelt and clicking it in place.

"That's it?"

"Well... yeah. What else do you want me to say?" she asks, her tone sounding a little snappy. "I'm sorry, Mum."

Jeanette waves away Carolyn's apology and clicks her seatbelt. "I'm just glad you actually decided to turn up today." She rests a hand on Carolyn's arm. "So where are we going?"

"Ashwood Forest," she says immediately.

"Ash... Ashwood Forest?" Jeanette asks, completely shocked. First Carolyn goes through with seeing the grief councillor, and now she's planning a visit to the forest.

"Wow... ok. Well done." Jeanette smiles. "Why Ashwood Forest?"

"Well, the grief councillor – her name is Maggie, by the way – *Maggie* suggested I visit places that Simon, Ryan and I enjoyed going. She said it'd help spark memories or something."

"Ashwood Forest. Well, I think a walk would do us great," Jeanette says.

"You don't mind coming with me?"

Jeanette looks at her daughter. "Of course I don't. Thank you for showing me. Let's go."

It takes Carolyn thirty minutes to drive to Ashwood Forest.

It would normally have taken longer, but this morning the lights and traffic are on her side.

The entrance on Barn Hey Road is leafy, and the tree branches overhanging from above make the entrance to the gravelled car park difficult to see. This is the entrance Simon and Carolyn would always use. The other one, on Brackenhurst Green, is a nightmare for parking, but the Barn Hey Road entrance always seems to have spaces. Simon would swear only a handful of people know of it.

Carolyn parks to the left and steps out as a silver Mercedes makes its way past, heading for the exit.

The trees are blowing calmly in the refreshing wind. The sound of the leaves moving, and the smell of the wet earth, bring a sense of relaxation to Carolyn. She closes her eyes and takes it in. Leaving Ryan's bedroom was definitely a good idea. She has always loved the beginning of Autumn.

She opens her eyes and looks around for Jeanette, then fixes onto the car leaving. It only takes one glance, but Carolyn sees him.

Ryan!

Her Ryan is sitting behind the woman driving the silver Mercedes.

Carolyn's eyes widen. The colour escapes from her face.

Why does this woman have her son?

"What... Ryan! Ryan!" Carolyn shouts as she chases after the car. The Mercedes heads onto Barn Hey Road and makes a turn. Jeanette rushes from the passenger seat of Carolyn's car and watches in horror as her daughter screams frantically. A man walking a Cocker Spaniel stops and pulls out one of his earbuds to listen.

"That woman has my son!" Carolyn shouts. She makes it to the exit and watches as the car heads further away, then turns and rushes to her own car.

"Carolyn, stop!" Jeanette says, standing in front of her and holding her hands up in a bid to slow Carolyn down.

The man with the dog runs over and pulls out his phone. "Shall I call the police?" he asks, concerned.

"Carolyn, Ryan is dead," Jeanette says, keeping up with

Carolyn as she heads for her car. "That wasn't Ryan. That wasn't your son!"

The man with the dog looks up from his phone and Jeanette fixes him with a look before saying she's confused, that she just lost her son, and that he shouldn't call the police.

The man nods and walks away, looking over his shoulder a couple of times before making it to his own car.

"Mum, that was him," Carolyn protests as she climbs into the driver's seat. "That was Ryan. I saw his face."

Carolyn starts the engine and Jeanette manages to jump back into the passenger seat before the car is thrown into reverse.

"Why has she got Ryan?" Carolyn says, unaware she is speaking out loud. "Why would she bring him to his favourite place?"

"Listen to me. That wasn't Ryan. You have to stop, now," Jeanette orders, but Carolyn ignores her. The car sprints back and swings around. Carolyn puts it in first and speeds out of the car park. She heads in the direction of the silver Mercedes, her foot down on the accelerator.

He's not dead! Ryan isn't dead. And if he isn't dead... where the hell is Simon?

Carolyn can hear Jeanette screaming in her left ear, but her mother's words are inaudible. She's too busy trying to piece together the crazy idea of Simon and this woman (possibly his lover) putting all of this together. Did they fake his and Ryan's deaths? Carolyn had never seen their bodies. Those coffins could have been filled with anything.

Did the woman driving that Mercedes bring Ryan here, to his favourite place, in a bid to gain his trust?

Carolyn can't think straight. None of those questions matter right now. All that matters is that she gets Ryan back, and that she proves her beautiful little boy isn't dead.

"Carolyn, STOP NOW!" Jeanette shouts.

Carolyn brings the car to a halt behind the Mercedes at a set of lights, pushes open her door and rushes from the car. She can see the woman driving the Mercedes watching in her wing mirror as Carolyn runs alongside her car and tries the door handles. They're locked.

"THAT'S MY SON. YOU HAVE MY SON!" Carolyn shouts frantically.

The woman in the Mercedes is watching her with horror.

Carolyn looks crazy, delusional even. She begins bashing on the windows and calling for Ryan. The boy in the back of the car looks petrified. Carolyn can hear him screaming for his mother.

Jeanette is holding onto Carolyn's shoulders and trying to pull her back, but Carolyn is stronger. She's full of energy in a bid to save Ryan.

"Ryan, I'm coming!" Carolyn shouts.

The traffic light turns to green and the woman in the Mercedes puts her foot down. The car sets off at speed.

"No, Ryan. NOOO!" Carolyn shouts. By now other people have stopped, some with their phones out, and others talking to each other in hushed voices. All are watching and pointing.

Jeanette turns and heads for Carolyn's car. The determined Carolyn realises that her mother wants to grab the keys from the ignition, and, without thinking, pushes Jeanette hard. Jeanette stumbles and falls to the floor, groaning as she bashes her knee. The onlookers gasp and point.

Carolyn stops and looks back to her injured mother. Guilt rushes through her. But at this moment, guilt is overpowered by determination. She climbs back into the car. She has to save Ryan. She has to protect her son and take him home.

Carolyn puts the car in gear as Jeanette gets herself up from the road, rubbing at her knee. Jeanette manages to rest a hand on Carolyn's car and slide into the passenger seat before her daughter can take off.

"I'm sorry, Mum. That bitch has Ryan!"

By now the lights have changed to red, though this doesn't stop Carolyn. She sprints through the lights and keeps her gaze straight ahead, in the direction that the silver Mercedes had headed.

Cars can be heard beeping and screeching to a stop. She doesn't even notice. "I'm coming, baby. Mummy's coming," she shouts.

Jeanette buckles her seatbelt and turns to Carolyn. "Please slow down. Think about it. That wasn't Ryan."

"It was," she snaps. "I saw him."

Her facial expression changes and Jeanette turns to see what she is looking at. Up ahead is the silver Mercedes. It is parked in front of a police car. The driver is speaking to an officer and is holding the young boy up to her chest.

Carolyn brings the car to a stop inches from the back of the police car. She dives out, almost falling over.

The officer turns and stands in front of the woman.

"Excuse me, Miss," the officer says as Carolyn charges for the woman. The officer, a redheaded man with a strong build, pushes Carolyn backwards.

"That's my son, officer. She has my son," Carolyn states.

Jeanette steps from the car and makes her way towards Carolyn.

"Mum, tell them. Tell them that's Ryan!" Carolyn looks to Jeanette for support.

Jeanette tells Carolyn again that it isn't Ryan. When Carolyn doesn't listen, she turns and explains to the officer what happened to Simon and Ryan.

The woman holding her sobbing son overhears. "Excuse me," she says, heading closer. "Please, take a look at my son." The woman turns the crying boy around to face them. He lifts his head from his mother's chest and looks at Carolyn, then Jeanette, and then to the officer before burying his face again.

"But…" Carolyn tails off. The boy is a little similar to Ryan, though Ryan was at least two years older and his hair wasn't as light.

"NO… I saw Ryan," Carolyn protests, looking at Jeanette. "I saw him."

The officer speaks with the woman, who tells him she doesn't want to take any further action. He tells Jeanette to take Carolyn home, and for Jeanette to drive.

Carolyn apologises to the woman and her son and climbs into the passenger seat. The thought runs through Carolyn's mind: *Am I going mad?*

The woman heads for her car, stroking a hand over the back of her son's head. Carolyn can't bear to look at her any longer. Shock and guilt fill her head as she looks down at her shaking hands.

Chapter Three

October 22nd

Jeanette is busy packing the last of Carolyn's cases into the back of her red Volkswagen Polo. After she finishes, she speaks to Carolyn's neighbour, Sara. Carolyn locks up and takes one last look around, making sure everything is switched off and the rubbish is taken out. She hands the spare key to Sara, in case she has to enter for emergencies, or check the electricity is still on, or that a pipe hasn't burst.

"How are you feeling?" Sara asks from over the fence. Sara is a thin black woman with short grey hair. She wears long, draped cardigans, held closed by hand.

"You know, it's hard, but…" Carolyn tails off.

"I can only imagine. You look well," Sara says. Carolyn knows this is a lie. She looks how she feels – awful.

"Thanks, Sara. And thank you for watching the place for me."

"Don't mention it." Sara drops the keys into the pocket of her knitted cardigan. "I'm happy you're getting away. You could do with the break."

Carolyn and Jeanette say goodbye and begin their way to Jeanette's home in Llanbedr, a small rural town near St Davids in south Wales.

Carolyn knows the break really will do her good. She needs to leave Leeds behind, get away from the traffic and the cake shop for a while, take time to clear her mind, and grieve properly. Part of the reason Carolyn had agreed to go is because her mother's constant prayers and the rattling of her rosary beads were starting to get under her skin, plus the fact that Jeanette wouldn't go home unless Carolyn went with her.

Carolyn's plan is to spend a couple of weeks away at Jeanette's, then she can get the train back home to Leeds and leave her mother in Llanbedr. Carolyn can be back home with Simon's jumpers and can sleep in Ryan's bed, surrounded by all his teddies and toys.

Jeanette had moved to Llanbedr ten years earlier, after her husband passed away from a heart attack. He is buried at his hometown's cemetery, between St Davids and Fishguard. Carolyn and Simon had tried to convince Jeanette to come and stay with them. At the time, they were renting a small apartment on Earle Street next to a strip of kebab shops and noisy student bars. But Jeanette has always been a strong person; she'd thanked them but politely refused. It hadn't been hard for Jeanette to sell the home she'd shared with her husband for all those years. She'd never really been the sentimental type.

With the sale of her home, to a young couple with two kids (the next-door neighbour had told her), she'd a decent amount of money spare after buying her bungalow. She'd used some of the surplus to help Carolyn and Simon with their deposit a couple of years later.

En route to Jeanette's, Carolyn offers to drive the rest of the way after they stop for food. Jeanette dismisses the gesture and tells her she's fine to do the other hundred miles herself. Carolyn shrugs and reclines her seat, closing her eyes. She pulls a stress ball from her pocket and squeezes at it as she imagines the events of the accident, or at least how it was described to her by the police. With a full stomach and a tired head, Carolyn drifts off to sleep and dreams of sitting in the passenger seat of Simon's car. Radio One is playing quietly. Ryan is screaming in the back and she turns to him and watches through the back window. A huge lorry is following their car, the bright headlights almost blinding, frowning and mimicking evil eyes. It's inches away from Simon's back bumper. She yells at him to speed up. His shirt is soaked with sweat, and he's panting frantically. She's never seen him look so worried before, at least not since the time Ryan fell and bumped his head on the concrete in the back garden and they rushed him to hospital.

Simon doesn't seem to hear her. He swerves the car from side to side in a bid to slow the lorry down, but it follows suit, as if attached to a tow bar on the back. Carolyn turns back around to hush Ryan. "Everything's going to be ok," she says, but the seat is empty. Not even his favourite toys have been left behind. She spins forward. Simon, too, has vanished.

She turns back to the rear window. The chasing lorry with its shiny metal is nowhere to be seen. The loud roars of the engine can no longer be heard. There is nothing but empty road. Scott Mills is in the middle of talking to a listener when the radio switches off and the car loses control and begins to veer towards the concrete slabs of the hard shoulder.

She wakes with a quiver.

"You're awake, finally. We're not far now," Jeanette says as they pass the sign for Llanbedr. Carolyn sits upright, rubbing her hands over the goose-pimpled flesh on her arms, her head groggy and damp with sweat.

"Bad dream again?"

"Yeah, I think it's them Mirtazapine drugs, Mum," she replies, feeling the cool breeze calm her forehead. "The GP didn't mention anything about nightmares, though."

They pull into Llanbedr, greeted firstly by the fire station, and next to that the police station with three panda cars outside. Chief Inspector Richard Williams stands outside smoking and holding a cup of coffee in his chubby hand, his face moist and pink. He acknowledges Jeanette's car and waves. She returns the gesture. Carolyn can see the happiness starting to creep slowly back into her mother's eyes. She's back with her own people, and back to the church she's missed so much.

Not long after the death of Carolyn's father, Jeanette had taken early retirement after working forty-two years as a nurse. A few weeks after moving to Llanbedr she'd got stuck right in to volunteering at the church. At the time she'd told herself it was to keep her mind occupied, and it was only supposed to be for a couple days a week, but she and Father

Joseph became good friends and now she's there every day.

They pass The Red Fox pub, just a little further down from the police station. It has a huge car park and beer garden with plenty of benches. Dead leaves are scattered across the grass outside the pub's wooden double doors.

"That's the only pub around here for at least fifteen miles. We should go one night, and introduce you to a few people," Jeanette says, cheerfully. "When was the last time you were down here, anyway?"

Carolyn rubs at her head. "Christmas, two years ago," she replies. She agrees to go one night, though she's not interested at all. She has no intention of meeting new people and making small talk with the locals. She just wants to get these couple of weeks over and done with so she can go home.

They pull onto the cobbled high street, which gives Jeanette's car's suspension a workout, and pass shops Carolyn remembers from her last visit.

"That candle shop has seen better days, hasn't it? Don't they ever change around here?" she asks, pointing to the battered wooden sign hanging from two rusted chains. "It looks as if a puff of wind would bring it down."

Jeanette chuckles. "No. People around here like things to stay the same. That's one of the reasons I chose to live here. I didn't want to be around people, always sticking their noses in…." She sighs. "Besides, what more do you need, apart from a good butcher, farm shop and church?"

Carolyn doesn't respond. She carries on looking out of the window, concentrating on the acres of fields and farmland that make up Llanbedr.

After a few miles, the car swings left onto Cherry Garden Lane where it's engulfed in bare overhanging trees and bushes. The lane goes on for three miles before passing the King family's pig farm. The stench can be smelled through the air ducts in the car. Carolyn frowns and switches off the air-con.

Jeanette chuckles. "You just need to get used to it, that's all. You'll be fine."

Carolyn gives an unenthusiastic grunt and tells herself she won't be here long enough to get used to it. Tears begin to form as she remembers passing the farm a couple of years back. She, Simon and Ryan had pulled faces at one another and made funny oinking noises.

Further down the country lane they pass a boarded-up building. It's the Sunlight B&B, which used to be run by Mr and Mrs Powell, a retired couple who had turned their five-bed home into a business.

Carolyn wipes at her cheeks. "What happened there?" she asks.

Jeanette frowns, "Ah, about a year ago now there was a small fire that burned through the kitchen. Luckily no one was hurt. I think it's going to be demolished. Shame really. They used to hold a coffee and cake morning every other Saturday. You would have enjoyed it." Jeanette tuts. "Why don't you join me in church this Sunday?"

Carolyn responds with another unenthusiastic grunt and watches as Jeanette fixes her hair in the rear-view mirror. "God. You're not still in love with Father Joseph, are you, Mum?"

Father Joseph is the long-serving priest at St Peter's Catholic church, which faces Jeanette's bungalow. He wears thick, black-rimmed glasses that make his ice-blue eyes seem small and beady. He reminds Carolyn of a much older-looking Dave Grohl, the lead singer of the Foo Fighters. It was Simon who'd first pointed out the resemblance when they were down visiting Jeanette for her birthday a few years back, and now Carolyn can't unsee it. They'd mentioned it to Jeanette once and she wasn't amused.

Jeanette pulls a face and waves away Carolyn's question. "Don't be so silly, Carolyn. We're friends. I help him out at the church most days and that's all," she replies hastily, but keeping an eye on the doors of the church, presumably on the off-chance that Dave Grohl – Father Joseph Coyle – might appear.

When he doesn't, she lowers her shoulders and Carolyn is sure she hears a sigh of disappointment, though this might have been her imagination. Jeanette turns the car up the path of her bungalow and applies the handbrake.

Jeanette unlocks and slides open the glass doors of the porch before unlocking the front door and holding it open for Carolyn to carry her suitcase through. She feels relaxed already. The plant next to the door reminds her it needs watering, and she makes a mental note to do so. Jeanette feels a sudden happiness as she sees her reclining armchair positioned in front of the television. Resting on the armchair is a TV listings magazine, now three months out of date. An unpleasant scent welcomes her back, not as revolting as the pig farm, but still quite nasty. It's the smell of rotting meat that pervades the front room and is coming from the kitchen.

Carolyn flings her suitcase onto the sofa and opens the windows, covering her nose with one hand. In the kitchen, flies are buzzing happily around a joint of lamb that's been left sitting in an oven dish on top of the work surface, along with what looks as if it used to be garlic cloves and rosemary. They both hold their noses as one opens a bin bag and the other chucks it in, dish included.

"When your neighbour rang me, what's her name again... Sara. When Sara rang and told me what had happened, I couldn't speak at first. I was just standing there frozen, then after crying for a while, I turned off the oven, threw a few sets of clothes and underwear in a case and dived in the car. I forgot all about the meat," Jeanette explains, trying her best not to throw up the sandwich they had bought from the service station a couple of hours back. Jeanette opens the fridge and also throws away the chunky milk and green spotted cheese and spoiled vegetables.

"I think this is a really good idea that you've agreed to come stay for a while," Jeanette says, still holding her nose as her stomach twitches. "It must be hard, to be reminded every day at home. It's not healthy for you." She hesitates for a moment before continuing. "I'm not saying any time soon, but when you're ready, you should think about donating the majority of Simon and Ryan's things to charity. I can help you if you like."

Carolyn just nods, and hopes her mother knows that when she heads back to Leeds, she'll be going alone. At this moment in time, she isn't ready to donate their things. She doesn't think she will ever be ready. She wants to be back home, to surround herself with Simon's clothes, to smell his shirt she'll be wearing as she cuddles Ryan's favourite teddy. To look at the sofa and picture Simon sitting there, totally engrossed in one of his historical fiction novels. She wants to look out into the garden and imagine Ryan sliding down the slide, laughing and mumbling to himself.

She just wants this nightmare to end so she can join them. She makes her way to the spare room, pulls off the dusty blanket covering the bed, fixes the new bedding her mother had got out of the wardrobe and unpacks her case.

In the kitchen, Jeanette pours two tins of soup into a pan and writes a list of ingredients that she'll have to get from town tomorrow. Not that Llanbedr has much of a town centre: just the one decent shop – Llanbedr Convenience – and a few other smaller independent shops, coffee houses, the police station, the fire station and The Red Fox pub.

They eat soup and watch Jeanette's daily shows, Jeanette slouching comfortably in her recliner and Carolyn on the sofa, yawning.

"Go and have an early night. It's been a long day. Once this show's finished, I think I'll be going myself," Jeanette says, fighting back a yawn. Carolyn accepts and changes into her pyjamas. She unpacks a picture of the three of them together. She and Simon are sitting with arms around each other as Ryan lies on his front resting on his elbows on top of a picnic blanket, with woodland in the background. She places it on the bedside table.

It's not long before her eyes are flickering. She doesn't fight it. She doesn't want to. At the moment, sleep seems to be the best cure for her. A minute later, she's dreaming.

Chapter Four

Carolyn wakes as the sun is setting, with the last remaining rays illuminating her room a cool pink through the thin curtains. Feeling flustered, she kicks off the quilt and sits up. It's time for her to take two Mirtazapine. She listens to her mother's snores from the other room as she heads quietly for the kitchen. The lid pops off her tablet case, and she swallows them with some water.

The key to the back door, leading to the garden, is hanging on a small wooden plaque that bears the words *MY GARDEN, MY RULES*. The plaque had belonged to her father. He was always an avid gardener. Jeanette had brought it with her when she moved from Leeds.

Carolyn unlocks the door and opens it. A refreshing breeze brushes past her, instantly cooling the thin cotton pyjamas she's wearing. Jeanette's slippers are on the shoe rack next to the door. She slips them on and steps outside, closing the door behind her. The abandoned garden which has stood alone for more than three months shows how nature has taken over. Weeds have sprouted through the cracks of the flags and covered the path leading to the old wooden shed in the corner. The shed was here when Jeanette moved in, looking as if any day now it would crumble to dust under a strong wind. The grass stands just below Carolyn's knees, hiding the various faces of the gnomes.

She steps out, flattening it as she creates a path and walks in a circle around the garden, examining the gnomes. A Grandfather gnome and a Grandmother gnome (a present last Mother's Day from Carolyn, Simon and Ryan) are standing side by side. He's holding a shovel and sporting a long white beard, while she holds a basket of eggs. Both have warm smiles painted on their faces. The other gnomes are what Jeanette has picked up throughout the years, including a fisherman sitting on a rock with a green hat, and a young princess wearing a long pink dress.

Birds tweet and land not so far from Carolyn before taking flight again, searching for their last meal of the day. She reaches the back fence, or at least, what's left of it. The six-foot fence runs around the perimeter of the garden. Cheap thin wooden slats that had fallen or been blown off by the wind lie behind the wild privets in front of it. An opening in the fence leads into the woodland behind. It's large enough for Carolyn to fit through. She looks down at her mother's slippers and examines the ground beyond the fence. It's a dirt track made up of fallen twigs and tree branches. The smell of wet soil and rotting tree trunk welcomes her. The woodland is beautiful; she doesn't see enough of this sort of thing in Leeds.

Carolyn stands and takes in the beauty. She imagines that Ryan would have loved it here, and feels a slight pang of guilt in her stomach. Carolyn and Simon hardly ever brought Ryan here. It would always be Jeanette travelling to them for visits.

The floor of the forest is covered with small yellow clover-like flowers, and the squirrels chase one another around a large thick tree. Carolyn could swear this might be a set from a Disney film. She kicks her way through the thick grass, stretches her arms out wide, and feels the bark of the elder trees in her palms. The sun setting and bouncing off the remaining leaves above gives her an autumnal feeling. She looks around her, taking in the bright colours of the many plants and bushes.

It is the dark-coloured brick that first catches her eye. Up ahead, to the east, stands a small brick structure.

Maybe it's an old wall, or ruins from an ancient castle that's lain in wait for a hundred years, just waiting for somebody to discover it.

With that thought, and knowing it's what Simon would have done, Carolyn begins heading towards it. She carefully avoids stepping on as many plants as she can, not to destroy this newfound haven at the back of her mother's home.

On closer inspection, Carolyn realises the small brick building is round with an open top.

"A well," she whispers to herself, smiling as she runs her fingers along the brickwork. Red dust flakes off and blows away.

Simon would definitely love this place.

Carolyn walks the circle around the well. Moss has overtaken a large portion of it. She begins to imagine what it could look like if she cleans it up, picturing herself sitting with her back against it, reading on a summer's day. She might wear shorts and a vest top as she sunbathes and could even bring a camping chair. She and Jeanette would bring sandwiches (not that Carolyn's planning on staying in Llanbedr much longer than she has to).

The small ball of excitement in her stomach is short-lived, however, when she peers down the darkening hole.

The well looks to have been filled many years ago with soil and crushed brick, though it's still at least fifteen feet deep. It's hard to say exactly, with the sunlight gradually fading and the thick, broken tree branches that fill the opening of the well.

Then she notices something else.

Carolyn can't move her face. Her eyelids won't blink. It is as if they have been superglued to her face. She is temporarily paralysed. The vision in the corner of her eyes turns blurry; only what is down the well stays in focus. The song of the birds singing above in the trees is muted, as if an evil dark cloud has formed above her, killing all the joy in Carolyn's little space. Her brain begins sending signals and making sense of what she is seeing. It is the broken and twisted remains of a young boy.

The flesh on the boy's skull has not yet fully decomposed, and he looks as though he's been dead no longer than a few days. His skin is dark, his body twisted with one of his legs bent behind him. Carolyn squints and can see a badge, a logo even, on the chest of his green jumper.

28

Carolyn's eyes water and her breathing becomes erratic. Finally she looks away, snapping her eyes closed. Ryan's face flashes in her mind. He calls for her in a loud, scared and lonely tone. She shakes her head and opens her eyes. Tears roll off her cheeks as the urge to throw up rests in her stomach.

Only a few minutes ago, Carolyn had considered this her new happy place; somewhere she could be alone with her thoughts, to forget the stresses of owning a cake shop, and (even if only for a moment) Simon and Ryan's death.

Now, next to an old derelict well, wearing pyjamas and her mother's fluffy slippers, she is standing on top of a potential crime scene.

Maybe the boy fell, and had got stuck and died from his injuries? Nothing sinister at all, just a young boy out exploring the way boys at that age do.

Carolyn doubts it. The world is never really that simple and innocent, is it?

She hears a twig snapping from somewhere behind and spins around, expecting to see people watching her, the killer or killers of this terrible act coming at her for exposing their dumping ground. She imagines them to be dressed in dark cloaks and clenching large pitchforks or machetes.

The tears on her cheeks turn to ice; the low refreshing breeze from before is now gripping hold of her spine and refusing to let go. She doesn't want to take another look, but she knows she has to. She has to be certain it is what she saw, and not her imagination playing a cruel trick. Her neck aches as she spins left to right, checking that she's alone, that there are no machete-wielding murderers behind her. Taking a large breath, she looks down the well.

Carolyn takes a step back and vomits on to the ground, not wanting to contaminate the crime scene any more than she has already. She's learned this from multiple episodes of *CSI* and other true crime documentaries she and Simon used to watch.

Behind Carolyn, bushes move. It's not from the mild breeze, either. Though Carolyn doesn't notice, her sides feel as though they're being squeezed by a vice as more vomit is brought up.

The woods are now a dull grey. The place no longer seems beautiful.

Her knees go limp and she drops to the hard ground. The thin cotton pyjamas offer no support to her kneecaps as small stones and twigs dig in, but she doesn't feel the pain. She feels dazed and nauseous. Her energy has been swept away. She tries shouting for help, but nothing more than a whisper leaves her lips. Her throat is dry, and she's now breathless.

She lies down on the uneven ground and looks up at the darkening sky. The trees seem to spin, laughing and mocking her with their bony structures.

There are no birds or squirrels around now. It's only Carolyn and the decaying corpse of the boy in the well.

Chapter Five

Two days ago, the freezer in which the body of the young boy down the well had been stored, broke. The first thing the killer noticed was the smell. Even now, standing in the bushes and watching as Carolyn vomits and lies down, that damn smell won't leave him. It's as if the scent has etched its way into his nostrils as a constant reminder of his crime. He stays back, standing motionless, with the ladder in one hand and heavy-duty bin bags in the other.

***

The ground beneath is cold on Carolyn's back. The chill has finally made its way through her pyjama top, giving her the energy to do what's right and inform the authorities. She rolls over onto her front and lifts herself up with exhausted arms, wiping the soil from her hands against her thighs. She spins around to find the path to home as she shouts for her mother. At first, no noise comes out, only air. With every step she takes, her voice returns, growing louder and louder. She rushes through the gap in the fence, trampling the plants before knocking over and cracking the princess gnome in the long dress. She leaps through the high grass garden taking huge strides.

Her heart is beating so furiously in her chest that she feels as if she's about to pass out, or will throw up again.

Carolyn continues to shout for Jeanette while at the same time trying to catch her breath. Jeanette has always been a heavy sleeper. Carolyn pushes the door of the spare room open and reaches for her iPhone. She swipes it open and dials 999. The phone is quiet as it attempts to connect. The top left of the screen is showing no signal.

"COME ON!" she screams at the screen, hoping this will entice it to work. She dials the number again, but nothing. The phone beeps and goes back to the home screen.

She throws it on the bed and runs to the living room, reaching for Jeanette's mobile. The same. No bars. Carolyn grabs her mother's car keys from the table next to the door. There's no time to wake Jeanette, or to even grab her coat. She dives into the driver's seat and starts the car. The small Polo's engine starts first time, releasing a cloud of black exhaust smoke behind her. Slamming the car into reverse with a crunch of the gears, she accelerates and backs out of the drive, skidding on the gravel stones and leaving an imprint on the path.

On the road, she slips into first and takes off with a screech, before turning on the headlights and fastening her seatbelt. The roads are quiet at this time of day. The clock on the dash tells her it's nearly half past six. Carolyn is used to driving in the bright lights of the city. The small amount of light supplied by the county roads makes her nervous. She switches on the fog lights to guide her.

Her hands are holding the steering wheel so tight that her knuckles are white, leaving moisture on the leather.

"Come on, come on, come on," she beckons the car to speed up. The daunting image of the young boy looking up at her is etched into her mind. She shivers, feeling a chill at her spine.

Ryan's face and the face of the boy down the well flash one after the other in front of her eyes. She wants desperately to close them and forget, but she can't. She has to keep her foot on the accelerator and inform the police. Her bottom lip begins to tremble and she cries out. Tears are streaming down her face as she approaches a sharp bend in the road, almost missing it and ending up through a wooden fence and into a dark field. She brakes and takes the turn, tyres screeching from the tarmac as the car's engine cries out in need of a gear change.

Carolyn continues for two miles, oblivious to the roars of the engine, before she finally shifts up a gear. On the cobbled high street the car bounces wildly, forcing her to slow down. Groups of people smoking outside The Red Fox pub turn and watch as the Polo approaches the police station and screeches to a halt a few feet away from the entrance. Onlookers watch with drinks in hand as Carolyn jumps from the car and falls to her knees. She loses one of her slippers, but straightens herself as she pushes through the glass doors of the police station.

The officer at the front desk, PC Ian Riley, watches as Carolyn, standing breathless and gasping for air in dusty, mud-stained pyjamas while missing a slipper, struggles to speak. PC Riley is looking her up and down as if she's crazy.

"There… is… a body…" Carolyn pants. Her complexion has gone white, and the nausea is back. "There is a body in a well… a young boy." She clutches at her stomach. Inspector Richard Williams is coming from his office. He sees the distressed Carolyn and steps in.

"Miss, are you ok?" he asks.

PC Riley looks at him and shakes his head. "She says there's a boy down a well, sir."

Richard Williams looks from PC Riley to Carolyn. His shirt is overhanging from his trousers and his tie is pulled loose from around his neck. A slight smell of body odour escapes him. Carolyn assumes he is near the end of his shift, and identifies his facial expression as annoyed.

"Ok, miss. Where is this boy? Is he still breathing?" he asks.

Carolyn shakes her head. "No, he's dead, I think. I can show you. It's at the back of my mother's house, facing the church. I'm Jeanette Stephenson's daughter. I'm staying with her for a little while." Carolyn pauses to catch her breath. "Follow me. I can show you," she adds, heading for the glass doors.

Williams says, "I know where the church is and I know your mother's bungalow. Is that your car outside?"

"Yes… no, it's my mother's car. My phone wasn't working, so I had to drive here."

"Okay, well leave the car here until later. You can ride with me." He turns and follows her out, then turns back to the

33

reception area. "Riley, park this woman's car up and get through to Hughes and Dixon. They're at that dispute over on Highfield Road. Tell them to meet me there, and get the fire brigade. We'll need them. It's the bungalow facing Father Joseph's church."

Riley nods and picks up the phone.

Carolyn is outside and slides the lost slipper back on. Richard Williams' car flashes as it unlocks, and Carolyn climbs into the passenger seat. She recognises the scent of old cigarettes and take-away food. PC Riley follows outside shortly after and climbs into the red Polo, parking it at the side of the station.

Blue lights flash further down as the fire engine joins the road just behind Richard Williams' patrol car.

"So you say the boy is dead?"

Carolyn doesn't respond. She's too busy watching the small gathering of people outside the pub. They are pointing and speaking, obviously not used to seeing such drama in their quiet town. Some take pictures which will inevitably be posted to social media within minutes.

"MISS!?" Williams shouts, snapping Carolyn from her thoughts. "You say the boy is dead? How do you know?"

"Yes, I-I think, anyway. He wasn't moving, and his eyes were... they were just staring at me..." she tails off.

Inspector Williams releases a sigh and nods his head. "We haven't had any reports of a missing child lately."

"That's just it. His skin was... well, it didn't look fully decomposed." Carolyn stops and holds a hand up to her mouth. The image causes her to fight down the vomit.

"Are you ok? Do you need me to pull over?" Williams asks, slowing the car.

Carolyn shakes her head. "No... I'm fine, sorry."

"There's nothing to be sorry for," Williams says, taking a bend of the road with the confidence of a man who has driven this route for well over forty years. "It must be hard seeing something like that. Can you tell me more? What does the boy look like?"

Carolyn closes her eyes and thinks. Nothing substantial

enters her mind, only the glazed white eyes appear.

"I'm sorry." She shakes her head again, then remembers. "He was wearing a green jumper!"

Williams nods. "Anything else?"

"I-I think it looked like a school jumper. There was a logo... maybe a crest on the chest... I couldn't see properly, but it looked like an S."

"An S?" Williams thinks for a moment. "That could be Silvis Primary. They have green jumpers as part of their uniform." He steps on the accelerator a little harder.

Carolyn is silent, her mind wandering.

"Jeanette tells me you live in Leeds," Williams says in a conversational tone.

"Yes."

"What do you do?"

"I own a bakery," Carolyn answers, and before Williams can ask why she is here, Carolyn adds, "I'm just here for a holiday and a visit for a few weeks." Richard Williams doesn't need to know the details of her visit, and Carolyn doesn't want to speak about them. Not yet, anyway. And not to a stranger.

As the car and the fire engine pass the pig farm, they are joined by DS Hughes' and DC Dixon's Hyundai.

They arrive at Jeanette's bungalow. Williams' car skids up the path and comes to a halt, making more imprints in the gravel as a small cloud of dust bursts from behind it. The fire engine and the other patrol car park on the road outside. The blue lights of the three vehicles light up the countryside sky like a busy fairground.

Father Joseph Coyle comes out and stands on the steps of the church, looking on. He wipes his glasses on his t-shirt and puts them to his face.

Jeanette comes out of the front door fastening her dressing gown. "Where have you been?" she asks. "I woke up to find you gone and my car was missing. What's going on?"

Before Carolyn can respond, Williams is standing in front of Jeanette, his considerable belly almost reaching her flat stomach. "Carolyn tells us she has found a body in the well...

35

behind your bungalow."

The rain has started again, but nobody seems to realise or care. Their attention is on the body Carolyn has found.

Jeanette's face, already pale as she isn't one for the sun, turns a ghostly white. She closes her hands over her mouth in shock and looks up to Carolyn. "Is this true? Are you sure?" she asks, her voice trembling.

Carolyn doesn't answer. She leads the way and heads through the front room to the kitchen, snatching a torch from the shelf as she passes. The three officers follow her through the house and out into the back, the firefighters following behind.

The bright LED torches illuminate the pathway to the bottom of the garden. Carolyn ducks and squeezes through the gap, Richard Williams pulls off some of the rotting fence panels and throws them onto the grass. One by one, each of them squeezes through and into the woodland behind Jeanette Stephenson's home. Jeanette herself stays in the doorway watching. She was never one for unpleasant sights, which is strange for a woman who spent her working life as a nurse. Instead, she watches with her hands clasped together, saying a prayer.

Carolyn continues leading the way. The idyllic scene from a short while ago, the one in which she imagined herself sitting and catching up on a bit of reading while sharing a picnic with her mother, has now been replaced by something out of a horror film. Moths flicker in front of her torchlight as she attempts to retrace the path she had taken earlier. Darkness has crept up out of nowhere.

She shines the torch left to right, left to right, and walks a few feet ahead, scouring the area. The footsteps of eight people following behind her, snapping twigs and bringing up earth, is loud and unsettling. Left to right, left to—

Carolyn points. "There it is. Up ahead," she says.

The well comes into view, housing the corpse that waits to be discovered. To Carolyn, it looks like the type of well you'd be expecting a goblin to climb from and chase you through the woods, snapping branches out of its way as it claws at your back with sharp nails.

"There, that's it. He's... he's down there..." Carolyn steps aside to allow the police to do their work. She's seen too much today already. Williams pushes ahead, the sweat and rain trickling down his flustered face. DS Hughes and DC Dixon follow behind, then the firefighters behind them. She leans against a tree as the crew run past, all eight torches shining down the dark hole, lighting the horror.

Carolyn sighs and looks up towards the dark sky in a bid to concentrate on something else, anything other than the decaying face she saw earlier. The vomit is trying desperately to break out again. She's lost in a train of thought. She doesn't hear the first question until she looks down and finds eight irritated faces staring back at her, expecting answers. The sound of night comes back, the hooting of an owl, the humming of the night, the angry tone of Richard Williams' voice.

"I asked, is this a joke?" His face is red with anger and his wide eyes focus purely on Carolyn. His forehead creases with frowning. The other two also demand answers. The firefighters shake their heads and begin walking back to their truck, frowning and muttering under their breath. Carolyn thinks she hears the one at the front, a grey-haired man, calling her a crazy bitch, though she isn't sure. It could just be the internal voice.

Carolyn watches as they walk back to the gap in the fence. She turns towards the three officers, confused, and walks towards the well. The morbid image of the poor boy who lost his life flashes in her mind as she heads over. DS Hughes lowers her look to Carolyn's chosen attire and grunts. She turns to her partner and mutters under her breath. He too inspects her clothing, the corners of his mouth lift as he smirks.

Inspector Richard Williams is holding his torch over the opening of the well. The bright beam illuminates through the cracks of the crumbling brickwork as his hand trembles with anger.

Carolyn reaches the well, the same spot she was standing

just an hour ago, a few feet away from where she threw up – now thankfully washed away by the rain – and looks from face to face. Disgust, anger, frustration and irritation all look back at her.

She leans forward onto the red brick, dirtying her pyjamas even further as she looks down the well. Feeling sick and speechless, she gasps.

There is no boy, no decaying body, nothing to even resemble a body. Sticks and bin bags entangled together, or maybe even a mannequin wearing a wig, would have made this an easy mistake, but there's nothing.

No corpse.

Chapter Six

"Well?" Williams asks, wiping the rain from his forehead.

The sick feeling is back in Carolyn's stomach, now even stronger.

How is it possible for a body to disappear? she asks herself.

You're crazy, Carolyn. Crazy old Carolyn, the internal voice replies. She almost yells back, ordering it to be quiet. She decides not to, as that's all they'd need to have her sedated.

The vision of the corpse comes back to her: the bruised, mangled body. There was no way she dreamt that up. Just no way.

"Well?" Williams repeats, this time angrier, his eyes focused on Carolyn's.

"I…" Carolyn begins. "I… I'm sorry… I really don't understand. There was a body down that well, I swear!" Carolyn can sense DS Hughes looking at her, feeling the glare burn into the side of her face, studying her. Carolyn turns to face the detective. DS Hughes clicks off her torch and places it back into the holder on her belt. She's a tall, stocky woman, and wears her hair in a thick plait. Carolyn thinks she resembles a female cage fighter, and is confident that in a one-on-one the DS would come off better. DS Hughes lowers her long face and mumbles something under her breath before nodding to her partner to follow. They turn, their shoes squelching in the wet grass as they head in through the fence, then into the bungalow by the back door.

"Do you think our police work isn't important, Mrs Hill?" Williams asks, wiping the rain from his forehead again. His face is back to its usual colour.

Carolyn feels nauseous and lightheaded. She pinches the corners of her eyes as she shakes her head. "I wouldn't waste your time like this. I'm telling you there was a body down there earlier. I saw it with my own eyes."

"Have you been feeling all right?" Williams asks. His eyes and facial expression show what he's really thinking: *Here is a crazy woman.*

"Don't do that," Carolyn says, giving him an annoyed look. Williams purses his lips and gives her a look that says, *I don't know what you're going on about.*

"I'm not crazy, and I definitely wouldn't waste police time like this!" Carolyn shouts.

The inspector turns his back on Carolyn and heads back inside.

Carolyn shines her torch down the well. The tree branches are in the same place, but there's still no body. She turns and follows behind Richard Williams. Hughes and Dixon return to their car to head back to the station, along with the fire crew.

Jeanette is sitting on the couch with Father Joseph, hand in hand as they say a prayer.

"Is it true, Richard? Is it a little boy?" Jeanette asks, wiping fresh tears from her shiny cheeks. "The other two officers wouldn't confirm it."

"There is no boy, Jeanette!" Williams barks. "Your daughter is a liar. She thinks it's funny to waste our time."

Carolyn enters after him, closing the door on the cold night air. The temperature has dropped, and the thin wet pyjamas are now proving to be unsuitable outdoor clothing. She steps inside, feeling embarrassed and confused.

Her mother looks at her puzzlingly, but before Carolyn can open her mouth, Williams speaks again.

"Whose are these?" he asks, holding up the tub of pills and reading the label. "*Side-effects include dizziness, drowsiness and weakness.*" His eyes lock smugly on to Carolyn's. "Label says these are yours, Mrs Hill. Do you think maybe you could have been tired and imagined the whole thing?"

"I know what I saw!" Carolyn shouts. "It wasn't my

imagination!"

"Carolyn!" Jeanette snaps. There's no mistaking the anger in her tone.

Father Joseph stands up and walks over to Williams, resting a hand on his shoulder. He's slightly taller than the inspector, and has wider shoulders. He takes off his thick-rimmed glasses, wipes them, and places them back on his face.

"She's had a long day, Rich. And with what's gone on lately... Maybe give her a free pass?"

Carolyn looks from Father Joseph to her mother with disbelief. "You've been telling him my personal troubles?"

Williams pulls a confused expression and places the tablets back onto the counter.

"I'll leave you to discuss it," Father Joseph says. "I'll see you tomorrow, Jeanette. Richard, have a good night." He nods at Carolyn and leaves the bungalow.

Carolyn watches him walk down the path and cross the road to the church.

"You told him?" Carolyn asks again, raising her voice.

Her mother avoids eye contact and doesn't reply.

"What's going on here?" Williams asks. Rain is falling from his police coat and forming a small puddle at his feet, along with the blades of grass and mud stains from the others.

"Father Joseph was wondering where I've been for the last three months, Carolyn," Jeanette explains. "I rang him from Leeds when I first arrived, but I couldn't tell him anything over the phone. He's going to say a prayer for Simon and Ryan tomorrow."

Carolyn turns and kicks off her mother's battered slippers before leaving the room. She sits at the bottom of her bed, trying to focus her mind on the memory at the well, just before she dropped to the ground.

Is it possible I imagined it? It could be the drugs taking their effect, she thinks.

Maybe she'd sleepwalked, or was low on sugar. She hasn't slept very well in weeks. She strains her ears to listen to her mother in the next room, telling Williams the events of what happened to Simon and Ryan. Her mother's voice is clear and audible. Williams' voice is deep, and it's hard to make out his short replies. She lies back and places a pillow over her face, trying to drown out the part when her mother mentions the lorry that had crushed her family. Not long after, she hears footsteps passing her room and then her mother's voice as she says goodbye to Williams at the front door.

Unable to shake off the image of the corpse, Carolyn reaches for her phone, connects to her mother's internet and opens the search engine. One article she reads is about hallucinations and how they can occur during times of stress and bereavement.

She shuts her eyes for a moment and thinks back to Ashwood Forest, and the woman driving the silver Mercedes with her son in the back. She pictures the fear and upset on the little boy's face as she bashed and yelled against the car windows, and remembers how certain she was that the little boy was Ryan.

You need help! the internal voice snarls.

"No, I know what I saw!" Carolyn says aloud.

"Carolyn?" Jeanette says, knocking on the door and stepping inside with two mugs of tea in her hand and a fresh pair of pyjamas under her arm. "Who were you speaking to?"

Carolyn doesn't answer. She just shakes her head.

"Change out of them dirty clothes will you, love? They're full of mud. And get this down you too, you'll catch a cold. You must have been freezing standing out there!" Jeanette puts the mugs of tea down on the bedside table before taking a seat at the foot of the bed. "I know what you're going through must be hard. I've never lost a child myself, so I won't say I know how you feel, because I don't, but—"

"Mum, I know what I saw. Something is going on around here."

Jeanette reaches for her cup and slurps her tea. "You've just lost your little boy, Carolyn." She begins stroking Carolyn's knee with her free hand. "That must be hard enough, never mind losing your husband too."

Carolyn picks her own tea up and holds it in two hands, enjoying the warmth of the mug on her fingers. She opens her mouth to speak, but Jeanette carries on.

"I know you've lost a son and a husband, but I've lost a grandson and a son-in-law. It's hard for us both. Please let me know next time before running off. I was worried sick. I didn't know what to think."

"I'm sorry. I think it's the pills taking their toll on me." Carolyn forces a laugh.

"I understand. Why not come over the church tomorrow? Get stuck in with some chores and take your mind off things."

"We'll see, Mum."

"Ok. It'll do you good though. Concentrate on something else for a change."

"Have you heard of Silvis Primary?" Carolyn asks.

"Silvis? Yeah, sure. It's a small primary school over on Black Lane. Why?"

"The uniform, do they have green jumpers with a crest on the chest?"

"Well, yeah. Why?"

Carolyn nods, she finishes the last of her tea and hands the empty mug over before picking up the new pyjamas. "I just want to go to bed. I'm shattered."

Her mother says goodnight and leaves her to change.

In bed, she thinks of Simon and Ryan, wishing she could be with them, wishing that she too had been in the car that day. She puts what she had seen earlier down to the drugs, or possibly a simple case of an over-active imagination. The stress of losing her family has taken its toll on her mind.

The green school jumper and logo is an easy explanation – on their way through town earlier she must have seen a child wearing it, and the logo with the S had managed to creep up in her mind. She will forget about it, and try to apologise to the police and the firefighters.

Guilt is resting in her stomach. She knows what the cost would be if there had been a fire or a police matter somewhere else, and they were busy dealing with the woman who'd cried wolf.

Chapter Seven

That was close, too close, the man thinks. He steps from his car and looks around. It's quiet, of course. He opens the boot of his car and pulls out the body wrapped in bin bags.

The stench is sickening. He'll have to leave the windows open for a week just to air it out. Climbing down that well earlier was one of the hardest things he's ever had to do. He'd almost vomited twice.

The man doesn't know why Carolyn hadn't simply called the police, instead of racing down there herself. But he's grateful. If she had called, the situation would have played out very differently for him.

He places the body gently on the ground, not that the boy would feel anything. It's a sign of respect… or that's what he believes. The man reaches for a spade and begins digging, using a small torch to guide him. He'll dig for a couple of minutes, then check his progress before switching the torch off again. He can't risk using the car's headlights, not out here at this time in the morning.

He digs and digs until he's standing in a hole three feet deep. He looks at his watch. 3 am.

"That'll do," he says, breathlessly.

He pats the last of the soil onto the grave and steps back, wiping his sweat-soaked forehead on the sleeve of his shirt. He places the spade back into the foul-smelling boot and rests against the car for a moment to catch his breath before heading home.

***

Carolyn tosses and turns. She's already missing Ryan's bed. She's missing his army of teddies that usually surrounds her. Restlessly, she's dreaming of being in the passenger seat of Simon's car again, and, as before, her family vanishes and the car veers into the concrete slabs of the motorway's hard shoulder. She wakes. Her hair is stringy across her sweaty face, and the collar of her pyjama top is damp. She wipes at her face before pushing herself upright and turning over the pillow to feel the benefit of the cold side. Reaching for her phone, she presses the *Home* button. The brightness of the screen burns her eyes. 3:11 am.

The image of the young corpse she had seen a few hours earlier returns.

The pictures flash in a cycle through her mind. Grass, yellow flowers, well, decaying body.

Resting against the headboard, she can hear the quiet rumble of her mother's snores through the wall. She draws in a deep breath, hoping the images will recoil to the back of her mind.

She asks herself again: *Is it possible I imagined the corpse? Did I sleepwalk to the well and hallucinate the body?*

In the three months since Simon and Ryan's death, she hasn't once hallucinated. Nightmares, sure, but no hallucinations. Especially so vivid. And if it wasn't her imagination, what the hell is going on? Who would leave a corpse down a well for somebody to find, then remove it again like some sick prank?

Carolyn closes her eyes tight and shakes her head. She feels like screaming to make the images disappear, but she can't. It would give Jeanette a heart attack. She's already caused enough trouble with the police, and she hasn't even been in Llanbedr for twenty-four hours.

The room is lit only by the light in the hallway, shining round the edge of the door. She can make out an old desk at the bottom of the bed. It has an old television on top, plus a DVD player, bin bags full of old clothes, and a couple of spare pillows. The clutter on the cabinet has taken a new

45

shape. Carolyn's psyche has manipulated the items into something else, something much less innocent. When Carolyn looks to the end of her bed now, all she can see is the silhouette of a monster sitting and waiting patiently for her to fall back asleep so it can devour her soul and chew on her flesh.

She turns her attention away from the monster and towards the window above the bed, moving one of the curtains aside. Peeping through the window, she watches as the bushes and flowers blow from side to side. The remaining fence panels move in and out as if breathing with lungs of their own. She concentrates on the large gap at the bottom of the garden, the black nothingness.

She watches it carefully, waiting as if at any moment a face will appear from the darkness and meet her gaze. The face will have an evil look and a sly grin, the type that a deranged killer might have. The killer would probably be in partnership with the binbag monster at the bottom of her bed.

She chuckles at the ridiculous thought and watches the dark gap for another moment before dropping the curtain back into place and slouching down onto the cool pillow, grabbing her phone from the bedside table. She presses the *Home* button, and the screen lights up the room. Her heart pangs as she admires the faces of Simon and Ryan, which are acting as her wallpaper. After a few seconds, the screen darkens, and then the room falls back into blackness. She presses the button again and repeats this for the next few minutes, before falling back asleep with the phone in her hand.

Chapter Eight

Carolyn wakes, her head pulsing with a migraine. The house is in complete silence. There's no mumble of game show chatter coming from the TV in the front room, and no noise from Jeanette doing housework. The bedroom door is ajar, probably from when her mum checked in on her earlier.

In the kitchen, a note is resting against the toaster.

Gone to pick up the car from town. Stay in and relax.
Won't be too long.
Love Mum x

Pouring herself a glass of water, Carolyn reaches for the tub of pills. They were still where Inspector Richard Williams had left them last night. Last night's events are fuzzy, apart from the judgemental eyes of the rescue party all looking at her for an explanation. The feeling of guilt returns, causing Carolyn to feel once again like a crazy woman; a crazy woman who turns up at a police station dressed in pyjamas and her mother's slippers and wastes everybody's time.

She unscrews the cap and tips two pills out into the palm of her hand. She stands there examining the red and blue casing, remembering the disturbing image of the young boy's face.

"Nope, not today," she says, throwing the pills (along with the tub) into the bin. She forces them down deeper, hiding them out of her mother's sight, under the old television magazine. If the pills have something to do with what she saw last night, then it would be best to stop taking them immediately, even if this goes against her GP's wishes.

Carolyn dresses and looks out of the window. Her mother's car is back, parked on the driveway. Father Joseph's white Volvo is at the church. She guesses her mother will be too.

She heads over.

Jeanette is kneeling next to one of the pew benches with a piece of sandpaper. She looks up and notices Carolyn standing in the doorway. She stands, resting her hands on top of her knees and grunts as she straightens, beckoning Carolyn over.

"Come to give us a hand?" Jeanette's voice echoes off the walls around the quiet building.

Carolyn looks around. "Where's Father Joseph?"

Jeanette doesn't have time to answer. Father Joseph speaks up as he gets to his feet from being crouched behind the first row of pews, and he begins walking over towards them. The heels of his shoes clunk against the hard wooden floor.

"Ah, Carolyn. I'm glad to see you up. You look better today," he says, stepping to the side of her mother.

He means that you're dressed and not crying for help, the internal voice tells her.

"Thank you," Carolyn replies, turning back to Jeanette. "Mum, can I borrow the car?"

Her mother looks down. There's an uneasy look on her face as she reaches for her bag.

"What's up?" Carolyn asks her.

Jeanette shakes her head and sighs. "I'd rather you just stay home. Why not put the telly on and watch a film? Or… or you could help out here? These benches need sanding and varnishing."

Carolyn feels the eyes of Father Joseph burn into the side of her face. She knows they've been discussing her. Discussing her loss, her unstable mind, her crazy imagination.

Carolyn convinces herself that Father Joseph has already made his mind up about her. She's the troublemaker, the sinner in this quiet town. Carolyn and Father Joseph have never been properly introduced. Whenever she, Simon and Ryan would visit, they never really had time to meet. Now they have, and his first impressions of Carolyn aren't looking too good.

Carolyn turns to face him before the holes in the side of her cheeks burn any deeper. He snaps his glare away. His beady eyes now look towards the door, and he heads back in the direction he came from, clunking on the floor as he goes.

"What's wrong, Mum?" Carolyn asks, feeling slightly annoyed and belittled.

Jeanette searches around the bottom of her handbag and pulls out the car keys with three colourful keyrings attached. "Father Joseph and I were talking this morning. He ran me into town to pick up my car, you see. You'll have to thank him, Carolyn."

"Why don't you want me to borrow your car?" Carolyn asks, raising her voice, not caring if Father Joseph is listening. He's probably watching from over his shoulder and reading her lips as she speaks.

"It's not that I *don't* want you to borrow the car. In town this morning I was getting milk and a few other bits. People were looking at me, some even ignored me completely." Jeanette pauses for a moment and looks down at the keys, visibly embarrassed. "This is a tight community." She leans against the bench. "News travels fast around here, you see. I like it here, and I don't want you to cause trouble with people. I want them to like you as they do me," she says with a pitiful face.

Carolyn nods, understanding her mother's point. Jeanette has made a life for herself here, and with the people of Llanbedr. Even if she herself doesn't like the place, her mother does. She wouldn't want to destroy the friendships she has made. Carolyn takes the keys and heads for the door. "I won't be causing any trouble. I just need a few bits. I'll pick something up for dinner too."

Out on the main road the radio is muted, giving her mind time to think. *Maybe Inspector Williams was right,* she tells herself. *Maybe I was exhausted and tired. I have been for weeks, ever since the accident.* Her mind wanders off and she begins to think about Simon and Ryan. Slowly she begins to

49

feel less angry and frustrated about last night. She forgets everyone's faces – the angry faces around the well, shaking their heads and tutting at one another.

"I made a mistake. Those tablets don't help either," Carolyn says as she takes the bend. She is so busy persuading herself that it was the side-effects of the tablets, she doesn't notice the horrific smell coming from the Kings' pig farm.

On the straight three-mile road leading into town, she examines herself in the rear-view mirror. The heavy bags under her eyes have grown deeper these past few weeks. Her skin colour, once a smooth and healthy glow, is now blotchy and pale, not to mention the weight she's lost. She decides to let go of the last few weeks. She will begin by sitting out in the sun for a few hours a day, whenever the unpredictable October weather allows it. She might even dye her hair and hide the roots, take it back to the shiny brunette she once was.

Carolyn comes to a stop at the lights on Baltimore Street before taking the left into Duke Street, and arrives at Llanbedr Convenience. She parks in the bay outside the shop and enters through the automatic doors, passing a group of lads in their late teens. They look at her in a strange way. She is the outsider.

Llanbedr Convenience is the only place in the town where you can get everything under the one roof, and today it's packed with shoppers. Carolyn enters the first aisle, pushing her trolley, and ignoring the faces she'd seen standing outside The Red Fox last night. Two young college girls are smirking and chuckling. They're probably laughing at a funny cat video on YouTube, but today Carolyn's mind tells her they're laughing at her. She keeps her eyes on the shelves, searching for what she came for. Perhaps she'll make cottage pie tonight. She briefly lifts her head to make eye contact with people walking past, and they murmur under their breaths.

"News does travel fast around here!" she says to the facewipes in her hand. Down the cosmetics aisle she finds the hair dye, and places it in the trolley before moving on. She comes to an abrupt stop as her trolley crashes into that of another shopper. A scruffy-looking man is now standing in front of her. He's wearing oily overalls and a thick mid-brown sheepskin jacket. His head is shaved, and he has a thick greying moustache with oil stains on his cheeks. Carolyn presumes he is around fifty-five to sixty years of age. His blue eyes are peering into hers with undisguised hatred. Carolyn remembers his face; he's another one of the bystanders from outside The Red Fox last night. The woman standing next to him is smaller, though she's roughly the same age. The woman's dyed blonde hair is thinning, exposing parts of her scalp and showing her roots. It reaches down to the shoulders of her long black leather coat.

Long cracks run up the arms of the leather, proving it to be well-worn. Underneath, she's wearing a white vest top exposing her belly, a short denim skirt which exposes her pasty bruised thighs, and black knee-high scuffed boots. Mascara is embedded in the deep cracks of her cheeks, and fresh tears are rolling off her chin. Inappropriate clothing for a woman of her age, Carolyn thinks. She also thinks that she looks like a woman desperately trying to hang on to her youth – and failing terribly.

The people around Carolyn turn into a blur. They stop to look on and watch. She hears them chatter to one another.

"That's the one who said she saw a body…" she hears.

The man in the dark overalls leans in closer. Carolyn can smell the stale scent of beer and cigarettes on his breath as he speaks.

"Are you the bitch that has been making lies up, saying you've seen the body of a young boy?"

Carolyn looks from him to his crying partner.

"I…" A rush of fear hits her. "… I haven't made any lies up. I don't know who you are or why you're asking me." Her voice is wavy and cautious.

The crying woman speaks out, but her voice is unclear, and the cries take over. Carolyn can't make out what she's saying, and the confusion must have shown in her face because the man repeats what she has said.

"She said you don't even live around here. Why are you

51

dragging up the past and creating lies?" The man stiffens his eyebrows and steps even closer.

"Now hold on, Frank!" says a whiny, high-pitched voice from behind Carolyn. The manager of the store is at his side. He's skinny, and possibly just hitting five foot six. He looks tiny next to Frank. Carolyn's face begins to feel hot and flustered.

"Don't be causing any trouble in here. If you have a problem with this woman, take it up with Chief Inspector Williams!" the store manager continues.

"Was he wearing a green padded coat?" The crying woman is wiping her face with a tissue. She's managed to calm herself enough to ask clearly. The two men stop talking and stare at Carolyn, waiting for her to answer, along with the rest of the shoppers that are standing by.

Carolyn's throat feels dry. If she's being honest, she really isn't sure what she'd seen. The image in her mind is dark. She'd spent most of last night, and the drive into town this morning, convincing herself it was all her imagination, or that it was the Mirtazapine tampering with her mind and creating things that weren't there. Now she's uncertain if she even saw a body at all – or even the well, for that matter. She might have been sleepwalking. *That sounds more of a plausible scenario*, she thinks.

The internal voice is now shouting at her. *Answer their questions, Carolyn. They're waiting.*

"I... I... really don't know. It was very dark. I'm not sure if I..." She tails off, looking from one shopper's face to the next. They're all standing around in a circle watching, as if witnessing a witch's final moment at the stake, waiting for the confession.

She braces herself, expecting that at any minute they'll start throwing rotting vegetables and spitting at her. The woman wiping at her face with the tissue begins to sob again. "Did you see his hair? Did he have blond hair?" she asks.

Again, Carolyn can't answer. Her throat won't allow her to speak. The image of the body is now non-existent in her memory.

"DID YOU SEE ANYTHING AT ALL?" the woman shouts.

At this point, the man in the overalls has abandoned his trolley and begins walking the woman out of the shop with his arm around her shoulders. The nosey shoppers stand aside, creating an exit, and the man and woman leave. Some of the customers are covering their open mouths. Carolyn turns her trolley around and heads for the till, ignoring the quiet remarks of the shoppers. She lifts two tins of soup into her trolley as she passes. *That's dinner sorted.*

The cashier is a redheaded girl, skinny and shy-looking.

"Be careful with them. Don't get yourself caught up with him," the cashier mumbles under her breath while scanning the items.

"Excuse me?" Carolyn says.

The girl looks around to be certain nobody is within earshot. "I said, don't get yourself caught up with him. He wouldn't think twice about beating you to a pulp. I've seen his wife in a few bad states in the past. He's... He's a very nasty man..."

Carolyn begins packing her bag. "What's their name?" she asks.

Again the skinny cashier turns and checks she can't be heard. She waits for an elderly woman to pass.

"That's the Lloyd family. Their son went missing a few years back."

Carolyn nods, looking down at the girl's name badge. "Thank you, Sophie." She pays for her things and leaves.

She unlocks her mother's car and places the shopping in the back, then heads to the driver's side and notices the long scratch in the paintwork which runs from the bonnet to the back door. She can only imagine how worried and annoyed her mother is going to be. A large pickup truck makes its way past behind her, the engine growling loudly under the bonnet. Its wheels slow down, almost coming to a stop.

Carolyn turns and sees the man with the greying moustache driving, his evil glare piercing her eyes. The crying woman in the passenger seat is wiping her face again.

The man driving keeps eye contact with Carolyn for an uncomfortable moment and takes off with a loud screech on the tarmac. She hurries into the car and starts the ignition. She wants to be gone from this car park and away from these people. She wants to be back in Leeds. She wants to be back with Simon and Ryan.

Carolyn backs out of the parking space and heads for home. She drives until she comes to a lay-by next to the old bed-and-breakfast, then stops. Her heart is thumping hard against her chest. She places her hands on the steering wheel, watching them shake and rattle uncontrollably. She has never been one for confrontation, and she isn't used to people looking at her with such hatred. She wipes at the tears running down her cheeks and restarts the engine.

Chapter Nine

Carolyn sits at Jeanette's kitchen table with a cup of tea, made with fresh milk. The one her mother had made last night was made with powdered milk, and it had tasted like warm cardboard.

Her hands have eased shaking enough for her to hold the mug in one hand and her worn stress ball in the other. She's wondering if it was Inspector Williams who'd told the first couple of people. Maybe it was the smokers outside The Red Fox last night, waiting for the police to return and find out the gossip. Or perhaps it was PC Riley. He'd given her a look of disapproval the moment she'd stepped through the doors of the station. She shakes her head with disbelief.

"Whatever happened to police confidentiality?" she grunts.

I must be crazy, she thinks, and drinks the last of her tea. She stands up, drops her stress ball onto the table and heads out to the back. She decides to check out the well again, to put her mind at rest and come up with a reason good enough to explain the hallucinations. It was almost dark, after all. There must have been a tree branch positioned a certain way for her to overreact and imagine the corpse. As far-fetched as that sounds, Carolyn needs something to justify what made her see a body. If she can't find anything, then maybe she really is crazy.

She heads through the gap in the fence and walks in the direction of the well, then stops, turns to her right and walks along the bushes at the back of her mother's bungalow. There must be another opening to this part of the woodland.

Carolyn heads straight on, keeping to the side of the bushes. After a five-minute walk, she comes to an opening between the trees. She pushes bare branches from her face and stamps down nettles to fit through the gap. Once out into the opening she can see a metal swing-gate with a rusted padlock. She climbs over it and steps out onto the concrete of a small road. It's cracked and filled with potholes and overgrown with weeds. It's also a dead end.

Some time ago it must have been an entrance into the woodland via the metal swing gate, but now people use it to dump their rubbish: old plastic Christmas trees and scattered bags of garden waste. Carolyn heads out onto the main road, then onto Alexandra Drive. The roof of St Peter's church can be seen not too far away. She wonders if this is the route taken by the person who'd dumped the body.

Carolyn heads back to the start, to the path just outside the gap in the fence, and begins walking in the direction she had previously taken. Standing a few yards away from the opening of the well, she braces herself for the gruesome, stomach-wrenching corpse her brain will imagine.

The sensation of anxiety is back, and her breathing increases.

"Come on," she says out loud. "This is silly. Get a grip."

She peers down. The well is empty, of course, just as it had been when Inspector Williams, the other two officers and the angry-looking firefighters had been here.

The feeling of relief strikes her, and she exhales, tears filling her eyes.

It must have been those damned tablets, she thinks.

Carolyn walks the circle around the well, admiring the beauty of this Disney-like place. She imagines herself and Jeanette bringing along some camping chairs and forgetting all about the hallucinated boy in the well.

Then, at the back of the well, she comes to a stop. She kneels down on the grass, examining the red brick that had caught her eye, and picks up her find. It's a melted lump of purple candle wax.

Her beautiful scenery is starting to chip away again. Very slowly, but it's happening, and she can feel it.

Surely there is an explanation for this. She looks up at the sky and waits for the clouds to turn an angry grey colour and for lightning forks to strike across, just like it does in the Disney world when evil is approaching.

Of course, it doesn't change.

Why would candle wax be next to a disused well in the middle of nowhere? Who would bring a candle out here? She tries, but fails, to think of a good enough reason. The only assumption she can think of is that somebody knew about the well. Somebody even cared enough to visit, enough to light a candle in the boy's honour. The idea of her being a crazy woman begins to drift away. On one hand she's happy; on the other, it means there really is a deranged killer out there, toying with her.

Maybe the deranged killer was on his or her way back to the well, Carolyn thinks. *To visit their kill, bringing with them a new candle to light, to sit and relive their horrific crime. Then I found their dumping ground and messed the whole thing up, and now they're not happy about that.*

The sensation of being watched hits her, and her arms and back begin to shiver. She hugs herself as she spins around to check there isn't anybody out there now watching from behind a tree, maybe even laughing at how silly she must look to the people of Llanbedr. Maybe the killer was even at Llanbedr Convenience earlier, amongst the crowd of bystanders and watching her lose her head. She steps to the side of the well, the spot where she puked the night before, now washed away by the rain. She looks down the well again, searching for anything she and the rest of the rescue party might have missed.

It was raining and dark then, after all.

She steps to the right, circling the well again. She feels the corners of her mouth rise. There, on the brick inside the well, are white scrape marks, presumably made by a ladder.

How did they miss this?

I'm not crazy. Once I show Inspector Williams this new evidence, he'll have to take DNA samples, return with a team of forensics, and climb down the well. The tests will show there was a corpse down there, a corpse of a young boy.

57

They'll find fingerprints from the bricks inside, and then PC Riley on reception will apologise for ever doubting me.

She races to the kitchen and searches through a drawer for a sandwich bag to place the lump of candle wax in – her newfound evidence – to take to the police.

Out in the car, she backs down the path. The sandwich bag with the candle wax sits on the passenger seat. She slips the car in gear and is about to take off when she hears her mother calling from outside the church.

"Where are you going now?" Jeanette asks, heading over. Carolyn winds the window down and beckons with her head. "Get in. I'll explain on the way."

Jeanette climbs in the passenger seat, moving the wax to the side, and fastens her seatbelt. "What the hell is going on?" she asks. "And why do you have… Is that wax?"

"It's evidence, Mum. I found it at the well. I'm taking it to Richard Williams. He needs to come back with a team of forensics and inspect the inside of the well."

"Carolyn… love, pull over and let's go back, shall we?" she insists, her face sympathetic, with questioning eyes. It is the same look Carolyn received last night from Williams, Hughes, Dixon and some of the firefighters.

Carolyn feels herself getting annoyed. "I know what I saw. At first, I thought it might have been the tablets. But it was too real, too vivid. There's no way I could have imagined something that gruesome." She takes a left turn, keeping the car at thirty now she isn't alone. "And then I find candle wax and markings inside the well."

Jeanette's face turns pale, and her eyes show confusion. "What type of markings?"

Carolyn goes on. "Something is going on. Do you know if there's a boy missing?"

Jeanette nods. "There are two boys missing. Elwyn Roberts was seven years old and Dylan Lloyd was fifteen."

"Lloyd… That's the parents I met today. They were asking me questions about their boy."

"You spoke with the Lloyds?"

"Well, it wasn't a planned visit. We sort of… bumped into

each other at Llanbedr Convenience. They don't seem like very nice people," Carolyn adds. She can sense Jeanette is thinking of something.

"That's because they are not very nice people. When their boy went missing, word got back to Frank Lloyd, the dad, about a man… What's his name now…? Juan? No… JULIO! That's it. Anyway, word got back to Frank that Julio has served time and is on the Sex Offenders' Register for being involved with kids. Police found him beaten to within an inch of his life. He never confessed it was Frank Lloyd. But we all knew." Jeanette looks at Carolyn. "Please don't stir anything up. It won't end well."

Carolyn ignores Jeanette and pulls into the police station car park.

***

PC Riley is on a call. He watches Carolyn come through the door, with Jeanette following behind. Rolling his eyes, he holds up his index finger indicating that they should wait. The glare he gives them is unkind, as if they've just trodden in a trail of dog mess under their boots. He ends the call and takes a long noisy slurp of his coffee, studying Carolyn and Jeanette over his mug. They look at each other and think the same thing: *Arsehole.*

Richard Williams comes out of a room behind the reception counter, accompanied by a man in a suit. They shake hands and Williams waves him off before acknowledging Carolyn and Jeanette.

"What is it today, Mrs Hill? We're very busy," he says, pulling at his tie to loosen it from his thick neck.

Carolyn steps closer to the desk. "I went back to the well earlier. You need to take another look. There's scraping on the inside brickwork." She lifts the sandwich bag from her pocket. "I also found this, at the side of the well."

Williams takes the lump of wax from her and inspects it. "Wax, so what? You want me to waste useful resources and valuable time because you've found a lump of wax?" He looks from Carolyn to Jeanette before going on. "I would have thought you would have spoken to her, Jeanette, instead of allowing your daughter to make a fool of herself again! I gave you the benefit of the doubt the other night."

Jeanette places a hand on Carolyn's shoulder. "Come on. Let's go home. He can't do anything."

Carolyn shakes her hand away, filled with anger that this man can't be bothered and isn't interested in looking into this any further, when it could potentially be a lead to one of the missing boys.

"It's not that he can't do anything, Mum. It's that he doesn't want to," she says scornfully as she brings her hands down, slapping the desk.

Williams' complexion turns an angry red. "I won't, because I can't, Mrs Hill. There is no body, nothing for me to go on or even look into."

Riley slurps his coffee again, loudly and with a smirk on his face, clearly enjoying the drama unfolding in front of him.

"Let's go home," Jeanette beckons, holding onto Carolyn's arm. Williams hands back the bag of wax, and Carolyn and Jeanette head for the door.

Carolyn turns before leaving. "Inspector, will you at least speak with that Julio person, and see his reaction? He might have something to do with this."

Williams stares at her, beads of sweat appearing on his forehead and dripping down above his eyebrows.

"Julio Alcala is the probation officer's concern, Mrs Hill, not yours or your mother's. Now how about you go home, stop interfering and let us get on with our police work? Oh, and if we need a cake baking, we'll give you a call."

Riley chokes on his coffee and almost spits it out over the reception desk. He wipes at his stubbly chin and looks up.

I bet that's going to be the joke around the station for the week, Carolyn. The internal voice tells her. She walks out to the car, making a mental note of Julio's surname. She figures there's no point in trying any more. The police have already made their mind up about her; she's the crazy woman who thinks she can lecture the police on how to do their jobs.

Jeanette is driving them both home, and with good reason; Carolyn's hands are trembling with frustration.

"How can he just push us away like that?" Carolyn says.

"Well, there isn't a bod—"

"And I've brought him evidence." She throws the bag of wax into the footwell. "If they just looked into it, and came to see the scrapings on the inside of the well... Surely that's enough evidence to run some sort of DNA test?"

"Carolyn, Richard did say that—"

"He's too lazy, Mum. Too lazy to even look into it and put my mind at rest. I'm not crazy. I know what I saw. You believe me, don't you?"

Jeanette is quiet for a moment and then releases a sigh.

"Doesn't matter. I know what I saw." Carolyn opens the glove compartment and rummages through, pushing an A-Z, takeaway menus and out-of-date shopping vouchers out of the way. She finds a small notepad and pen and tears out the last shopping list, crumples it and drops it into the footwell. At the top she writes *Julio Alcala* and then turns back to Jeanette. "What were the names of the two missing boys again?" Jeanette tells her as she slows to give a tractor space. Carolyn writes the names down. *Elwyn Roberts and Dylan Lloyd.*

"Why?" Jeanette asks, watching her. "Why are you writing them down? Can't you just forget about it? You're going to get yourself into trouble."

"I'm sorry, but would you want somebody to forget about it if it were Ryan missing?" Carolyn doesn't give her mother time to answer. "No, I'm too emotionally involved now. I saw something I wasn't supposed to see, and if the police can't help me... I'm going to do what I can to make things right."

Jeanette is silent for the rest of the journey home.

Chapter Ten

Carolyn had hardly slept last night. The smirking faces of the officers played on her mind throughout for hours. A few times she'd felt the urge to open her phone and search for the names of the two missing boys, but she knew that once she started a search she'd be up all night, reading article after article on various online news websites.

No, she'd decided to leave it until today. But she needs a place with a printer. The closest library is in St Davids, so the internet café in town will have to do. Carolyn had been surprised that internet cafés still exist, and had first thought the address she'd found on the web must be out of date. That was until she turned up and saw it with her own eyes.

From outside, the grimy-looking windows make the place look closed or under refurbishment. The crinkled blinds are also shut, though this seems a pointless attempt to close out the light, given the amount of slats that are missing.

Carolyn approaches the door and peers through the glass. She sees a small room with at least six elderly-looking computers positioned around the wall.

There is movement to her right. It is a young man wearing a beanie hat pulled down to just above his eyebrows. Thick strands of greasy hair dangle from the front of his hat and reach his spotty cheeks. He's jumping up and down in his chair with excitement at his computer screen. Carolyn can hear him mumbling into a headset as she pushes the door open. A little chime rings out above her.

The smell of chip fat, sweat, crisps and marijuana stings her nostrils, and Carolyn has to fight the urge not to cover her nose. Her first thought of the place is that it's being used as a cover for the marijuana that they probably store in the basement. The man pauses his game and removes his headset. He stands and straightens his stained t-shirt before brushing the crumbs off his lap in a bid to show some professionalism.

"Welcome to Ray's Internet Café. How can I help you?"

Carolyn wonders how many times he says that line in a week, or a month, or even a year.

"Are you Ray?" Carolyn asks.

The gamer shakes his head and points to his chest to indicate his name badge. When he doesn't feel it, he begins searching around his cluttered desk, which is filled with empty pop cans and sweet wrappers. He eventually unearths the badge and pins it back in place.

"No, I'm Terry, the café manager," he says proudly.

Carolyn explains she'd like to use a computer. At Terry's request she opens an account, then sits down at the computer at the back of the room and takes out the notepad from her bag. The outdated machine comes to life making a whirring noise and eventually prompts her for the login details.

She gives the dusty screen a wipe with her sleeve and logs in.

Waiting for the computer to register her username, Carolyn looks around. The carpet feels sticky under her shoes. The tables the computers sit on are also grimy and stained with circles from mugs. The wallpaper has started curling at the corners, as though trying to free itself from the walls and escape this joyless place.

The computer screen flashes and a search engine appears. She types in the name *Julio Alcala* and waits for the results. It appears Julio Alcala shares the name with a famous movie stuntman who was known for his daring motorbike stunts. She types in *Julio Alcala, Llanbedr*. There's a small article dated some six years ago, stating that a forty-six-year-old man had been arrested by police after they randomly searched his house and found child pornography in his possession. He was also linked to numerous other investigations about a man exposing himself to children in a nearby park. There's no picture of Julio, and no address for

63

Carolyn to write down.

She clears the search and types in *Dylan Lloyd, Llanbedr*. A result appears at the top of the screen. She clicks the link and is directed to *The Llanbedr Times* online paper. The story appears underneath a thumbnail picture. She clicks the thumbnail, and it expands across the screen. When the pixels clear up, the image shows a smiling boy with someone's arm slung across his shoulders. The person next to him has been cropped out. She hits the *PRINT* button, and a loud grinding noise comes from the desk next to Terry. He looks up from his screen and tuts, before returning to hitting the keyboard in an attempt to save the world from flesh-eating zombies.

The article is dated a couple days after Dylan was last seen, on 23rd February 2016.

THE TOWN OF LLANBEDR IN SEARCH FOR MISSING TEEN.

Search parties worked throughout the night in search of the missing teen, Dylan Lloyd. The fifteen-year-old was reported missing by his mother, Gwen Lloyd. Dylan Lloyd is the second boy to have gone missing since 2011, when Elwyn Roberts disappeared.

The search for Elwyn Roberts is still ongoing with no new reports. The Lloyd family have spoken to friends of Dylan but they have so far had no positive leads. The father, Mr Frank Lloyd, told The Llanbedr Times that his son is a happy child with a good home life and that there is no reason for him to run away or want to leave. Anyone with any information should contact the police.

Carolyn opens a new tab on the internet page and types in *Gwen Lloyd*. The results come back with a few Facebook profiles, but none were of the woman she met the other day. Next, she searches for *Frank Lloyd, Llanbedr*. A search box loads with the results: *Frank Lloyd, cheap and reliable mechanic. Green Farm Lane*. Carolyn scribbles down the address and goes back to the website for *The Llanbedr Times*.

In the search bar at the top of the page, she types in *Elwyn Roberts*.

As before, the page loads, and shows a small thumbnail picture above the headline with the date of the article: 6th October 2011. She clicks it, and it expands. Once the picture is fully loaded and becomes clear on the screen, Carolyn gasps.

It is the face of the boy in the well.

Chapter Eleven

If it wasn't for the strong back of the computer chair, she would have fallen backwards onto the sticky carpet. Terry doesn't look over this time. He's too engrossed in his game.

Confusion sweeps across her, boggling her mind. The corpse she had seen in the well looked as though it had been dead for no longer than a week, possibly even just three to four days. How does that make sense?

She searches online for any other reports containing missing children in or around the Llanbedr area. None since 1968: a young girl whose body was found in the river. Her foot had become snagged on a weed and she'd drowned. *A freak accident*, the online search states.

How could the boy in the well be Elwyn Roberts? He's been missing for eight years.

The gamer at the front desk shouts at his screen again, which looks to have explosives going off and debris flying around. It snaps Carolyn out of her confused daydream. She clicks on the picture and selects *PRINT.* As the printer screams into life, she reads the article on the screen.

CHILD VANISHES PLAYING IN STREET

Heather and Kelvin Roberts, the parents of missing eight-year-old Elwyn Roberts, reported their son missing yesterday afternoon. Elwyn was playing out at the front of his home on Jarrett Lane.

Mrs Roberts told our reporter at The Llanbedr Times that the young boy was kicking his ball as she was inside doing housework. "Our house on Jarrett Lane never gets any visitors or cars. Even the main road outside is quiet the

majority of the time," Mrs Roberts said. Elwyn Roberts'
father, Mr Kelvin Roberts, works at Sleepy Nights mattress
factory.

The parents of the missing boy are offering an £8,000
reward for anybody who comes forward with information that
leads to the finding of their son. Anyone with any other
information should contact the police.

Carolyn makes a note of the address for the Roberts family
and signs out of the computer. Looking forward to leaving
the shop and using some hand sanitizer, she heads over to the
front desk. Terry has got the pictures she printed.

"That'll be sixty pence for the prints," he orders. Carolyn
reaches for a pound in her purse.

"What do you want pictures of dead kids for?" he snorts,
moving a strand of greasy hair away from his eyes.

"How do you know they're dead?" she asks.

Terry shrugs. "How often do missing kids show up?"

Carolyn feels the urge to slap the ignorance out of him.
She thinks quickly.

"I am... I am a Private Detective. I've been asked to look
into it by the family."

"Oh... right," he sneers. "A Private Detective, wow."

"What do you know about a Julio Alcala?" she asks,
folding and sliding the pictures into her bag.

"What do you want to know?" he says, taking a seat back
at his computer and feeding his mouth with crisps.

"Do you know where he lives? Or where I can find him?"

"I know exactly where he lives," Terry replies.

"Great," Carolyn says, waiting for him to continue. He
doesn't. "Want to share it?" she asks.

"Information isn't free, Miss Private Detective," Terry
says, chomping on the crisp in his mouth. He looks at her,
pushing the thick greasy hair from his eyes again, and
smacks his lips. He types at his computer keyboard quickly
and hits *PRINT*. He reaches for the printed page and walks
towards Carolyn.

"That'll be a tenner," he says, holding the paper close to

his chest and smudging cheesy crisp stains on to the back of the printout.

"Ten quid? For information?"

Terry doesn't answer. He just stands there and stays quiet.

Carolyn reaches for her purse. "You found out his address from using the web that quickly? That's impressive." She keeps herself calm and fights the urge to not call him a thieving bastard. Her knowledge of computers is limited. She knows how to order stock and file invoices at home for Happy Bakes, but that's all. She hands over the tenner from her purse.

Terry laughs. "I got that information from passing his house every day on the bus into work. I Googled the bus route and found out the name of his road."

She shakes her head and snatches the printout from him.

Terry chuckles, shoving more crisps into his mouth. "Oh, and it's the house with a dick spray-painted on the front wall."

Chapter Twelve

The pictures of the two missing boys are laid out on the passenger seat of Jeanette's car, and the creases where they had been folded into Carolyn's bag are now roughly straightened out. Carolyn stares at each of the boys, studying their faces one after the other.

She's parked in the car park of a closed function hall, across the road from Julio's house.

The house hasn't been as easy to find as the greasy-haired Terry had claimed. Carolyn has already passed it a couple of times before turning around at the top and giving the road another scan. It's 5:30 pm, and the lack of sunlight makes it hard to see the spray-painted dick on the wall. Also it is faded into more of a purple cloud, from past attempts of getting rid of the graffiti. Words have been scrubbed away above the lewd artwork, making it hard to spell out. Carolyn thinks she can picture the words *Scum* and *Paedo*, but she can't be certain.

Julio's house looks scruffy. An old petrol scooter with a ripped leather seat is chained to the wall next to the front door. Though the owner needn't bother; the green bodywork is dinted and battered, and the handlebars are corroded with rust. Bin bags sit around and on top of the already-full wheelie bins, suggesting he's too lazy to pull them to the kerb to be taken away. Empty beer cans and food tins are scattered around the garden, half-hidden in the overgrown grass. The windows of the house are streaky and smudged, with a build-up of years of mucus from wet dog noses pressed against them. The small window next to the front door has been replaced with a plank of wood. The curtains are almost fully closed, blocking out the majority of daylight.

Carolyn spots a face in the upstairs window, poking

through the gap between the curtains. Its owner's eyes meet hers, but the face disappears before she is given a chance to see if it's male or female.

The front door swings open. A moment later, a man with bronzed European skin exits. He crosses the road, zipping up his hoodie as he approaches Carolyn's car. Her chest tightens and her jaw clenches. She reaches for the keys in the ignition, ready to turn the engine on and make a swift escape if he becomes aggressive. He stands next to the car window, evidently waiting for her to wind it down. Her brain is screaming at her to turn the key and to leave the car park, watch him disappear in the rear-view mirror and head back to her mother, where she'll be safe in the house, and take Jeanette's advice to forget all about this before she gets herself into serious trouble.

Instead, she breathes out and lowers the window a couple of inches. Julio stares at her for a moment in silence, clearly expecting her to speak. He's a short man with an athletic build, and a deep scar running across his left cheek. Carolyn wonders if Frank Lloyd was the one who gave it to him. As his brown eyes move to the passenger seat, Carolyn notices the change in his expression. Though it isn't the expression of a man who has recently moved the corpse of a boy pictured in one of the printouts, but more of a frustrated sigh.

"Why are you watching my house?" Julio asks.

A noisy white van pulls into the car park and a big man climbs out, the metal from the suspension creaking under his weight. He heads to the doors of the function hall and bangs loudly to be let in, watching the agitated Julio as he waits.

Carolyn opens her mouth to answer, but a huge lump in her throat stops her from speaking.

"You're a private detective, aren't you?" Julio asks.

She looks in the rear-view mirror and can see the midriff of the man at the doors behind her car. The sound of large steel bolts unlocking the doors of the function hall is heard, and the big man steps in after giving Carolyn another glance.

That prick charged me a tenner for information, then got straight on the phone to his friend Julio to warn him to look out for me, she thinks, silently furious. She opens her mouth again.

"I... Mr Alcala. I am—"

"Save it," he interrupts. "I know you've been hired by the family of one of those missing boys. They've hired many private detectives in the past, and they always approach me. I have nothing to do with their disappearances." Julio looks again at the pictures on the passenger seat, and then back to Carolyn. "I've been questioned, and I have my alibi. Now please, tell whoever hired you to leave me the fuck alone!" He turns and heads back across the road, holding out his hand to stop an approaching bus as he crosses into his garden. The bus driver gives him an angry look and shakes his head.

Carolyn rests back into her seat. The van is still parked to her left. She figures the owner will be out soon. Wiping her sweaty palms onto her jeans, she turns on the ignition and pulls out of the car park and heads down the road before pulling into a gap between parked vehicles. She folds the pictures back into her bag and imagines what DS Hughes would do next. For starters, she probably wouldn't have shown weakness, or been unable to find her words in front of Julio like that. And DS Hughes, unlike Carolyn, is built like a brick privy. She's twice the size of Julio. Carolyn imagines DS Hughes would probably speak with the parents of the two missing boys. But she's not DS Hughes; she's Carolyn Hill, a cake decorator from Leeds.

If you show you're not interfering, just trying to come to terms with what happened to the two boys, you shouldn't piss anybody else off, the internal voice convinces her. Today it seems to be helpful. She decides to not go into detail about what she had seen in the well. She will keep it formal and just show an interest in them, then the parents should be happy to speak with her. As she writes down the plan to visit the two families, she's disturbed by the hum of a scooter's engine. It is Julio's scooter.

Carolyn watches him ride away. Before processing her decision, she pulls out and begins to follow. Although there are now two cars between her and Julio, she still has a clear view of him.

They head out of the housing estate and into a more open space. The scooter doesn't go very quickly, so Carolyn stays back a fair bit, not to spook Julio, as now they are the only people on the road. The rest of the cars have either turned off onto other side roads or reached their destinations. The sky has quickly darkened, and Carolyn hesitates, turning on the main beams. She keeps the side lights on and stays a hundred yards behind. There aren't many roads Julio is able to take, so Carolyn concentrates on the hum of the scooters engine, sounding similar to a petrol lawnmower, only louder. They drive on for another fifteen minutes.

Carolyn toys with the idea of calling the police, to tell them she's got a bad feeling. But she realises how pathetic that would sound. She imagines the laughter at the other end of the phone. No, she will follow and observe, to see if there is anything that looks out of place. She could phone in and report it without giving her name.

The scooter finally takes a left turn into a small metal-fenced industrial site. There are six units, with banners pinned above four of them. The other two show *TO LET* signs. Holding back outside, she kills the engine and slouches down in her seat.

Julio takes off his helmet and hangs it from the bars. He walks over to the second unit in. The banner on the top reads *P's Party Accessories,* and like the other three occupied units, it seems to be closed for the day. Julio bangs on the shutters and they slowly open, but only enough for him to squat under and head through the door.

"What the hell are you doing?" Carolyn says. She wishes she had a set of binoculars and a handheld sound amplifier. She writes down the address of the party shop in case it has some significance, and also the time: 7:00 pm.

Until now, Carolyn hadn't noticed how long it had taken them to drive here. The thought of it being a trap to lure her here races through her mind.

Maybe he does know something about the body, but he doesn't have any emotions, or fear, to change his expression.

She grips the steering wheel a little tighter, her palms

beginning to sweat. She looks in all three mirrors, expecting to see a man crawl up alongside her car, pull her out and beat her to within an inch of her life.

Out here, nobody would be along for quite a while. That would give her plenty of time to bleed to death.

Carolyn reaches for the ignition and prepares to leave, but then the shutters open. Julio crouches underneath and heads for his scooter, placing something in the inside chest pocket of his coat. Carolyn can't see very clearly from the distance, but it looks like a small brown envelope. She reaches for her phone and begins to dial the police. Hesitating, she sighs and wonders what she could tell them. Instead, she locks the phone and watches as Julio starts the engine and takes off, passing her car without showing any interest in it. Carolyn decides not to follow. She assumes he's probably going home, and she has the address anyway.

A couple of minutes later, an overweight man exits, closing the shutters down to the ground and locking up. He walks slowly to a van with the party shop's logo printed on the side, and each step looks to be causing him a great deal of pain. Carolyn can see the sweat on his face glimmer from the orange street lights around the industrial site. He climbs into his van and drives out of the site, heading in the opposite direction from Julio.

Carolyn doesn't follow. This time of night on a quiet road like this will surely raise his suspicions. Could the body from the well be hidden inside that unit? There must be something shady going on, for the two men to meet at this time of night. But could they have anything to do with the two missing boys?

Carolyn watches as the low, red sidelights of the van move out of focus. It takes a turn up ahead and is hidden behind trees. She turns on the engine and pulls the car into the industrial site, parks where the van had been, and walks over to the front of the shop. The shutters are electric, and she knows she wouldn't be able to prise them open without the key. She'd already tried once with her own shop after the shutters malfunctioned. It wasn't worth the effort, or the dirty hands. She rests her face against the shutters and peers through the slits between the metal. It's pointless; the shop is in complete darkness. She'll have to come back during the day.

She heads round the back in search of another door, even though she knows it will be locked. There is just a fire exit, which has no external handle and is flush against the brickwork. She digs the tips of her fingers in the gaps, but nothing. She slams her hands against the door.

"SHIT!" she shouts. The condensation of her breath lingers in front of her face, reminding her of the foggy night, and immediately causing her to feel uncomfortable.

She heads back to the car and makes a note of tonight's events before heading home.

Chapter Thirteen

Carolyn starts the day late – or at least, later than she'd planned. She's made a note in her pad to revisit P's Party Accessories, though she feels it's best to leave it for a day, in case the owner spotted her car last night, or Julio had described her to him. So first on the list is the Roberts family, the boy who went missing in 2011. The address she got from *The Llanbedr Times* shows it to be just outside Llanbedr. The sat-nav says it is a twenty-two-minute drive.

Out on Alexandra Drive, Carolyn heads east. Father Joseph is out brushing the steps. He waves, and Carolyn waves back. Carolyn wonders what he must be thinking. *There goes crazy Carolyn. Off to cause more trouble,* she presumes. Passing the rusted gate surrounded by dumped rubbish, Carolyn can't help but look. She imagines the night the killer dumped the body; her mind immediately visualises the killer as a mountain of a person with a disfigured face. They'd be climbing from a van in the early hours of the morning, holding the lifeless body over one shoulder and carrying a torch to guide their way. Carolyn shudders and brings her attention back to the road.

During the drive, the radio is off, and she rehearses the questions she is about to ask, saying them out loud. She tries to ignore the thought of having the door slammed angrily in her face.

On her way through Llanbedr town centre, she stops at The Coffee Shack, an independent business. It isn't Costa Coffee or Starbucks like she's used to in Leeds, but coffee is coffee, and today she's in need of some. It's already 1:15 pm, and of the eight round tables in the coffee house, at least five are occupied. Her eyes fall on a man who is sitting alone near the front and eating a sandwich. He is watching her. He's huge, and his thick fingers are wrapped around a coffee mug as

75

though it's an espresso cup. Even sitting, Carolyn can tell he'd be at least 6'6, maybe 6'7, and strong-looking – not particularly muscular, but chubby and broad-shouldered, like a rugby player who holds his weight well. She remembers that he was the man who'd been knocking on the function hall door yesterday when she was speaking with the frustrated Julio Alcala.

The man is dressed in white overalls which are full of rips and splashes of paint. Carolyn orders her latte and turns to see if he is still staring, but the table is now empty, and the man is heading through the door. He's left half of his sandwich uneaten, and steam is still escaping his cup.

"Who's that man?" Carolyn asks the barista, pointing through the window towards him.

"I think his name's Barry. Usually comes in for lunch most days," he replies, before turning back to the attention of the coffee machine. Carolyn watches him climb into a battered white van. She thinks that it's same van that pulled up yesterday, though she'd hardly paid it much attention at the time. On it are the words:

B. Cookson.
Painter and Decorator, Llanbedr.

Carolyn pulls out her notepad and writes down the name before she forgets it. She feels awkward about the way the man left immediately, discarding his full mug of coffee and his half-eaten sandwich.

Carolyn thinks about sitting down and taking a seat by the window for half an hour, to watch the people of Llanbedr shopping and taking their lunch breaks. But she knows she would just be procrastinating, nervous to speak with the grieving families.

***

The Roberts' house is a semi-detached in a row of six, down a tight leafy country lane which faces acres of field.

You wouldn't know the homes existed if you didn't have the postcode.

Carolyn approaches the gate and pushes through it. A woman is kneeling beside a rose bush and turning a trowel through the soil. The garden is well cared for, and Carolyn wonders if this is the woman's way of dealing with the disappearance of her son, or whether she has always been an avid gardener.

Carolyn begins to imagine what she will do once she's back home, no longer under the watchful, caring eye of her mother. She has never been one for gardening herself. The grief counsellor had suggested she find herself a hobby, maybe knitting or crocheting, but anything, really, to occupy her mind for a few hours a day.

The woman turns and jolts at the sight of Carolyn.

"I'm sorry, Mrs Roberts?" Carolyn asks.

"Yes, I'm Heather Roberts," she responds, standing and brushing the dirt from her knees. Her Welsh accent is strong. "Who are you?"

Carolyn gives the woman her best trustworthy smile and walks up the path. "Hi, I was wondering if I could ask you a bit about Elwyn—"

The woman cuts her off and drops her trowel onto the grass. "Are you another journalist?"

A black man with a balding head and deep eye sockets appears in the doorway of the house. He's wearing a blue jumpsuit with a small logo across the chest. He stands and watches, waiting for Carolyn's answer.

She shakes her head. "No, I'm not a journalist. I'm here staying with my mother, Jeanette Stephenson. My son was killed in an… an accident, and I was just wandering if it's possible to ask you a few questions about the day Elwyn disappeared." She can't believe how quickly the words have left her mouth, or how open she has just been with a couple of complete strangers.

The man turns and heads back inside. Heather Roberts pulls off her gardening gloves, dropping them to the grass next to the trowel, and gestures Carolyn to follow her.

Inside the house, the Roberts offer her a cup of tea. Satisfied from her latte, but not wanting to sound ungrateful, Carolyn accepts, and is left alone in the front room as the pair of them head into the kitchen to make it. She hears them whispering, but the sound of the boiling kettle masks their conversation.

She passes the time by examining the wall, which is full of pictures of a young Elwyn. Each frame is the same: stylish, thin black wood and plain glass. The grey wall – more of a shrine really – is dust-free and is obviously cleaned regularly, and a strong scent of glass cleaner lingers in the air. Carolyn looks to the chair and sofa in the corner. Both look old – there are clear signs of wear and tear on the floral fabric, and the cushions are sloped and no longer have any bounce. The dusty television, with its bulky back, sticks out noticeably from the wall. The curtains at the window are frayed and tatted at the bottom. The ancient table next to the sofa is cluttered with small glass figurines, and shows signs of woodworm infestation. Carolyn looks back to the pictures. Two wall lights, positioned level with the top of her head, give a low glow from the middle of the wall.

The majority of the pictures show the boy looking happy. He is either laughing or giggling at something. Carolyn can see they've been arranged to show that each photo is a year older than the previous one.

One photo in particular catches Carolyn's eye: the final one in the sequence, on the bottom right of the wall. Presumably this is the last picture ever taken of Elwyn Roberts before he was reported missing. He must be about seven years old in this picture. He's sitting on a rock next to a river, holding up the line of a fishing rod with a pleased smile, displaying the silver fish he had just caught. His hair is short, and his face is round, and Carolyn estimates the boy to be around four feet tall. Then her eye is caught by the picture to the left of this one. Her stomach drops and goosebumps begin to surface on her skin, sending a shudder through her spine. Elwyn is wearing a green school jumper with a logo on the chest. A large S is stitched into the crest.

Carolyn now knows for certain. This is definitely the boy she saw in the well.

"We went fishing that day. It wasn't long after his birthday," a voice says from behind, startling her.

Kelvin Roberts places the tray of mugs onto the coffee table, shoving a stack of envelopes out of the way. He walks around the table and sits on the sofa, leaving a space at the end for his wife to join him. Carolyn takes a seat in the chair opposite.

"Mr Roberts, I know this must be hard for you and your wife, bringing all this back up again. I'm just wondering if there's anything you might have left out of your statement from that day, anything you remember. In Leeds, I work... I work as a private detective, you see, and I'd really like to help."

Kelvin shakes his head and rubs at the two-day-old stubble on his cheeks. "So... you're here for money. Freelance I take it. You're looking for a job?" His voice is raised and agitated.

Carolyn frowns. "No, no. Nothing like that. Just with losing my own son, I know it must be hard for you not to have answers. I'd really like to help, for free... of course... though I can't promise I can bring you anything you haven't heard already."

Kelvin rubs his hands together and sighs. He lifts his legs up as his wife squeezes past him and takes her seat.

"Good. Because we don't have any money left to pay you. We've spent it all on private investigators, and they all came up with nothing. No idea what happened to our boy. They all tell us the same. Anyway, if you think it could help, I'll tell you what I told the rest." He sits back and takes Heather's hand. "It was a Friday, and I was working in the factory. I'm still there, as you can tell from my uniform." He smiles, but there's no joy in his eyes. "From what I remember, it was around five when I got the call. Heather rang the office, and they shouted me up to take the call. Wasn't allowed phones on the factory floor, you see. I hung up and drove home as fast as I could. When I got here, there was a police car parked outside the house and officers taking statements."

Carolyn looks at Heather Roberts. Her eyeliner has run, and she now has dark streaks around her eyes and running down her cheeks. She pulls out a tissue and wipes at them.

"It's…" Heather sobs as fresh tears appear. "It's my fault he went missing, you know."

Kelvin squeezes her hand and shakes his head. "Don't be silly, love. We've spoken about this, remember?"

"Mrs Roberts… Heather… What do you mean by 'It's your fault'? How could it be your fault?"

"I should have been watching him. I should have…" She sinks her face into her hands, and Kelvin rubs the top of her shoulders.

"Elwyn was playing outside, after school. He was kicking his ball against the front wall. This lane is a dead-end, and we're the last house, so nobody really comes in or out without any of the neighbours seeing. He's always played out front. He knows he isn't allowed to kick the ball in the back, you see." Heather releases another cry.

"Heather likes to take care of the garden," Kelvin says. "You know, plant flowers, trim the bushes. There are lots of painted ornaments out at the back."

Carolyn nods. She guesses Heather must feel she is to blame because if she wasn't an avid gardener, maybe Elwyn could have been playing with his ball in the safety of the back garden.

Heather looks back up towards Carolyn, her eyes red and bloodshot. Carolyn wonders how many nights this woman's eyes have been in this state. She imagines Heather crying herself to sleep, face pushed into the pillow to muffle the sound. Carolyn's concentration is side-tracked for a minute as she thinks of her own many sleepless nights spent screaming at the ceiling in agony, asking why it was her son, why it was her husband.

Heather speaks again, breaking Carolyn's thoughts. Her voice is low as she catches her breath through the sobbing.

"I was listening… to the sound of his kicks, of the ball hitting the wall every two or three seconds at a time. I… I told him to come in some thirty minutes earlier because it

80

was October and it would be getting dark soon. His tea was cooking in the oven, so I told him half hour more then come in." Heather wipes at her eyes and continues. "I'm not sure how long it was that I didn't hear the thumps of the ball against the wall. I was doing the dishes at the time and was tapping my foot to each thump. Like I was in sync with the noise... and with his kicks." She frowns, sniffing and wiping at her nose. "My mind must have wandered off, as my foot was still tapping on the floor, but I couldn't hear the thumps any longer. It was the oven timer that snapped me out of my daydreaming. I dropped the cup I was washing into the sink, and I ran out of the front door. I knew, then, I just knew at that time my little Elwyn wouldn't be outside." She breaks down again.

"Did the neighbours see or hear anything, maybe felt like something was off about that day? Any strangers they might have seen hanging around? Any suspicious-looking vans or cars?" Carolyn asks, thinking up the questions as she goes along.

Kelvin shakes his head. "The police have spoken to them all. At the time, the first house as you enter the lane was empty. The other four families didn't see or hear anything. Elwyn used to play with Josh, the young boy from next door, but after what happened... Well, the family didn't feel safe anymore, and they moved not long after. I can't say I blame them."

"I think about that day every single waking minute," Heather begins. "And I ask myself, what kind of mother am I?" Her cheeks are shiny with tears.

"Mrs Roberts, you can't blame yourself for this, what—"

"I hope that... I *pray* that one day I'll be out there, doing the gardening, and the gate will open. I'll turn to find my son, my Elwyn, has returned to us, instead of police or a journalist or somebody else that wants me to keep reliving that fucking day!" Heather barks at Carolyn, then stands up and runs out of the room, heading up the stairs.

Carolyn gives Kelvin a sympathetic smile, closes her notepad and stands up. "I'm sorry again. I'm sorry to come here and bring all this up. Please apologise to your wife for me."

"Don't worry about it. We'd like to know anything you find, even if it's not the best news... We'd still like to know, please!" Kelvin begs. He stands and shakes her hand, looking towards the ceiling. "Heather doesn't mean to be rude. She knows you mean well. She's just upset, you understand."

Carolyn nods. "Oh, one last thing. That picture there, on the rocks with the fish... When exactly was that taken?"

"About two weeks before he went missing. We gave the police a copy of that one. It's the last picture we have of him." Kelvin smiles proudly. "It was the first fish he'd ever caught. After I got home that night, I drove there, half-expecting him to have been sitting on those rocks with his rod in his hand and a tackle box at his side, watching his float bob up and down, all excited. I wanted nothing more than to run over and shout at him for the trouble he's caused, hug him so tight and call him an idiot." Tears are beginning to trickle down Kelvin's cheeks. He wipes them away with a finger, his stubble rasping against his skin.

"I'm sorry, again. Thank you. Thank you both. I'll see myself out."

Carolyn drives away from the Roberts' home, but before she turns back onto the main road, she pulls over at the start of the lane. The image of the boy in the well flashes in her mind. She feels anger build in her stomach and squeezes the steering wheel. The leather squeals in her grip and she thinks, *Elwyn went missing eight years ago this month.*

The image of the corpse looking up from the well implants itself in her mind again, almost turning her stomach. She closes her eyes and concentrates, forcing herself to remember that horrific scene. She imagines herself back in the open, walking along the yellow flowered bed of the forest in her mother's fluffy slippers, passing the squirrels that chase one another around the thick tree, then walking up to the well and peering down into the dark. That was the moment her happy place was destroyed, the moment her time to grieve for

Simon and Ryan was over… for now at least.

She locks eyes with the boy. He stares back up at her with eyes glazed and lifeless, pain etched into his young face, questions in his innocent eyes. His skin is dark!

His father being a black man and his mother a white woman, it would mean Elwyn would have been mixed-race.

It must have been him in the well. It was his face she had seen before, sitting on those rocks feeling chuffed with his catch of the day. It was definitely the same logo she'd seen on the jumper. There's no way she could ever know what Elwyn had looked like, or his school's logo. She'd never seen this boy before.

The internal voice speaks up. *But the lack of decomposition of his body doesn't make sense. That wasn't the corpse of a boy who has been dead for eight years.*

She hushes the voice and opens her pad to make a note of it, and just in time, too. She pushes open the car door and leans over as far as the seat belt will allow to throw up the combination of coffee and tea. Wiping at her mouth using a napkin, she decides to apologise to the Lloyd family and tell them she must have been hallucinating, or that maybe she was confused. They're sure to believe she's a private investigator, and that she does wants to help them. She'll do this today before looking more into the man at the coffee shop – Barry Cookson.

Chapter Fourteen

The sat-nav takes Carolyn to the Lloyds' address, the message *Arrived* filling the screen before turning itself to standby. The road is long and winding, with trees at each side. There are no signs of a home. She turns the sat-nav back on, and punches in the postcode to make sure she entered it correctly. *Arrived* flashes again before turning itself off. Carolyn slips the car in gear and proceeds down the road. It's now almost half past four, and the sun is setting slowly, hiding behind the trees, causing her to flick on the headlights. Up ahead there are two cars parked on the side; both have lights, bonnets, doors and radiators missing. Just past the cars is an opening, a dirt road leading up towards a farmhouse and some large sheds. A wooden sign at the start of the dirt road reads *Lloyd, Green Lane Farm.*

Carolyn turns the car to head up the road and stops, hesitating. She wonders if it's best to leave it till another day, maybe earlier in the afternoon, and possibly bring someone with her. But who? She remembers what the skinny redheaded cashier told her, the shop girl – Sophie. She'd said to be careful, not to get in the way of Frank Lloyd. "*He wouldn't think twice about beating you to a pulp…*" And then there's the unpleasant scar across Julio Alcala's face.

She sits, watching the house in the distance.

Maybe he isn't home. Maybe it's just the wife, Gwen. I can try to get her to understand that I'm here to help, she tells herself. Deciding she can't delay any longer, she drives up towards the house.

The path is cluttered with rusting cars, now nothing more than shells hoisted up on logs and bricks, with parts missing from all of them. The pickup truck is parked at the side of the house. She remembers it humming past her in the car park of

Llanbedr Convenience.

"Shit," Carolyn says out loud. Her heart begins thumping hard as she approaches. Her palms begin to sweat, and she comes to a stop again, thinking about whether to go back down the path and return another day. But she's already too far up. She gives her pockets a feel for the stress ball. Empty. She's left it at home, not that it does much to calm her any other time.

The doors of the largest shed are open, and inside is a black van. Sparks are flying out from behind it as the man welds on a replacement panel. The man stops, takes off his helmet and heads towards the entrance of the shed. He's young. His face is dirty, oil stains are smeared across his acne-scarred cheeks, and his forehead is damp with sweat. He smiles an ugly smirk at Carolyn, showing a mouth full of yellow teeth, and watches as she exits the Polo and approaches the front door to knock.

The combined stench of animal urine, rotting food and body odour can be smelt from outside the door. A dog barks loudly, jumping up at the glass and smearing its wet nose along it, leaving streaks.

Carolyn begins to think it's a bad idea, and turns around to leave. She hears a man's voice inside, shouting and swearing at the canine to quiet down and move away from the door. The young man from the outhouse is still staring at her and wiping his hands on an oily rag. From the look in his eyes, Carolyn knows he is thinking rude, grotesque thoughts.

The door swings open and Frank Lloyd stands in the frame. He is wearing blue jeans, battered black boots, and a crinkled green shirt that has food stains down the front. The stench is now revolting.

"You must be fucking kidding me. You're the crazy bitch from the shop," he shouts, the smell of beer strong on his breath. He steps forward. The dog, a tall black German Shepherd, is standing behind its owner, ears tilted back, cautiously watching the stranger at the door. It begins barking again, loudly and furiously. Frank Lloyd's eyebrows lower and his forehead creases. He moves back into the house and grabs the dog by the collar. Carolyn steps aside as he pulls it out into the front. The dog runs down the path. "Put that thing on the leash!" he yells toward the young man – his son, Carolyn presumes. He looks back to her. "I said, are you fucking kidding me?"

Carolyn takes a step back to escape the sour smell of old beer. "Mr Lloyd, I've come to apologise for saying what I thought I saw the other day. I'd like to have a chat, and possibly ask you some questions about your son."

Frank stays quiet and only stares. Carolyn keeps his gaze.

"Well, go on then. Apologise to me." He stands upright and folds his arms, and a small smirk appears at the corners of his mouth.

"I'm sorry for causing you or your... wife, I presume, trouble. I'm here trying to find out what happened to Dylan. If you want me to go... I will," Carolyn says, a small part of her hoping he orders her to piss off. She doesn't want to be around these people, on their isolated property, where they could easily beat the life out of her, and where nobody would hear her cries for help. A chill runs down her spine, and for a second, she feels faint, as the realisation hits her that she hadn't told anyone she was coming here. That could have been a mistake. The look she'd encountered in the eyes of the son tells her he'd probably enjoy inflicting pain on her.

It'll be easy to find a spot to bury her body out here. Or would they drive her back into town and throw her from the pickup truck?

Gwen appears at the side of Frank. Her eyes narrow as she looks Carolyn up and down.

"Mrs Lloyd, I'm not here to cause trouble. I don't mean to bring up the past. If you don't mind answering a few questions, it would help. I'm looking into the disappearance of your son."

Carolyn stands upright, waiting for the tired-looking woman to slam the door in her face. She imagines scrambling back to her car as the Lloyd family watch from the windows, laughing. Maybe they'd even set the dog on her. But instead, the woman with the straw-like bleached hair steps aside and beckons for her to enter.

Inside the house the smell is even worse. The carpets are faded and torn. Their patterns have been replaced with oil, grease and mud stains, and they look as though they've never been hoovered or cleaned since the day they were laid. The furniture is damaged, and splinters hang off the wooden tables, possibly from the dog chewing the legs. Carolyn is led into the kitchen. The sink is rusted and worn, and looks almost as old as some of the cars out at the front. Every cabinet surface is piled high with dirty plates, cutlery, takeaway plastic containers and beer bottles, all balancing on top of one another like a bad version of *Jenga*. The bare concrete floor is littered with beer bottle caps and cigarette butts.

Carolyn resists pulling a sour face. She steps over piles of clothes which are full of black dog hairs and yellow piss stains that she hopes are from the dog. The stench of urine is multiplied in here, and it takes all of her willpower not to cover her nose. She can taste the smell and wonders why the man and woman standing in front of her seem not to notice. The kitchen table is small and square, clothes half-folded on top. It's hard to tell if they were clean or dirty, though it doesn't matter as Frank Lloyd pushes the pile onto the floor with the rest of the piss-soaked garments. Carolyn takes a seat and Gwen Lloyd sits opposite, the chair next to her left empty. Frank remains standing and leans against the sink.

"Thank you for agreeing to speak with me. I know we didn't—"

"Did you actually see a body or not?" Gwen interrupts. Her face is stern and unblinking. Carolyn looks from her to the man by the sink. She notices they both look tired and worn out.

Before Carolyn answers, she tells them about the deaths of Simon and Ryan, and how much stress she has been under lately. She wants to say it could have been her imagination playing tricks on her that day, or that she was drunk or extremely tired. But she doesn't. She tells them the truth, that she saw a body. She hopes this will stop Frank Lloyd

87

thinking of her as the crazy bitch he insisted she was.

The man and wife both look at each other in amazement, exchanging looks of sorrow.

"How come you're looking into this? Are you a private investigator?" Frank Lloyd asks, standing a little taller, furrowing his eyebrows. His arms are folded against his chest again and he's stroking the end of his grey moustache. "Did the parents of the other missing boy hire you?"

Carolyn shakes her head and tells them she hasn't been hired, that she feels passionate about finding out the truth, and that in any case she would like to help. She'd like to think somebody would do the same for her son.

The young man from outside walks in, pulls out a chair from the table making a dreadful creaking noise along the kitchen floor, and takes a seat.

"And I believe," Carolyn says, looking from one to the other, "that the police haven't done nearly enough. They don't seem to care or want to help." This sends Frank into a blubbering frenzy. The words *pigs*, *lazy* and *fat* are used numerous times, and not necessarily in that order. Gwen also joins in with the insults. Carolyn nods and smiles as if in agreement, knowing that this will probably get them to open up to her. After all, she is here to help them. What's a little white lie?

The man sitting next to his mother is in his late twenties. His skin is blotchy and oily, and his thick hair looks uncombed and unwashed for God knows how long. His eyes are dark and slightly too far apart. Carolyn can feel him leering at her, undressing her in his mind. She avoids eye contact. Feeling his eyes on her skin is bad enough. She ignores him and proceeds with her questions, now that Mr and Mrs Lloyd seem to have relaxed a little.

"So what can you tell me about that day?" Carolyn asks. "Do you have any enemies, anyone who might have wanted to see Dylan hurt?"

The Lloyds look puzzled, scratching their heads.

"Can you imagine anyone, Owen?" Frank asks his son, who is now smirking at Carolyn and licking his lips. She

88

keeps her feet firmly under her chair, after feeling his boots rub against her ankles one too many times for it to be an accident. His glare is making its way from her eyes down to the opening of her shirt.

Owen answers in a bored tone without blinking or shifting his gaze. "Nope. I can't think of anybody."

"He would sometimes be out for hours on his own," Frank begins, unfolding his arms and placing his hands in his pockets. "He wasn't interested in learning how to fix cars or anything else I tried to teach him. He would just pick up and take off. We were out that day at a family party; we'd left the boys at home. And when we got back, well, we thought maybe at first, he might have been staying with one of his friends. Maybe he'd told us, but we forgot or something. We drove around all of the friends' houses we know of, and the police did too. Nothing."

Carolyn makes some notes, imagining that's what a private detective or even DS Hughes would do. *Had done.*

"You want to write down my number, sexy, and maybe we can talk in private?" Owen sneers at Carolyn. His mother brings her arm up so fast Carolyn almost doesn't see it happening. The slap echoes off Owen's cheeks.

"She's trying to find your brother!" Gwen shouts. Owen stands, pushing his chair away with his legs, and it hits the grimy counter behind him. Beer bottles fall to the floor, clinking against the concrete. Owen clenches his fists.

"What the fuck do you thi—" the young man snaps as Gwen flinches away. Frank takes his hands from his pockets and grabs Owen by the top of his shirt, pulling him out of the kitchen and through the front room, out into the garden. Carolyn can hear the two of them arguing outside. The dog starts barking again.

"Does he do that a lot? Is he usually violent towards you?" Carolyn asks.

Gwen doesn't answer. Her head is resting in between her arms on the table, and she is silently crying.

"What can you remember about that day?" Carolyn continues. "Anybody around that you hadn't seen before?

89

Any strange vans or cars?"

The woman lifts her head and wipes at her face using the sleeve of her top.

"It wasn't unusual for Dylan to be out on his own. He and Owen would argue all the time, and Owen would end up hitting him and going too far, really hurting him. Dylan isn't like Owen, he's a good boy. He wanted to study. He was respectful. He had dreams and ambitions, not like *him*," Gwen snarls, looking towards the noise of the men arguing out at the front.

"Did he ever talk about friends he might have gone to?" Carolyn asks, unsure what else to ask. What good she thought she was going to achieve, she didn't know, but she knows she needs answers – and that, corpse or no corpse, she isn't crazy. Whatever the internal voice might say.

"No, he never had many friends. Owen would make sure of that." Gwen reaches for a box of cigarettes that lies hidden between a pile of plates and glasses. Carolyn stares bemused at how Gwen knew they were there. Gwen lights one and blows out smoke, the hand holding the cigarette shaking slightly.

After writing down the events of that day, Carolyn decides there isn't much left to ask and stands to leave.

"If you find anything… anything at all, will you let me know? I'm not sure how much longer I can wait," Gwen sobs. She stands and searches through some papers next to the toaster, pulls out a yellow flyer and hands it to Carolyn. "I need to know… I… I can't stay here forever."

Carolyn thinks about asking what she meant by *how much longer I can wait*, but the woman's expression looks as if she didn't want to repeat it – and in any case Frank Lloyd has just walked through the door and taken a seat at the square table. Carolyn looks down at the flyer. It reads, *Frank Lloyd, Auto Repair Centre* in a thick bold font, along with pictures of cars that are no longer in production and the address and phone number of Green Lane Farm, the same as Carolyn had found online. She nods and makes her way to the door.

Outside, the fresh air hits her, and she wishes she could

lean back against the front door and take in as much of the glorious clean air as her lungs will allow. Instead, she sucks in what she can as she heads for the car.

The visit leaves her feeling dirty and in desperate need of a shower. In the car, she pulls out the flyer. It has ketchup and grease stains on it. She adds the number to her phone memory and crumples the paper for the bin. As she turns the car round before heading down the long driveway towards the dirt road, she hears whimpering and looks around. The black German Shepherd is on a long chain leash, attached to one of the dismantled cars. Owen stands a couple of feet in front, a safe distance from the dog's snout, holding a long thick branch and poking at it. The dog is going berserk, running the length of the chain in an attempt to defend itself and attack back.

Owen watches as Carolyn turns the car round. He continues to prod the branch into the dog harder and harder until it stops barking and accepts defeat. It cries in low scared squeals, curling in between two of the vehicles in an effort to shield itself.

The enjoyment on Owen's smiling face upsets Carolyn. How is he feeling joy from torturing the family dog? She wonders if he could be involved in the disappearance of his brother. Perhaps he's not a killer, but is it possible he's done something evil enough to have made Dylan want to leave home? His own mother cowered away from him in the kitchen. Gwen did say the two used to argue a lot, and now here he is prodding their dog and enjoying its cries of pain.

Carolyn stops the car, takes off her seatbelt and opens the door. She wants to snatch the stick from him and shove it somewhere it belongs. He's watching her, his mouth twitching with every strike of the stick, taunting her to get out of the car. His dirty face is begging her to. But Carolyn leans back in against her seat and closes the car door. She doesn't want to ruin the progress she has made by getting the Lloyds to trust her. Any good she has done by offering an apology (which they seem to have accepted and welcomed her into their home) would all have been for nothing.

91

These last few months have been really hard. First she'd lost her family, and now some insane killer is out there, toying with her. She'd enjoy nothing more than to take out some of that anger and frustration on a low-life like Owen Lloyd. She breaks her gaze and drives out of the Lloyds' property, praying that the chain breaks and the dog finds it within itself to tear him to pieces.

Chapter Fifteen

Excitement and fear rush, simultaneously, through Carolyn. She looks at herself in the mirror again and again, to make sure she looks like a normal customer. Today she will go back to P's Party Accessories, step inside and scope the place out. She doubts that Julio has described her to the owner, and even if he has, she's pretty average-looking, with no distinct physical attributes that might cause her to stand out.

She'll have a look at the place from the inside, and try to see if it has a back room or any other kind of storage. The unit itself is small, so if the body of a young boy is in there, it shouldn't be hard to find. She guesses the killer hasn't brought the body back there, though the shop might provide other evidence. After all, she has nothing else to go on.

Carolyn drives into the industrial unit and takes a parking space next to the door of the party shop. She leaves the car facing the exit, to make a quick getaway if needed. Clouds are starting to form, and the atmosphere has a grey and miserable feel to it.

Carolyn figures the place might have looked gloomy and depressing the other night because of the time of day and circumstance. The sign above the door looks bleak, dull and worn. Nothing that screams 'party' at all.

Inside, the unit is even smaller. Boxes of new stock haven't been opened or stacked on the shelves that run along the walls. And with the amount of unstacked items, you wouldn't get more than two customers in at a time.

At the back, placed on the counter, is an old-style cash register. The overweight owner is sitting on a stool, and behind him is the fire exit Carolyn tried the other night. The owner looks up from his newspaper and nods hello to

Carolyn before he returns to circling horses' names.

Carolyn's nerves ease slightly. If Julio has described her to the owner, he seems not to recognise her.

She scans the room quickly. There is no storage room behind the man, and nothing out of the ordinary; no shovels, ladders or plastic sheeting that's visible. There are only inflatable Teletubbies and Peppa Pig balloons. Nor is there any horrific smell of a decomposing body. A door is to Carolyn's left, next to a display of Halloween costumes in plastic packets. Though the room behind can only be slim, it doesn't look as if it would store much; the walls come out about two feet less than the average coat cupboard at home. There is no other storage space at the back.

If the body is here, it would have to be inside this cupboard. The door is locked. Carolyn stands next to it, pretending to look through the funny black-and-white birthday cards with googly eyes.

The padlock attached to the door is thick and bulky. It's the type you would use for shutters outside. It isn't for a simple storage cupboard.

The thought of a decaying corpse behind that door, wrapped in plastic sheeting, sends a chill through Carolyn. The smart thing to do would have been to bury the body somewhere else. She has no idea if that's what they've already done. She doesn't know anything. She only knows that something suspicious is going on with Julio Alcala, and her grieving mind is jumping to conclusions that involve this overweight owner. The idea that the party shop owner had anything to do with the missing boys is pathetic. And to be honest, the man behind the desk – wheezing and struggling to breathe – isn't capable of digging a hole, or even of carrying a body. He looks as if ascending a single flight of stairs would bring on a heart attack. No wonder the stock is still waiting in unopened boxes. So if there was a digger involved in the crime, it would have to have been Julio.

She has to find out what's behind that door. What needs hiding so much that you'd use such a big padlock? She wanders off, thinking of ways to gain entry.

Then, as if an unknown force has answered her wish, the door of the party shop opens and a workman decorating one of the unoccupied units sticks his head in.

"I take it that's your van outside?" he says.

The obese man behind the counter looks up from his paper. "Yeah, it is. Why?" he wheezes, catching his breath.

"Just to let you know, you've got a flat tyre, mate." The man behind the counter sighs "Shit" and follows the workman out of the door without paying any attention to Carolyn, leaving her alone in the shop.

Now's her chance. But now that it's here, her heart is beating fast. She pauses for a moment, then races through the path of boxes on the floor to the counter. She searches through the shelf underneath, pushing invoices and receipts out of the way. Under the mess of paperwork are nude magazines; a few of them centre on Asian women and women with large breasts. Carolyn picks one up: *Uniform Specials*. She grimaces and carries on searching, not looking at the titles of the rest.

Finally she discovers a small wooden box. She opens it and finds the padlock key inside. She looks up to the window and can see the obese man still hasn't yet reached his van. His poor health and inability to walk has worked in her favour today. She runs to the locked door and slips the key into the padlock. It scratches around before sliding in. What is usually a simple task has proved to be difficult by her nerves and her trembling fingers.

Her accusations of Julio and the shop owner come flooding back. Expecting the worse, Carolyn braces herself to come face to face with the body again.

She pulls open the door.

The room is how she pictured it: only big enough to store coats or a mop and bucket. It smells of sweat and fast food, like the internet café. On the back wall is a corkboard, pinned to which are magazine clippings of young girls wearing summer dresses and bikinis. Nothing illegal, but definitely not right either. Secured to the wall under the corkboard at about waist height is a plank of wood that acts as a makeshift desk. On it is a grey laptop. Next to that is a box of tissues and hand cream.

Carolyn's face tightens, and she realises she's pulling a face of disgust. There's no way the party shop owner could sit at this laptop and close the door behind him. She imagines him wheeling over his swivel stool from behind the counter and sitting at it with the majority of his body hanging out. It would explain why he'd close the shutters, obviously for privacy. But what was Julio Alcala doing here?

She desperately wants to open the laptop. The magazine cut-outs above have already stirred things up in her mind. You don't have to be a rocket scientist to guess what kind of man he is, or what type of sickening things he is into.

For a split second, Carolyn debates starting up the laptop and searching the hard drive, the files, even the internet search history, but she knows there isn't time. She's sure that the obese, wheezing man isn't going to change the flat tyre himself, which means he'll soon be back to call a tyre fitter, and then he'll catch her snooping around.

After seeing the clippings on the wall, the tissues and the hand cream, and the fact that the laptop is heavily guarded behind a locked door with a padlock, Carolyn feels uneasy. She knows she has to find out more.

She imagines the embarrassment of being arrested for stealing in her mother's town. Richard Williams would love that.

No, she'll have to find another way of seeing what's on this computer.

Looking out of the window, she sees that the party shop owner is now bending over, leaning down as he examines his tyre. She closes the door and clicks the padlock closed again, and rushes over to the counter, hitting her shin on a box as she goes, and replaces the key. Then she straightens the papers and nude magazines back on top of the box and selects a *Get Well Soon* card with a picture of an elephant in bed, a bandage wrapped around its huge head, and a thermometer hanging from its frowning mouth. She waits at the counter as the owner comes back through the doors, with sweat running down his face. He looks at the price tag on the back and holds out his hand for payment, too breathless to speak. Carolyn hands him the correct amount and leaves.

She pulls out of the gates of the industrial unit, and then parks in the same spot as the other night and writes down what she has found: the locked door with the heavy-duty padlock, the laptop, and the clippings on the corkboard. Her heart is thumping wildly, and she's full of adrenaline. It feels good to be doing something out of the ordinary like that, something to occupy her mind and not think of Simon and Ryan's deaths.

Without clouding her mind too much with how she would manage to see what's on the laptop, she Googles *Barry Cookson, Llanbedr Painter and Decorator.* His business address also acts as his home address, and Carolyn makes a note to visit him tomorrow. Tonight, she is going home to celebrate her small victory with a bottle or so of red, even if she can only celebrate alone.

***

The man tosses and turns a lot that night. He's been thinking of how much he could have lost if only somebody had turned up unannounced and discovered that foul smell for themselves.

How stupid he has been to keep the body all this time.

Stupid, he thinks, shaking his head and thumping his pillow. What he has done is stupid, idiotic even. Like serial killers who keep trophies of their victims. He knows better than that. How could he have risked it all?

What's done is done. They'll never find the body now. Never.

Chapter Sixteen

October 24th

Jeanette has already thumped on Carolyn's door three times, urging her to wake up. The smell of eggs and sausages cooking has enticed Carolyn to push the duvet off, but it's the smell of fresh coffee that makes her stumble to her feet. Jeanette likes to make coffee in the morning. She's confessed numerous times that she wouldn't go back to the instant stuff, not after Carolyn, Simon and Ryan had bought her an electric coffee grinder for Christmas a few years back.

"What's the rush?" Carolyn says, looking at the clock. "It's only eight-fifteen… and it's a Saturday. Why don't you try sleeping in sometime?" She slumps into a chair at the small kitchen table.

Jeanette sets a plate in front of Carolyn and pours her a mug of coffee before taking a seat facing her.

"I need the car today. I've got a thing on," Carolyn says.

"No. That's not going to happen."

"I need it today. I've got an important thing to do," she insists, slurping her coffee and taking a bite from a sausage.

Jeanette places her cutlery down onto her plate and gives Carolyn a quizzical look. "What important thing would that be?" she asks. Carolyn finishes chewing her food and goes to answer when her mother speaks up. "Is it too important to visit your father's grave on his birthday?"

Carolyn looks at the puppy calendar on the wall next to the door leading out into the garden. *October 24th.*

"That's today?" Carolyn asks as she finishes chewing.

"Yes, it is."

"I'm so sorry, Mum. I've been so caught up in all of this

shit that I completely forgot. I'm sorry." She remembers past birthdays. Her father had never been one for celebrating and making a fuss of himself. He'd rather be left alone to sit in the ugly reclining armchair and read his paper while smoking his pipe, as if it had been the same as any other day. Jeanette isn't very sentimental, and after his death she'd made an exception to bring the chair with her when she moved to Llanbedr. It had spent a couple of days at the upholsterers for some new fabric, and now she sits in it to watch TV.

"It's fine, love. I understand," Jeanette says. "I know it's not a priority at the minute with everything you're doing. But I just wish you'd stop and relax. That's what you're supposed to be doing here, remember? Relaxing. Not out following people and causing trouble."

Carolyn nods modestly and starts on her eggs.

"So, after we've been to the cemetery, how about joining me at the annual Halloween fair in Fishguard? I've been going since Father Joseph told me about it. I haven't missed a year yet." Jeanette slurps her coffee before adding, "I love that it's based in your father's hometown, where he lived when he was a boy. It was before we met, of course, and before we decided to move to Leeds." She looks down and smiles. "I visit his grave and wish him a happy birthday, and I tell him about everything that's going on. I sit there for a while before I go and spend the afternoon at the fair, drinking tea." She smiles into her cup.

"Of course, I'll come. I'd love to. Thanks, Mum," Carolyn decides that speaking to Barry can wait for another day. Today will be about remembering her father, spending quality time with her mother, and forgetting about this mess. Just for today.

The cemetery is a forty-minute drive from Jeanette's bungalow, and she enjoys the journey. It's one filled with country lanes and scenic views. The cemetery is a huge and peaceful place, well-kept by the full-time groundsmen, who today are gathering up the golden autumn leaves. Carolyn and Jeanette arrive close to eleven, having stopped for

99

flowers on the way. The air is crisp, and condensation leaves their mouths as they walk to the grave. Jeanette crouches down, puts on her gardening gloves and pulls out the dead flowers and weeds, fixes the stones around the headstone and picks up the smoking pipe that's left under a small painted pebble Ryan had done. She tips out the debris from the chamber of the pipe, pulls out a pouch of tobacco from her coat pocket, pushes a small pinch into the pipe and sets it back in place.

Carolyn watches and smiles. "How long have you been doing that for?"

"I come on his birthday and close to Christmas before I make my way up to yours. Oh, and on our anniversary, of course. I think it would be something he'd appreciate." Jeanette kisses the top of the headstone. "Have you got anything to say to your father?"

Carolyn wishes she could tell him everything that has been going on, and talk to him about how much she misses Simon and Ryan and her search for the missing boys. She wants to tell him about what she saw down the well and about her suspicions about the owner of the party shop. Her father would have known what to say and what would be the best thing to do next. Instead, she says she misses him and hopes he's looking after Simon and Ryan.

The comment makes Jeanette smile, and she leans in, resting an arm around her daughter. They sit for thirty minutes before leaving and heading for the Halloween Fair.

They pay their fee at the gate and head straight for a drinks stand. Jeanette slurps a hot chocolate while Carolyn decides to try a *Witch's Heart* cocktail, served in a plastic glass, with a jelly worm hanging over the brim. Jeanette gives her a raised eyebrow.

"I'm not driving today. You are." Carolyn laughs, hugging herself. Jeanette purses her lips, smirks and shakes her head. She points to a huge tent across the field, a pop-up bar with heaters, tables and chairs. They find an empty table in the corner, next to a young couple engrossed in each other's eyes. On the table between them, two straws stand out of a plastic skull that is filled with ice cubes and a colourful blue and green liquid.

Carolyn notices a few faces from Llanbedr. Possibly from the day at Llanbedr Convenience, though that incident with Frank and Gwen Lloyd has now been forgotten about, at least for now. Today she's here to drink Halloween-themed cocktails, indulge in pumpkin-flavoured pies, and judge the outfits of the vampires, werewolves and bear-mauled victims walking around them.

"Carolyn, Jeanette, nice to see you here." Father Joseph joins them, pushing his thick-rimmed glasses back up his nose. He's wearing a flour-stained apron and a chef's hat sporting a huge smile, though Carolyn can still feel his dislike for her through his beady look.

"Father, good to see you. How are the cookies selling?" Jeanette asks, taking a sip of hot chocolate.

He looks from Jeanette to Carolyn, down at Carolyn's *Witch's Heart* cocktail and then back to Jeanette.

"Great. I'm almost sold out. Thank you again for helping. I wouldn't have had nearly enough if it wasn't for you." He pauses and looks at Jeanette. "You really are a saint. Come over and taste a few when you can. I'll save some under the counter, just for you."

Jeanette's cheeks turn a rosy red colour, but Carolyn knows her mother can't use the excuse of alcohol today. Father Joseph gives Carolyn another disapproving look before turning back to Jeanette. Carolyn feels the urge to ask what his problem is. It's gone half past twelve, and she's an adult enjoying a cocktail in honour of her late father. She's tempted to open her mouth and tell him that if he doesn't like her company, then maybe he should leave, and let her and Jeanette get back to enjoying their day.

The words burn her tongue and ache to be released into the air. Instead, she puts on a brave face and smiles. "I'm going to the bar. Would you like a drink?" she asks.

"I no longer drink," he says. "I had a problem and I got help. I've been sober for eight years now. Today I just keep to the boring stuff." He chuckles, with a fake grin on his face.

"Oh, well done. You're really doing well," Jeanette says, resting her hand on top of his on the table.

Carolyn fights to not let her emotions show, despite the sickening feeling in her stomach. Although now lapsed, she knows from her Catholic upbringing that their priests are supposed to be celibate. But Father Joseph appears to make absolutely no effort to discourage Jeanette's attentions.

She walks to the bar and leaves them to talk. From there, she watches the movement of her mother's lips. She tries to figure out their conversation, but it's pointless. The young couple sitting next to their table are now chomping on each other's faces. Carolyn can imagine the wet smacks, how she and Simon had been the same when they first met, with not a care in the world about the people standing by and watching in disgust. She turns away to be served.

She heads back over to her table, this time clutching a *Zombie Finger* drink, with an eyeball floating on top, and a hot chocolate for Jeanette.

"Gone back to his cake stand, has he?" Carolyn asks.

"Yes, we'll have to head over and see him soon. He's saved us a few cakes. I helped bake most of them, months ago though, and we'd freeze them."

Carolyn picks out the floating plastic eyeball and places it on the table, rolling it back and forth under her finger.

"Father Joseph doesn't like me very much, does he?" she says.

Jeanette looks shocked. "Of course he likes you. He just hears a lot of things that are going on, like you causing trouble with the Lloyds the other day." She sighs and lowers her voice. "Not to mention the police."

"I know what I saw. It wasn't my imagination!" Carolyn barks, sipping her drink and pulling a sour face.

"Well, let's not get into that today, shall we? Besides, you should stay away from the Lloyds. They're not nice people. Take it from me, they won't be too happy with you if the rumours start again."

Carolyn looks up from her drink and turns to face her

mother head-on. She wonders if she heard correctly. "Rumours? What rumours?"

Jeanette lowers her body closer to the table and looks around. Carolyn does the same.

"Well, their boy that went missing. Dylan. Anyway, apparently, he's not Frank's son. His wife, Gwen, she had an affair some time back. When Dylan went missing, it all got brought up again. I heard it from Anne at the shops. People say, and I don't know how true it is, but people say it's the man who owns the candle and fragrance shop on the high street." Jeanette pauses as the young kissing couple stand up and leave. "There's no doubt he's the father. They look so alike!"

"Who look alike?" Carolyn asks, intrigued.

"Dylan and the candle shop man. Everyone must know." Jeanette blows on her drink and takes a small sip.

Carolyn reaches into the inside pocket of her coat and pulls out her pad and pen. She jots down the information her mother has just given her and replaces the pad into her coat. That's the last she will think of this today. The rest of the day is for celebrating her father's birthday and for talking about their memories of him.

Chapter Seventeen

Today Carolyn decides to investigate the candle shop owner first – Dylan's apparent real father – and find out how he feels about the missing boy, before visiting Barry Cookson, the painter and decorator. She learned the name of the shop owner from Jeanette last night. He is Mark Buckles.

On her way into town her head throbs, and her stomach makes her grimace from the feeling of the *Witch's Heart* and *Zombie Finger* cocktails sloshing about and mixing together. The night comes back in parts: the conversations about visiting Spain, France and New York as a youngster, and speaking about the silly things her father would do to impress Jeanette. She remembers a part of the night, near the end as places were starting to close, of her spilling a drink across the table and laughing uncontrollably while Jeanette, sober as a judge, had pulled her usual embarrassed expression and apologised as the annoyed waiter cleaned up the spillage. She remembers a look of annoyance from Father Joseph.

God, I must have been a mess, she thinks, leaning her elbow on the driver's door as she rubs at the top of her head.

The wind, icy and carrying specs of rainwater, blows through her hair, keeping her alert. She pulls the pad from her handbag on the passenger seat and reminds herself of the name. *Mark Buckles.* The writing looks wiggly, as though Ryan had got into her bag and left her a note, or drawn a penguin on stilts.

She arrives at the candle shop just after half past two. The sign, *Buckles Candles and Scents,* looks decades old, with most of the paint missing from the letter B. The red paintwork outside the shop is also starting to peel away, exposing the old brick underneath. A brand-new Mercedes is parked outside the shop in the only private parking space, *MB-01* in fancy lettering across the licence plate. Carolyn assumes it belongs to Mark Buckles.

She pushes through the door and a little bell rings out above her, alerting the shopkeeper in the back. She looks around, waiting to be welcomed. The shop is immaculate, there's a fresh smell of lavender in the air, and the wooden floor is shiny and scratch-free. Carolyn's first impression of the place is that it looks as though it doesn't do a lot of business.

A man comes from the back and steps behind the counter, with a white cat following behind as though he's carrying catnip in his pockets. He's wearing an expensive tweed suit with a silk tie around his neck, dark slicked-back hair and a clean-shaven face. He reminds Carolyn of a lawyer or an accountant.

This surely can't be the man who had an affair with Gwen Lloyd, she thinks. *This must be the accountant. That'll at least explain the flash Mercedes outside.*

"Can I speak with Mark Buckles please, the owner?"

The smartly-dressed man looks her up and down, and she's sure she sees him smirk at the corners of his mouth, though this might have been her imagination.

"I'm Mark Buckles… *the owner*. What can I do for you?" he asks. His accent is different from what she's been hearing lately. London, perhaps.

"You're not from around here, are you?"

He leans over the counter and straightens some papers next to a bunch of candles. She sees that the price on these starts from £62.99, and widens her eyes.

"Neither are you," he says, and smirks (there's no doubt about it this time). The white cat meets Carolyn's ankles, brushing its long bushy tail across the inside of her jeans, leaving hairs behind. She stoops to stroke it, and reads the name tag: *Bella*. The cat purrs, and continues moving in and out of her legs as she stands.

"No, I'm not. Leeds, actually. I was wondering if we could speak about Dylan Lloyd."

He shrugs. "What do you want to know?" Bella makes a meowing noise and runs into the back. "If I'm honest, I've actually been expecting you."

Carolyn steps forward, brushing away the cat hairs from her trousers. "You have?"

"Yes. When I was told you where looking into those missing boys, I knew it wouldn't be long until you paid me a little visit and the rumours would start again." He steps from behind the counter and turns to face her. "It's the last thing I need right now." A worried look creeps onto his face.

"And who told you I was looking into the missing boys?"

"This is a small town. People talk. You hear everyone's business."

"Those rumours you speak of, are they about how you and Gwen were once an item, and how Dylan could be your son?"

He sighs and pinches the corners of his eyes, as if her voice is sending painful signals through his skull.

"We were never an *item*," Mark says, making imaginary quotation marks in the air with his fingers. "Not properly, anyway. She and Frank were on a break, or so she told me. I was down at the time, and spent most of my evenings at The Red Fox, drinking myself to death. My father had recently died, and I wasn't coping with it very well. Gwen and I got talking one night and, well… One thing led to another, and for the next couple of weeks we were… you know." He shrugs, as if embarrassed to say they were sleeping together. "So the rumours of Gwen cheating on Frank for one random night with me is all a lie. It wasn't like that at all."

Carolyn can't see any resemblance between Mark Buckles and Frank Lloyd. They're both completely different in every possible way: physical appearance, personality, even accents. She presumes that this is what attracted Gwen Lloyd to the man in the suit in the first place. Frank, after all, does have a temper. Mark Buckles seems calm and composed. She wonders if the candle shop owner received a large inheritance after his father died and spruced up his shop, bought nice suits and paid for that Mercedes out at the front.

"Do you believe Dylan could be your son, Mr Buckles?" She has no idea what she's doing here, and even what her question might accomplish. But sitting around Jeanette's bungalow only leads to thinking of her dead family, and that's something she really doesn't want to be doing.

Mark shakes his head immediately. "No. No way. Gwen assured me that Dylan wasn't mine. And even if he was, I'm happy to sit back and believe her lie. Gwen knew I didn't want kids, and I still don't. I really don't need these rumours to start up again. After their boy went missing, I offered to help search with the party. When it got too dark for us to go on, I came back here to grab my cat and head home. That's when Frank turned up. He stood where you are now, pushing my stock off the shelves and stomping on them. I tried to push him out of the shop and was about to call the police. Then he punched me and I went down like a sack of potatoes. He threatened me, said not to bother helping again, that Dylan had nothing to do with a queer-dressing bastard like myself, and they didn't need my help. He warned me to stay away, and before taking off, he left a large scrape down the side of the car I had at the time."

Carolyn looks out of the window. Another time she's been reminded of Frank's temper. "He likes leaving scrapes along cars, doesn't he?"

Mark looks at her quizzically.

Carolyn shakes her head. "Doesn't matter. So did you phone the police after that?"

Mark lowers his head and brushes a hand through his hair. "No, I just left it there. He hasn't been back since, and when we see each other in town, we just pass without making eye contact. Who knows what he'll do next? Burn my business to the ground, most probably."

"I'm sorry for asking and going off the subject, Mr Buckles, but it doesn't look like you do much business here. The flashy suit and the new car out there... All this from owning a little candle shop in the middle of nowhere?"

"I don't see how my finances have anything to do with you searching for two missing boys. But if you must know, after my father died, he left me a bit of money. Nothing substantial, but a fair amount. I used most of it to pay off bills and credit cards, and to take my business online. I do very well on the web."

Carolyn nods, realising his tone is beginning to sound annoyed and he's had enough of her questions. She takes one last look around the shop of the overpriced candles and incense sticks and decides to leave. She thanks him for his time and heads for the door, turning before she goes.

"Oh, one last thing. The shop looks to be recently furnished. The car and the chosen attire are flashy. I'm just curious. Why leave the battered sign?" she asks.

He places his hands in his pockets and takes a moment to reply. "As I said, most of my business is now online. The sign? It adds character, I guess," he says, then turns his back and heads through to join Bella in the back office.

Carolyn leaves with the sensation of being watched.

Chapter Eighteen

Barry Cookson's flat is above a betting shop on Hardman Street. Next to that is a greasy spoon café. Carolyn pulls into a space and kills the engine. The road is quiet, filled with parked cars and vans, presumably from the people working at the Sleepy Nights mattress factory across the road. The café is empty and looks as if it'll be closing soon. The skinny elderly woman inside is lifting chairs on top of tables and preparing to mop.

Carolyn heads around the back. The van she'd seen at The Coffee Shack is parked in a garage that's missing a door. On the wall of the garage, spray-painted in white, is *3B*. She heads through the gate and is faced with an alleyway. She turns to her right and sees a flight of steps. A wooden plaque attached to the wall reads *Deliveries left, Flats 3A and 3B right.* The small thick heels of her boots clang as she climbs the metal stairs.

3A is evidently empty. Carolyn looks through the window next to the door and can see empty cupboards with doors wide open. She approaches 3B and knocks, placing her face against the frosted glass on the front door. Coats and different coloured objects can be made out behind it. A movement appears, then disappears behind the door frame at the end of the hall. Carolyn squats and lifts open the flap of the letter box. Noises from the TV in the front can be heard.

"Mr Cookson, I know you're in," Carolyn shouts. "I just want to have a chat, that's all. I'm the woman from The Coffee Shack the other day." She stands up and lets the flap fall closed.

No reply.

Her stomach rumbles and she begins to feel slightly

nauseous, though the breeze from the wind feels good. Specks of rain begin to hit her face, and she hopes the occupant will answer soon.

She knocks again and waits. Nothing. She squats and lifts open the flap again. The noise from the TV is now much louder. He's deliberately ignoring her.

"Barry, I know you're in. Your van is parked outside. I just want to chat. Can you please open the door? I'm not going anywhere. I'm wondering why you took off." She steps back and takes a seat on the metal step.

As the rain falls, she's taken back to a day at Ashwood Forest, a few months before the accident.

Carolyn had been swamped at work, unable to take a day off in two weeks. Ryan had talked about going on an adventure, like Dora the Explorer. To make up for her absence over the last couple of weeks, Carolyn had bought him a new backpack, just like Dora's. They packed a lunch and put on their hiking boots. Ryan wanted to carry his sandwiches in his new backpack, along with his magnifying glass and, of course, his favourite tiger teddy. They had bought it for him from the zoo a year earlier.

The weather was overcast, with threats of rain, but that hadn't stopped them. After a morning of hiking, they decided to eat their lunch sitting on a couple of fallen trees. Halfway through his sandwich, Ryan had jumped up with excitement, spitting soggy bread from his mouth as he shouted, "Look, Mummy, a snake!" He'd quickly dropped to the floor and pulled out his magnifying glass to get up close to the 'snake' – which was in fact a caterpillar. Carolyn and Simon had been bent over with laughter. Carolyn had managed to stop laughing for long enough to snap a picture of the three of them huddled around the caterpillar.

Later, when the exhausted Ryan was home and asleep in bed, Carolyn and Simon had snuggled on the sofa. James Morrison was playing quietly on the radio. Simon had got up and topped up their wine glasses. He'd looked at her with admiration in his eye, as though nothing else was happening in the world. Just him and Carolyn, sharing a bottle of red.

"What?" Carolyn had asked.

"I've been thinking," Simon had taken a large gulp of his wine before placing the glass on the table. "I think we should give Ryan a baby brother or sister."

"I agree." They'd kissed some more before heading to bed.

During the following weeks she'd done numerous tests, and felt a little pang in her stomach when they'd all come back negative.

Carolyn breaks out of her daydream as the rain has now increased. The skinny elderly woman from the café comes out of the back door. She is wearing her coat and holding a bin bag of rubbish. She throws the bag in the bin and pulls down the shutters, then gives Carolyn a shy smile and walks over to her.

"Go home," she says. "It's going to rain pretty heavy. Don't be sitting out here all night waiting for him. If he wants to speak, I'm sure he'll ring you, and you both can talk through your argument."

Carolyn is about to explain that they're not a couple, but the woman turns immediately and heads for her car. She's gone within the minute, leaving a cloud of smoke evaporating into the cold afternoon air.

The sky has darkened even more, and the temperature has dropped.

Carolyn stands and heads back to the door. She stoops and peers through the letterbox flap once more. The colours bouncing off the wall and the loud chatter from the television in the far room are all she can see and hear. She pulls up the hood on her coat and heads back to the Polo, her boots clanging on the steel steps as she descends.

She turns up the car heater to de-mist the windows, and the wipers sway left to right at high speed. The rain soon turns torrential, the car wheels hitting potholes with force and sending the car off-track. Carolyn slows to a safe speed and concentrates on the road ahead. Her head is pounding again. She wants to be safe at home with a cup of tea and to chat with Jeanette.

A vehicle joins the road behind. It accelerates until it is a few feet behind her. Dazzling lights shine in the rear-view mirror. Carolyn slows down and pulls to the left, a couple of inches away from the slope leading down to the ditch. The vehicle behind is large, possibly a van or a jeep. She waits for it to pass, but it doesn't. Instead it speeds up further until it is barely a foot away from the rear bumper.

Even with the heavy rain hitting the back window, Carolyn can hear the engine behind. She winds down the driver's side window and puts out her arm, motioning the driver of the vehicle behind to overtake. Rain soaks her sleeve instantly. She watches and waits, but the person driving the van stays behind, revving the engine and jerking forward. She closes the window and steps a little harder on the accelerator.

"You've got plenty of room to overtake, so overtake, you idiot!" she yells into the rear-view mirror. Her eyes flick from the mirror to the road ahead, desperate to not lose control of the car and hit the potholes too hard. She thinks back to when she was leaving Buckles Candles, and the sensation of being watched sweeps over her again.

It's Frank Lloyd. I bet he was watching you leave that shop, and now he's come to silence you, to make sure the rumours don't start again. He doesn't want his wife to be branded a whore. You've fucked up now, Carolyn.

The vehicle behind crashes into the back of Jeanette's car. Carolyn almost loses her grip on the steering wheel and cries out with shock.

"What the fuck are you doing?" she shouts. "Crazy bastard!"

It's definitely a van. She notices the shape of its bonnet. Her mind begins racing again.

It's Barry Cookson. He didn't open his door. He didn't want to kill you at his property. That would be stupid. He'd sat waiting for you to leave and has followed you on to this country lane in the middle of nowhere.

She is breathing heavily, and her palms are beginning to sweat. She reaches for her mobile from the pocket of her jeans and pulls it out, swiping to unlock the screen and tapping the keypad while watching for more bends in the road. The thought of breaking the law by using her mobile while driving doesn't even occur to her. Not while there is a lunatic behind her. The air-con blows loudly, fighting off the mist at the windows. The engine roars and the tyres are fighting to keep their traction on the wet surface. It's not long before the side of the wheels skid along the embankment that lead to the ditch. She wrestles the car back to the centre of the road. The van behind crashes into her once more, forcing her to drop her phone and swerve across the road. The phone lands in the passenger footwell, out of reach.

"SHIT!" Carolyn screams. She slows the car slightly, hoping for the van behind to slow with her so she can get out and face Barry, or Frank, or whoever the hell it is, directly. A stupid idea, she knows, but right now her judgement is clouded.

The van doesn't slow. Instead, it crashes into the back of the Polo, sending sparks into the air. The screeching of metal scraping on metal sends a sharp pain through her ears, though this is the least of her worries.

She puts her foot back on the accelerator in a bid to outrun the maniac behind her. The engine of the small car offers the best it's capable of giving. She keeps it in gear as long as she can before having to change up.

The van slows.

She watches the lights move further away from her mirror, allowing her to see more clearly. Her heart is pounding against her chest, blood beating in her ears.

She swallows with a dry throat, sending shooting pains through her rib cage as she pants. Stupidly, she reaches into the passenger footwell for her phone.

The car sways from side to side and hits a pothole in the middle of the road before bouncing up. She sits upright, clutching the steering wheel with both hands in a bid to save control.

It's no good. The back tyre of the car hits the top of the embankment and begins sliding down, bringing wet earth up into the air and across the back window.

Carolyn stomps on the brakes, but they do nothing. The car collides with a small brick wall, flips over and rolls onto its roof as the windows shatter and implode. Carolyn screams, but her voice is drowned by the sound of crunching metal.

The car slides down further before coming to a stop. Luckily, Carolyn is strapped in by the seatbelt. Her ribs ache, she can feel thick blood running down the side of her face and across her nose, and there's a loud ringing in her ears. She looks around, shocked and dazed. The headlights flicker. The car is facing a hill of mud, and she watches the radiator hiss white smoke. The malfunctioning *beep, beep, beep* is coming from the dashboard. She closes her eyes.

"Simon!" she calls. She needs him now more than ever.

Chapter Nineteen

The wind whistles loudly, blowing the rain at Jeanette as she runs across the road to her bungalow. She turns and waves goodnight to Father Joseph as he closes his door and locks up. Jeanette steps indoors and shouts for Carolyn, though she knows she isn't in. The car is gone... again.

She isn't in the mood for cooking tonight. Her back and feet hurt, and the last thing she wants is to be standing at the stove. She decides on having a Pot Noodle and a cup of tea before taking her seat. She leaves Carolyn's Pot Noodle on the counter next to the kettle for whenever she decides to come home, then kicks off her shoes and gets comfortable on the recliner, just in time for her nightly TV shows.

Jeanette looks at the clock and sighs. 6:35 pm. She hates Carolyn being out of her sight, especially when it's dark and when the weather outside is so bad.

And Jeanette isn't as stupid as Carolyn appears to think. She knows she isn't at the shops, or out for a drive to clear her head, or any of the other many excuses she's told her. When Carolyn has been showering, Jeanette has read the notebook Carolyn keeps in her handbag. Of course, she isn't proud of going through her daughter's things, but she has to keep an eye on her.

She knows Carolyn is out watching and mixing with people she should be staying far away from, such as the Lloyds. Jeanette has seen for herself many times that Frank Lloyd is a bully who enjoys watching other people quiver. She also hears a lot of what happens around Llanbedr, and especially of what happens in the only decent supermarket in over twenty miles. She understands that she can't have Carolyn under a watchful eye every minute of the day as though she's still a child. But the idea of Carolyn coming here had been for her to treat Jeanette's bungalow as a sort of retreat, to take baths and to pamper herself, even to try out some new cake recipes if she's feeling up to it. At least it would give Jeanette a rest from worrying about her whenever she leaves the front door.

She reaches for her phone and calls Carolyn. The call goes straight to voicemail. Phone reception in some parts of Llanbedr is very poor, so she messages her, hoping the text will get through.

Where are you? It's getting very dark. Emmerdale is starting soon, hurry home. x

She places her mobile back on the side table and watches the rest of her show, keeping an ear open for the sound of her car making its way up the path.

It isn't long before Jeanette is falling asleep in the comfortable reclining chair.

Chapter Twenty

Carolyn doesn't know what else to do other than to close her eyes. She hopes that, by closing them for a moment, when she reopens them, everything will be fine, that she'll be in her bed and that this whole thing would be nothing but a nightmare.

Of course, that isn't the case.

Her shoulder and neck are now in agonising pain. Her breathing is harsh, and the seatbelt is still strapped across her waist. The engine has cut out. She looks around to assess the damage. There is broken glass and bent metal. The airbags had deployed, probably saving her from breaking her neck. She wonders if the car will explode, like they normally do in films. That thought sends panic rushing through her. She shouts at herself to stop being ridiculous.

She pushes the button on the seatbelt clip and it releases her body. She drops to the roof of the upturned car, groaning in pain. Lying in a shallow puddle of muddy water, she feels around her aching body for any damage. Apart from the cut on her forehead – which she flinches as she touches it – she's confident she isn't bleeding anywhere else. From what she can feel, nothing appears to be broken.

Her hands are in the muddy puddle as she searches for her phone. She begins pulling out clunks of squishy earth and drops them behind her. A ping noise sounds and a dim light flashes above. Miraculously, her phone is safe – when the car turned over, it had landed in the space between the passenger seat and the car floor. She reaches up and grabs hold of it.

A message from Sara appears across the broken screen. The first lines of the message can be seen on the lock screen.

HI HUN. HOUSE IS FINE. JUST CHECKING IN. HOPE YOU'RE ALL RIGHT. SPEAK SOON X

Carolyn wants to reply that she isn't all right: that she's seen the corpse of a young boy down a well and nobody believes her, not even her own mother. Oh, and she is currently fearing for her life in an overturned car.

Of course, she doesn't reply. She will at a later date. If she's still alive.

Right now, she needs to call the police. She begins pressing 999, then her phone freezes. A white light fills the screen before returning to the home screen and showing no signal.

It's that mountain of a man, Barry, the internal voice tells her. *He's going to snap your spine without even breaking into a sweat... And if it's Frank Lloyd, he's going to feed you to his dog.* Then her thoughts are interrupted as a vehicle approaches from above the ditch and comes to a halt. The loud engine shuts off with a rattle as it cools.

Time to die, Carolyn.

She struggles to lift her neck as ferocious pain stabs at her legs and back. She holds onto her side as if her guts will flop out into the muddy rainwater. She hears a door opening, then slammed shut again. Boots kick at the wet road surface as the person walks over to the top of the ditch.

Carolyn opens her mouth to shout for help, but then closes it again. What if it's the person in the van that was chasing her? They wanted to hurt her, and push her off the road. What if they've come back to check if she's still breathing? So she stays quiet, and looks up from the shattered window.

She can see boots and dark jeans, and she cautiously edges closer so she can see the top half. The car creaks and shifts slightly. She holds a hand over her mouth and shuts her eyes, fighting back a scream. She opens them again and looks up. The person turns and heads back to their vehicle. A slight spell of relief warms her. She silently exhales, thinking she will wait until she hears the motor start and the person take off before even attempting to escape from the wreckage. She hopes the person thinks she's dead.

She hears the sound of the door opening and closing again, then the sound of metal being scraped along the road.

"I know you can hear me down there. Get out of the car!" It's a man's voice. The grass squelches under the man's boot as he reaches the top of the embankment.

"GET OUT OF THE FUCKING CAR!" the man screams, his voice echoing around the quiet night air.

Her heart is beating so fast that she can hear the thudding in her ears. She taps at her phone again, almost dropping it in the muddy water. The screen still shows no signal. Her head feels faint, and for a second she thinks she is going to pass out from the nausea.

"If I come down there and get myself dirty, you're not going to like the consequences. So do yourself a favour and get out of the car," the man orders.

Carolyn coughs, clearing her dry throat. "Ok... ok. I'm coming. Don't hurt me." She pushes the phone into her back pocket before lying down on her front, then knocks the remaining glass from the window using her elbow, and begins climbing through on her belly.

Outside, she stands up and leans against the car. It's still raining, but not as heavily, and it cleans the blood from her face. The bitter night air nips at her wet cheeks. She wipes her muddy hands on her jeans and holds them up to her eyes. The headlights from the van are on full beam, hiding the figure in front like the silhouette of an alien descending from a spacecraft. The figure lifts a bar and rest it on his shoulders. Carolyn can now see it's a crowbar. Her knees begin to lose their strength as she imagines being beaten to a pulp, then left out on this quiet country lane to be discovered by a dog-walker some time tomorrow morning.

"Get up here. Start climbing this ramp. Come on," the man orders, condensation leaving his mouth like a cloud of smoke.

Carolyn is reluctant. She stares at the shadow on top of the ramp, not knowing what awaits her. She slides her hand into her pocket and clutches hold of her phone. She knows there's no point in trying it again. Even if she can get a signal, she knows the police wouldn't get here in time – and in any case she isn't entirely certain what road she's on. She wonders, for a split second, if she could get hold of her mother and listen to her voice, for one last time. She'd tell her how sorry she is for all the trouble she's caused her, for not listening to her, and how she wishes she'd forgotten all about this silly thing.

"Get your hands out of your pockets and start climbing."

"I know your voice. Who are you?"

"I'm the one holding a crowbar and telling you to get up here!"

Carolyn staggers towards the bottom of the embankment, but her foot is immediately swallowed by the sloppy mud. She falls to her hands and digs them in too. Her legs are shaking, and she isn't sure whether it's the cold of the night and the wet clothes clinging to her skin, or the fear of what's going to happen once she reaches the top. Probably both. Her elbows buckle, and she falls flat on her face. The man standing above laughs an evil hyena giggle. Carolyn wipes the thick mud away from her eyes, nostrils and mouth, before carrying on.

Her first attempt is pathetic. Her foot slips and she slides back to the bottom. Her shirt catches on a branch and tears open, exposing her black bra.

The man laughs again.

The pain in her leg fills her with anger and determination. She stands and digs her foot in deep and tries again.

Eventually, with a lot of effort, she reaches the top, panting for air. Her head is lowered, and she's on her hands and knees. She looks up to face the man who has caused all of this.

Chapter Twenty-One

The smirk on Owen Lloyd's face grows even wider as Carolyn stands upright, his eyes instantly falling to her breasts, now visible through the torn shirt. She covers herself with an arm.

"You!" Carolyn says.

She wants to pounce at him, wrap her hands around his throat and throttle the bastard, but the pain at the top of her leg and across her back argues otherwise. Plus, Owen Lloyd has a weapon.

"I bet you want to play footsie with me now, don't ya, bitch?" Owen chuckles, exposing yellow teeth as he steps closer to the edge. He places his free hand into the pocket of his tatty hoodie and peers down at the battered car.

"If I'm honest, I didn't mean for that to happen. I only wanted to scare ya a little. Shake ya up, that's all."

"You... you wanted to shake me up? Why? I told you, I was trying to find your missing brother." Carolyn shakes her head, trying to make sense of it all. "Why on earth would you try to stop me?"

Owen circles her slowly, unfazed by the rain that showers his face.

"You won't find him. All you're going to do is to cause trouble around here for my family."

"Trouble? In what way? I'm trying to help—"

"The rumours will start again!" he barks, his eyebrows furrowed. "After you went round telling people how you saw a body last week... my mum... she... she went straight back to locking herself away again. Staying in her room and drinking herself to death... And then my dad, he'll take it out on me, again."

Carolyn knows how Owen's mother, Gwen, must be feeling. It's all she wanted to do after Simon and Ryan's death. She still wishes that she could just lock herself away, not face the world and the responsibilities that come with it.

She attempts to speak, but decides not to. Owen seems to have picked up his pacing with angrier steps. The crowbar drops to his side and is brought back up to his shoulder again.

He goes on. "It's old news. He probably ran away after we argued, and I... I really can't blame him for not wanting to come back here. To all this shit. It's probably my fault he went..." he tails off.

Carolyn speaks softly, but tries not to sound patronising. "What do you mean, it's your fault? I'm sure that's not true."

Owen spits and goes to answer, but stops and watches in the distance behind her.

Headlights are approaching.

Carolyn and Owen look at each other. She shifts her weight from one leg to the other to ease the pain. He stands still, frozen. The vehicle in the distance is approaching too fast for either of them to make a decision.

It reaches them within the minute and screeches to a halt on the wet road, a couple of feet behind Owen's van. The driver steps out and rushes over, leaving the engine running, blowing smoke from its exhaust.

"Barry?" Owen says, examining the man's face.

Before he replies, Barry is in front of Owen and swinging a fist to his face. Carolyn hears the whack echoing in the quiet night. Owen drops the crowbar and it hits the road with a ringing noise, followed then by the sound of him hitting the ground while holding his nose. Blood gushes down his face and on to the front of his hoodie.

"You all right?" the big man asks Carolyn.

She doesn't respond. It's all happening too fast. She's watching the blood leave Owen's face, and her stomach turns a little.

"Hello... Are you ok?" Barry asks again, waving a hand across her vision.

She just nods, still speechless.

Owen groans on the ground. He rests on his hands and knees and attempts to stand.

"What the fuck... wh—" He breaks off as Barry grabs at the hood on the back of his top and pushes him back down.

Carolyn watches as Barry handles Owen with ease.

"W-why... H-how did you know?" Carolyn asks.

Barry squats, resting a thick, heavy knee on Owen's back, and Owen cries out, struggling to breathe from under Barry's weight. Carolyn guesses he is twenty stone at least, though with the physique of a rugby player rather than just overweight.

"I watched you leave my flat," Barry explains. "A few seconds later, I saw his van follow behind you. I just had a bad feeling, I guess. I knew you'd be heading this way."

"How did you know I'd be heading this way?" Carolyn asks.

"Your mum lives facing the church, right?" he asks over Owen's cries of pain.

She nods again, and clears her throat. "Yes, she does," she says. "Thanks. I don't—"

"Do you have your phone?" Barry interrupts.

Carolyn pulls it from her pocket. It now has signal as she's above the ditch, though the home screen is dull with a horizontal orange line across the faces of Simon and Ryan. She unlocks it. It's still usable through the damaged screen.

Owen begs to be let go. Carolyn walks away to use the phone, so not to hear Owen's yells of pain.

"What's the name of this road we're on?" Carolyn asks.

"Wilson Drive," Barry shouts back, keeping his eyes on Owen.

"Ple... please, I can't breathe. I think you've broken my nose," Owen says.

Barry looks over to Carolyn. She shrugs. "Maybe let him sit up a little."

Barry lifts his knee from Owen's back and stands behind him. Owen sits up and uses the sleeve of his hoodie to wipe the blood from his nose.

"You said it was your fault," Carolyn says, returning from

123

making her phone call and stooping down to Owen's height.

"What?" Owen replies, his voice sounding nasal.

"About your brother. You said it was your fault. What did you mean by that?"

Owen looks from Carolyn to Barry. He pulls his sleeve away from his nose and checks to see if the bleeding has stopped.

"The day he went missing," Owen begins, turning his head away to spit. "My mum and dad were at a party, a christening... I think. Or an engagement, I don't really remember. Anyway, Dylan's heard the rumours going around, people in school joking about how our mum is a slut." Owen spits out a mouthful of blood and saliva. He goes on. "The rumours stopped a few years back, but when kids learn it from their friends or overhear other people speaking, they bring it to school. They started calling him a bastard and other names. Anyway, our parents were at that party, and Dylan and me were fighting. We'd always fight. Dylan said something about my teeth, that they looked dirty or horrible... Something stupid like that. I shouted that Dad wasn't his real father, and he went berserk, kept asking me was it true. I realised I was being a twat and told him I was just saying it to make him mad. I don't think he believed me though."

"That's it?" Carolyn asks.

"Yeah, he stormed out. If we hadn't argued, he'd have been at home, safe," Owen says, tears starting down his cheeks.

Carolyn nods. "What were you going to do tonight if Barry hadn't turned up?" she asks.

Barry looks from her to Owen, then into the distance, as if waiting for the blue flashing lights to appear.

"I just wanted to scare ya off. I told ya I didn't mean for your car to go over like that. I just wanted to give ya a little bang and hope that you'll leave looking into Dylan. I... I'm sick of the rumours. I hear them around town. All sniggering behind my back. All because somebody started a rumour that my mum had an affair with that queer-looking fella in town."

Owen sniffs with one clear nostril; the other is still blocked with blood.

Carolyn and Barry stand for the next fifteen minutes as Owen is ordered numerous times to stay on the ground. Carolyn can't stop watching Barry, this mountain of a man who has saved her. She's grateful it wasn't the other way around, that Barry had been the attacker and Owen had turned up to save her. The two of them wouldn't have stood a chance against him. But Carolyn thinks Barry doesn't look the aggressive type; when he speaks, his voice is low and gentle. His eyes meet Carolyn's and he gives a warm, shy smile before fixing his gaze back down to Owen. She's still curious about why he hadn't answered the door to her earlier, and why, in The Coffee Shack, he'd picked up and taken off without finishing his lunch. But these questions can wait until Owen's prying ears aren't listening in. She hugs herself and shivers as her wet, torn clothes cling to her skin. Barry takes off his checked fleece and hands it to her. Underneath he's wearing a worn t-shirt, the type you only wear to lounge around the house.

"No, it's fine," Carolyn says.

"You'll freeze out here. Please, take it," his soft voice beckons. Carolyn accepts and slides it over her shoulders before zipping it up. The fleece feels like a tent on her, but warm, very warm. She can't wait for tonight to be over, and for her to be in bed sipping tea.

Headlights bounce in the distance as a vehicle hits the potholes, racing towards them. But it's not a police vehicle, and the speed of the car shows it's not a passer-by either. The person driving can only be heading for them.

Barry strains his eyes and watches as the vehicle comes into focus, then shoots Carolyn a quizzical look.

Chapter Twenty-Two

"Are you fucking joking me?" Frank Lloyd asks as he steps down from his pickup truck and heads towards the three of them.

Owen is still sitting on the ground.

Carolyn had remembered that she'd saved Frank's number in her phone from the flyer Gwen had given her, and had decided to leave the police out of it. Though now she wonders if she's done the right thing by not calling them. Barry looks at her, still with the questionable face, and draws himself up to his full height.

"Get up off the road, you fucking idiot," Frank shouts, giving his son an evil glare. "Get the winch attached to that car, and start pulling it out of the ditch. NOW!" He murmurs something else under his breath that Carolyn and Barry don't hear. Carolyn sees Owen's face turn pale, and she knows that whatever his father whispered isn't going to be pleasant for him.

Owen stands up, brushes the mud from his bottom, and heads straight over to the pickup. The winch makes a whirring noise as he pulls on it and slides himself down the muddy embankment.

"Thank you for not calling the police. It's the last thing that idiot needs right now… Thank you," Frank Lloyd says, examining the car as Owen attaches the hook of the pulling winch to a place near the wheel. "It's not that bad. Looks worse than it is, I swear."

"So you'll fix it?" Carolyn asks, standing next to him.

"Oh yeah. It'll take me a couple of days at least, but I'll get it back to you good as new. He'll be doing most of the work himself. I'll see he's punished properly."

126

Carolyn doesn't like the sound of that. She wonders what Frank's punishments would be. Thinking back to the scar on Julio Alcala's face, she feels a slight chill. A small part of her actually feels sorry for Owen, being the talk of the town whenever his back is turned, and paying for a mistake his mother had made years earlier.

"Frank, go easy on him," she says. "I felt like strangling the life out of him before. But I think he's just angry and upset that Dylan is still missing. I think it was just his way of expressing it, and me poking my nose in probably didn't help either."

Frank's eyes are fixed on his son as he climbs back from the upturned motor. He looks back at Carolyn and gives her an expression she can't make out. Is Frank wondering how much she knows? Has she heard the rumours about Mark Buckles and Gwen Lloyd?

Frank turns and looks at Barry. "What are you doing here?" he asks.

Barry steps forward, his big frame making Frank look small. "I was heading back from a job and saw what had happened. I had to interfere. Sorry about his nose."

Frank smirks a little. "He deserved it. Lucky you turned up. Thanks. Are you ok driving her home?"

Carolyn looks from Frank to Barry, then back at Frank again. She is about to refuse, but Barry gets in first.

"Of course. I can get her home." Barry smiles at her. The questions she has for him swim around her head.

They walk over to where Barry's van is parked and Carolyn is about to climb in when she remembers her bag. The battered car is now at the top of the ditch, and the sensation of anxiety hits her. She wonders how she is going to explain this to her mother.

"I need my bag from the back," Carolyn shouts, and Owen pulls it from the back seat and jogs over. It's a little scuffed but not drenched with water.

"I... um... I'm sorry. Thank you for not calling the police. I'm sorry." Owen says. He turns to walk away.

"Owen," she shouts. "I did you a favour so your dad will

go easy on you. Now you must promise to do me a favour. Stop beating that dog."

He agrees before looking back down to the road, then walks over to his father.

It's cold in Barry's Ford Transit van. It would be a lot colder if Carolyn weren't wearing the thick fleece. The heater is on high, but it's only producing cold air and is making a wheezing noise like an asthmatic struggling to breathe. It's also very noisy. Tools, ladders and planks of wood rattle and bounce around the back with every pothole and bump in the road. After briefly examining the cut on Carolyn's head, Barry insists she should go to the hospital and have it looked at in case of concussion. The hospital is based in St Davids. Llanbedr only has a medical centre, which closes at five. Carolyn agrees. This way, she gets to question him a little. A slight wave of shame clogs her mind at the way she'd stereotyped him only a few days before. She can see he's thinking of something to say, to break the silence, so she decides to go straight in with it.

"How come you lied back there?"

"Lied about what?" Barry asks, looking insulted.

"You told me that you saw Owen following me as I left your flat. You told Frank that you were just passing through after finishing a job."

"I didn't think you'd want Frank knowing you were at my flat. He's aggressive and usually jumps to conclusions without thinking them through."

"So you were home, then? How come you didn't answer the door to me?" Barry looks at her and then back to the road. He blows out his cheeks and takes a moment to answer.

"I have a criminal record... for abduction."

Carolyn straightens in her seat, her fingers hovering over the door handle as the internal voice speaks again. *What have you done? You must be the easiest person in the world to abduct. You freely climbed into his van, literally.*

"Let me explain," he says. Carolyn listens through the rattling of the van. Barry starts from the beginning, telling

128

her about his ex-wife, Lisa. They'd originally lived in Fishguard, and she'd always had an addictive personality, whether that be chocolate, coffee or booze. At the local pub she met this woman, Johanna, who had recently moved to the area, and Lisa and Joanna had become close friends. Things just escalated from there, Barry explains. After their daughter, Amy, was born, Lisa calmed down on her partying for a while.

Barry, thinking the birth of Amy would stop the arguing and the fighting between Lisa and him, was proved wrong. Lisa got back in touch with Johanna one night after the pair had an argument, and she took off, leaving Amy alone with Barry for three days. Her phone had been turned off and Barry was worried sick. He'd contacted the police, the hospitals and even Lisa's parents, and he'd driven around town with Amy in the baby seat next to him, asking whether people had seen Lisa.

On the fourth day, when Lisa finally returned home, wearing the same clothes and stinking like an old forgotten gym bag, she had confessed that she'd been at some derelict house with Johanna and a few old friends. People she knew from her past, she'd said. She admitted sleeping with a man she met there, and for three days they'd shot up heroin and drank cheap cider. When Barry attempted to take Amy away to stay at his own parents with her for a while, Lisa broke down in tears, swore it was a mistake and it would never happen again. Barry decided to stay, but he'd sleep on the sofa, and they would only share the home for the sake of their daughter.

Lisa's addiction for heroin grew stronger. She'd passed out one day on the sofa, leaving Amy in her cot starving while Barry was at work. Soon after that, he'd filed for divorced, left Fishguard and moved to Llanbedr.

Lisa was very crafty at hiding her addiction from the social services, and it was agreed that Barry would have Amy at weekends. That agreement lasted for five years, and Barry watched as Lisa deteriorated more and more. One night, Amy called Barry as he was finishing a job painting a ceiling. Amy was crying down the phone, saying that she could hear her mother fighting with a man as she listened from the top of the stairs. Barry assumed it was about drug money, and raced over. By the time he arrived, Lisa was high and had passed out. He took Amy over to his flat. When Lisa woke she'd called the police, claiming that Barry had forced his way into her house and taken their daughter. The police arrived and demanded to know why he had taken her out on a night when he was not entitled to have her. The officer, PC Alan Raines, had accused Barry of acting aggressively towards him as he tried to escort Amy back to her mother. The statement from the officer, together with the lies Lisa made up about Barry beating her in the past, worked in Lisa's favour and she was granted full custody. Now Barry can't contact Amy until she's at least sixteen, which is two months away.

His massive hands tighten around the steering wheel, and his face is as red as a London bus.

Carolyn shakes her head and apologises. "That still doesn't really answer my question though," she says, trying to smile and lighten the situation. "How come you never answered your door to me?"

He answers calmly. "I saw you pull up outside the function hall I'm working on the other day. You know, when you were speaking with that Spanish guy?"

Carolyn nods.

"I heard him call you a private investigator. Even people in the pub are speaking about a woman going around town in a red Volkswagen, questioning people about those boys that went missing. I saw you that day at The Coffee Shack and I wasn't in the mood to be questioned. It started when the first boy went missing years ago. I don't know how they got my information… Probably have a friend working in the police or something. Anyway, I've had a couple of private investigators in the past watching me and trying to question me. They see I have a criminal record for abduction, and that's it, you're Suspect Number One. It's not good for business, you know? I don't need people watching me from their cars as I'm working on people's homes. And I didn't want to have to explain that my criminal record is for trying to abduct my own daughter to keep her safe from her drug addict mother. I'm sick of it." He slows the van down as they take a corner.

"I understand," Carolyn replies.

"Anyway, I watched you leave my flat and get back into your car, then that scumbag Owen started following you. I had a bad feeling, and it took me a few minutes to decide to follow him. Lucky I did, hey?"

"Yes, it was. Thank you again. Oh, and I'm not a private investigator. I don't know if Owen did just want to scare me, but it worked." Carolyn shifts her leg as cramp sets in.

Barry looks at her with that same questioning expression. "You're not a private investigator?"

Carolyn shakes her head. "Nope."

"Then why the hell are you going around looking into the missing boys?"

She looks at him and sighs. "I saw a body down the well behind my mother's home—"

"What?"

"Nobody believes that I saw it, but I did. The police think I'm crazy, my mother thinks I'm crazy, and everybody else in Llanbedr thinks I'm crazy."

The van turns a corner and the hospital comes into view a hundred yards down, the entrance lit up with dim blue lighting.

"Well… If you say you saw it, then I believe you." Barry smiles.

"You do?" Carolyn asks. Hearing the words *I believe you* feels magical.

"Yeah, you don't seem crazy to me. I'm not trying to question you…" Barry stops.

"But?"

"But doesn't there have to be a body first?"

Carolyn sighs. It sounds louder than she intended, but is mainly for the ache in her leg as she shifts to face Barry. "I did see a body. That's the craziest thing about it. I wasn't dreaming or imagining it. I saw the body… his eyes were looking up at me. It was real. I could never have imagined anything that... I'm sorry... but it was too real."

Barry parks the van and shuts off the engine. He nods at Carolyn. "Okay then. Well, until I see any evidence of you being crazy, I believe you fully. You think it's one of the boys that went missing?"

"I'm almost certain it is, yes. I believe it's Elwyn Roberts."

"You think after you saw the body... that what, somebody else moved it?" Barry sounds sceptical, and, in all honesty, Carolyn can't blame him. If it was the other way round, and Barry was telling this story to Carolyn, she would probably try to stay well clear of him!

"That sounds like the most likely explanation, I guess. I really don't know, Barry. But I do know that I saw a body down the well, and when I came back with the police it was gone."

"I'm surprised you haven't spoken to Sophie yet."

Carolyn looks at him, puzzled. "The girl who works at Llanbedr Convenience? Why would I speak with her?"

"When Frank's boy went missing, Sophie went to the police and told them she saw something. But I guess it must have been nothing..." Barry shrugs.

"Hmm," Carolyn replies, unclipping her seatbelt. "Do you know what it was that she saw?"

Barry frowns and shakes his head. "No, sorry. Listen, it's going to take Frank a few days to get your car sorted. I can drive you into town tomorrow if you like. You know, to speak with Sophie." His day-old stubbly cheeks begin to blush.

Carolyn thinks about it for a moment. "Only if you don't mind," she says. "That would be great, thank you." She hesitates for another moment. "Also, I may be able to use your services tomorrow night, if you're up for it."

Barry pulls a confused look and slides out of the van.

The hospital discharges Carolyn just after eleven. She has a bruise in the shape of a rugby ball on her leg, and her shoulder hurts from bashing into the side of the door, but luckily there are no broken bones, fractures or concussion.

Carolyn had told the nurses that she'd swerved to avoid hitting a fox in the middle of the road, and Barry, who had been driving behind her, had backed up the story.

Barry drops Carolyn off at home. She feels excited to have somebody on her side, someone who believes her story and is keen to find out the truth.

As Carolyn comes through the door, Jeanette, who had fallen asleep on the recliner, wakes and rubs her eyes.

"It's very late. Where have you been?" she asks, showing Carolyn a worried look after hearing the loud engine from Barry's van take off.

"I was driving home, and a fox ran out in front of me. I swerved not to hit it and the car ended up down a ditch. I'm sorry, Mum."

"Are you ok?"

Carolyn says that she's fine, but the car is damaged and that it is being repaired by the rescue guy. She just hopes Frank Lloyd's work is as good as Barry had promised.

"Your head?" Jeanette runs a hand over the bandage. Luckily Carolyn hadn't needed stitches, but she does flinch as Jeanette's finger touches the swelling.

"I bumped it on the steering wheel, but it's fine. Stop worrying and go to bed," Carolyn replies, taking her weight on her good leg and trying not to show that it hurts. That would only make her mother worry more.

Carolyn can see that Jeanette is sceptical at first, but after she smiles and tells her mother that she's already been the hospital to be checked over, Jeanette eventually heads for bed.

Chapter Twenty-Three

Carolyn waits in the front porch for Barry. Her mother had left half an hour ago for the church. She can hear the loud rumble from the van's engine before he comes into sight. Carolyn climbs in and is welcomed by a strong-smelling aftershave. She's smelled it before. Simon had the same one.

Barry is wearing a grey jumper with a blue shirt collar poking out of the neckline, dark jeans and smart boots. A little too smartly dressed for running a 'friend' into town. The van has also received a cleaning. The dash is now clutter-free and there are no empty wrappers or cola bottles in the passenger footwell. Carolyn hopes Barry doesn't see this as a date. She isn't ready for dating. She's not sure if she will ever be ready for it again.

"Hi. You look smart for interrogating a shop girl," Carolyn jokes.

"I like to make an effort on my days off, you know. I'm always wearing paint-stained scruffs," Barry replies, his cheeks turning a slight pink, though now there is no stubble to conceal the blushing. Today he's clean-shaven.

"You look fine. I was just joking," she says, holding up a hand. "Just don't think this is a date." They both laugh and head for town.

Carolyn hadn't mentioned Simon and Ryan to Barry last night. She thought that there was no need for it to come up, but then she thought she ought to explain why she's so eager to figure out what had happened to the disappearing body she seen in the well. She decides she'd tell him later over a coffee. Although Barry doesn't appear to need any explanations. It seems he's already on board.

Carolyn is more relaxed on their drive into town. It feels

more comfortable than last night. Barry keeps apologising over the broken heater and the worn shock absorbers. As they hit bumps in the road, his face blushes a darker shade.

"I think it's time for a new van. I've had this for the past five years and it was already ten years old when I got it," Barry chuckles. "I bought it for a bargain though."

Carolyn tells him again that it's fine, and she's very grateful for his help.

At Llanbedr Convenience, Barry says he'll stay in the van and wait. He doesn't want to seem intimidating towards Sophie. Carolyn agrees it might be a good idea.

Sophie is starting her lunch break as Carolyn approaches and asks if they can talk. The skinny redheaded girl ushers her around the side of the building to a part that has a sign reading *EMPLOYEES ONLY*. They sit on a wooden picnic bench, surrounded by plastic coffee cups. The surrounding floor is cluttered with dozens of cigarette butts. Sophie reaches into her bag and pulls out a box of cigarettes. She offers one to Carolyn, and when she refuses, she puts one to her lips and lights up. Sophie tilts her head up to blow the smoke away from Carolyn's face.

"So how come you want to talk to me?" Sophie asks, taking another drag of her cigarette. "It's about those missing boys, right?"

Carolyn nods.

"It's about time somebody decided to do something about it. After I told the police, the old fat one who is always sweating didn't even write anything down. He just listened, staring at my tits the whole time, then thanked me and left." Carolyn guesses she's talking about Inspector Richard Williams. Not wanting to give the same impression as him, she reaches into her own bag and pulls out the pad, turns to a new page and puts pen to paper.

"So, what did you tell the police?"

Sophie stares straight ahead, holding her cigarette in one hand and twisting a strand of her long red hair in the other. She begins.

"I was twenty-two when it happened. Rhodri and I had

only been together for a couple of months. My dad didn't like him at the best of times, because he smoked weed and was mad for motorbikes. So we'd go camping you know, so we could... do it." She flusters.

Carolyn nods, and writes this down.

Sophie continues. "I didn't feel comfortable doing it at his parents' house, and there was no way Dad would allow him to stay at ours. So I'd say I was staying at Rachel's, my friend. I don't want to sound like a slut to my parents. But instead, we'd go camping at Sandle Moor. We'd hike up the mountain and find a desolated place overlooking Llanbedr. We'd sit up all night smoking pot, and drinking, and making love."

Carolyn smiles at the *making love.*

Sophie goes into a stare again, as though remembering their romantic time together. Carolyn waits, and after a moment, the girl looks back up at Carolyn and smiles, taking the last drag of her cigarette before flicking it away and lighting another, all in the space of five seconds. Carolyn makes a few notes and gestures for Sophie to continue.

"Well, anyway, it was so quiet up there, and after we'd smoked a few spliffs, Rhodri would always go silent and watch over the town, you know, daydreaming? He was always so deep and meaningful."

Carolyn conceals another smirk and nods.

"We both heard it: a twig snapping and bushes moving. We looked at each other. Rhodri jumped up ready to catch somebody watching us, but we didn't find anyone."

Carolyn writes it down. "Go on," she urges.

"Then we went to sleep, after some more lovemaking, but later that night... I woke up to go for a pee. I think it was around half four, maybe five in the morning. It was all misty outside and really cold, and I swear to God I saw the back of somebody's shoulder walking away from our tent. I almost choked on my breath. I panicked and ran back in the tent to tell Rhodri, but he wouldn't wake up. He just kept telling me to leave him alone and go back to sleep... but I couldn't. I stayed awake for hours listening in case there was a killer after us. It wasn't long after that boy went missing. I had to wait until Rhodri woke up before I could pee." Sophie inhales deeply.

Carolyn looks up to Sophie, then back down to her pad with the useless information she's been given.

"That's it? That's all you told the police?" Carolyn asks, trying not to show frustration at a wasted journey.

"Well, I didn't tell them about the weed we smoked... but yeah. I told them of the person I saw the back of. But they told me it wasn't helpful," Sophie says, her cigarette smoked almost to the butt. "Oh, and now we've broken up."

Carolyn thanks Sophie for her time, and heads around to the front before the girl can light another cigarette.

"Well... That was a waste of time," Carolyn says, climbing into the van as Barry is in the middle of checking his teeth in the sun visor mirror. He slams it closed as she gets in.

"What happened?" he asks.

"Sophie and her boyfriend went camping. Sophie thought she might have seen a Peeping Tom watching them, and now, sadly, she and her boyfriend have broken up." Carolyn drops her bag into the footwell. "That's it. That's the whole story."

Barry stays silent, his cheeks twitching as he fights back laughter. When Carolyn looks over, they both open up.

"What's this thing you might be able to use me for then, other than my taxi service?" Barry says.

Carolyn looks at her watch. "Soon."

"Come on. I've been wondering all night what it could have been. Tell me."

"I'd like to buy you a coffee as a thank-you for saving me yesterday, and I can explain then. Is that ok?" Carolyn asks.

At The Coffee Shack, they both order large lattes – Barry's plain, Carolyn's with a shot of caramel syrup – and take a seat at the window. It's a quiet afternoon. Two elderly women sit three tables away, not speaking. A man and his daughter are sitting at the back, next to the door for the toilets. It's the table Carolyn would have chosen as she thinks it looks more private.

Barry's huge hand cups his mug, almost hiding it in his palm. He looks up at the man and his daughter, who are colouring pictures, and sighs. Carolyn acknowledges his sadness and shows a sympathetic smile. She spends the next half hour discussing Simon and Ryan, telling him about the accident and about the woman driving the Mercedes that she was sure had Ryan strapped in the back seat, that day in Ashwood forest.

"Wow. So that's why you're in Llanbedr then. There I was feeling sorry for myself because I don't have contact until Amy is sixteen, which is pretty soon." He smiles at the thought, but quickly the smile drops. "I'm sorry."

"Its... okay," Carolyn says, though she knows it isn't *okay*. None of this is *okay*. She shouldn't even be here in Llanbedr. "Thank you for listening and for helping me."

"So," he says, holding open his hands, "what you got so far?"

She tells him about her visit to the Roberts' home and the pictures she saw of the young boy, especially the one of him sitting on the rock, fishing.

"But Elwyn Roberts went missing about seven years ago."

"It was eight, actually. And that's what's getting to me. Not only does the body vanish, but it's supposed to belong to a kid that went missing eight bloody years ago."

"It doesn't make any sense."

"This is what I've got so far." Carolyn pulls out the pad and places it on the table in front of Barry. "I literally have no idea what I'm doing. I'm just making notes, pissing people off, and hoping for the best." She finishes the last of her coffee.

"You feel really passionate about finding out the truth," Barry says, looking up from the pad.

"It's something I'd hope another mother would do, if it was my son."

Barry flicks through the pages. "Julio Alcala?" he asks.

"The guy you saw me speaking with the other night... outside that function hall you were at."

Barry nods. "P's Party Accessories. What's a party shop

got to do with any of this?" he asks, intrigued.

"The day you saw me talking to Julio Alcala. It must have been roughly ten minutes later, he left his home, and I don't know why, but I followed him, and he went to that party shop. He was in there for about half an hour."

"So?"

"So, it might be nothing, I guess. I paid the party shop a little visit the other day. There's this locked storage room." Carolyn goes on to explain how she got the key and what she found. She tells Barry about the cork board with cut-outs of young girls, the laptop, the tissues and hand cream.

Barry grimaces. "And Mark Buckles, the candle shop owner?"

Carolyn nods. "Apparently he's Dylan's biological father, or so the rumour goes. I thought I'd go and speak to him, to see if he could shine some light on what's happened or what he thinks might have happened. But to be honest he was quite rude."

Barry flicks through the rest of the pad and pushes it back over. "You still haven't told me what you need me for tonight."

Carolyn lowers her voice and explains her plan to him.

He leans in closer to the table and keeps his own voice low. "You want me to break into the party shop using the tools in my van and steal the laptop?"

She explains her gut feeling is screaming at her that something isn't right with the owner, or with whatever it was that Julio had picked up the other night.

"Why would he drive such a distance if it wasn't important?" Carolyn asks.

Barry rests back in his chair, looking thoughtful.

You're completely crazy, the internal voice shouts. *He's going straight to the police!*

Barry leans back in, looking side from to side, and smirks. "I'd say it's still far too early and far too bright to go breaking into a party shop," he says. "You go and get us another coffee and we'll discuss our plan... Oh... and we're putting the laptop back once we've searched through it."

139

Chapter Twenty-Four

Barry parks his van next to the cars for sale and turns off the ignition. The van is in roughly the same place where Carolyn had parked the other night, after following Julio. It's gone 6:45 pm., and according to the shop's website, the shop closes at 5:30 pm. The shutters are three-quarters of the way down, but the lights are still on and the party shop's van is parked in its designated spot. Barry watches his wing mirrors and is beginning to breathe nervously. His index finger taps agitatedly against the steering wheel.

"Don't worry. Try to relax," Carolyn says. "Even if he does spot us, we're not breaking the law by being here, are we? Besides, if he drives past, we'll pretend that we're kissing. I saw that in a *Mission Impossible* film."

Barry doesn't answer. Carolyn doesn't look at him, but she knows he's blushing again.

"Okay, I think he's leaving," Carolyn says, watching as the shop lights switch off.

The obese man drops the shutters to the floor, locks up, and heads for his van. He starts it and pulls towards the entrance of the industrial site.

"We'll give it a few minutes before going in," Barry says.

"SHUSH!" Carolyn holds a finger up, as though the party shop owner can hear them from over a hundred yards away. They both watch as the van comes to a stop, then its reversing lights come on and it backs into the parking space. The party shop owner gets out and reopens the shutters, flicks on the lights and disappears inside.

"What's happening?" Carolyn asks.

"Do you think he saw us and is calling the police?" Barry asks nervously.

"Calling the police about what? That you've driven me here to look at these cars that are for sale, after I swerved from hitting a fox and ended up down the ditch?" Carolyn replies. She wonders if Barry has always been like this, a worrier. For a man of his size, she would never have guessed he'd feel nervous, not when he looks as if he works for security at night clubs.

Whilst the obese man is in the party shop, Barry and Carolyn sit with their eyes glued on the shutters, watching. After forty seconds which feel more like five minutes, the light goes out and the obese man, now sweating considerably more from the walking, comes back into view holding a leather case. It's the laptop.

"SHIT!" Carolyn whispers. "He's got the laptop with him. Why?" she asks.

Barry sighs, keeping his voice down too, the same way you do when standing in a lift with strangers.

The party shop's van starts up again and heads out of the industrial grounds, this time making it to the road and heading away from them.

"Follow him!" Carolyn orders.

"What?"

"Follow him!" she orders again, this time more assertively.

"But he *has* the laptop, Carolyn. What's the point?" Barry argues.

"Please, just follow him. Follow him."

Barry pauses for a second, then he turns the engine on, looks in his mirrors and joins the road, keeping a safe distance behind the party van.

"What are you expecting we do here?" he asks.

"I… I don't know. I just want you to follow him and see where he goes. I don't think he suspects us. It's just a strange coincidence that he went back in for it," she says, trying to sound confident and keep Barry focused. Although while saying this, she feels the knot in her stomach tighten.

"He probably takes it home every night. Why leave a laptop in there? It could get nicked."

"It was locked behind a door with a thick padlock. Why

141

would he lock it away like that? He'd keep it under the counter he sits at, surely. I have a laptop in my shop in Leeds. I never take it home. Ryan would want to play on it if I did and probably give me a virus." She falls silent and watches the van in front. A car is waiting to pull out from a side road and Barry slows down and flashes it out, creating more of a distance.

"Well, I think it's normal to want to bring your laptop home. I wouldn't want to leave mine in there," Barry says.

Carolyn doesn't reply.

They watch the van take the next turning, and after the car carries on they turn after it. They're heading down a long open lane, passing a farmhouse then a landfill a few yards down. Apart from a lorry that had just passed, the road is quiet. Finally, the party van slows and indicates right into the driveway of an old cottage. The grounds around the cottage are unkept and the wild hedges stand tall, almost completely hiding the two-storey building.

Barry drives past the cottage, finds a lay-by further down the road and parks. The cottage lights can be seen through the bony, leafless bushes.

"So what's the plan now?" Barry asks, shutting off the engine.

Carolyn shrugs, looking from him to the cottage. She wishes she'd taken the laptop with her the other day, while the obese man was busy looking at his flat tyre. That was a silly idea; if the place had CCTV that she hadn't spotted, or even if he'd described her to the police, she knew Inspector Richard Williams would happily take her in for the owner to confirm it was her. She's come this far, and no way is she going to give up now. One way or another, she's going to have a look at what's on that laptop.

Barry turns to face Carolyn. "Go on. What's on your mind?" he asks. "I can see you're concentrating on something."

She is, in fact, concentrating on something: a plan. She pulls in her tongue from gritted teeth and meets his gaze.

"I'm going to find a way in and get hold of that laptop tonight. I understand if you want to leave me here and head home. It's not a problem." But even as she speaks, she knows only too well that it would have been a very big problem if he did decide to take off and leave her all alone out here.

Barry shakes his head. "I'm not going to leave you here by yourself, am I?" he says, a slight tone of annoyance to his voice. "I think we might have passed a fish and chip shop not too far back. I'm starving. Want to go grab something to eat, and give him time to settle in?"

They order a sausage each and a portion of chips to share, then head back to the cottage. There is a dim light in the front room, and they can also see flashes from the TV bounce back through the crack in the curtains.

"He's still up, watching TV," Carolyn says.

Barry parks back in the lay-by. "Give it time," he replies with a smile.

"It's such a nice little cottage, isn't it?" Carolyn says, keeping her mind occupied on anything other than what she has planned.

Barry agrees. They finished their food and play I-Spy, and talk more about Simon, Ryan and Jeanette. They speak about Carolyn's plans once she heads back to Leeds, and whether Barry is planning on moving from the flats above the betting shop and café. It's now just after half past nine, and the light in the front room has gone out. They watch carefully, but can't see any flashes from the television either. A lamp in the top window of the cottage switches on, and a few moments later it flicks off.

Barry urges Carolyn to give it another half hour. A lorry passes them quickly, with the driver not showing any interest in the lay-by or their van. They watch in silence for any other life in the cottage, then Barry turns on the engine and creeps forward. He bumps the tyres onto the kerb outside the cottage and shuts off the engine.

"Shouldn't you have stayed in the lay-by?" Carolyn asks.

"I'm not taking any chances if something goes wrong and he calls the police. I want us gone out of here, quick. I don't want to give him the time to see our faces or my van as we run back to it across the road. Besides, here it's hidden behind the bushes."

143

They climb from the van and close the doors, careful not to slam them shut. Barry takes a couple of screwdrivers, a small LED torch and a metal rule with him, and they walk slowly into the front garden. Their steps crunch on the stones in the drive.

"Wait… does he have kids?" Barry asks, stopping Carolyn with his arm held out. She steps closer to him, squinting her eyes as she hears the stones crunch under her boots.

"I don't think he does. And the place was in darkness when he got home, remember?"

"Okay, but any sign of him having kids in there, I'm out!"

"Agreed. Now come on. Be quiet."

They head to the side of the cottage and into the rear garden. An old Ford Mondeo estate with deflated tyres is rusting against trees at the back of the property. Carolyn notices an old sign on the bonnet. The faded balloons and pointed party hats imply it's an old company vehicle.

Barry keeps the torch in the palm of his hand and only points it towards the ground. Carolyn heads over to a window and peers through it as he keeps his eye on the top floor windows.

Carolyn is looking into the kitchen. Like the Lloyds' place it is small and messy, with the work surfaces covered with dirty dishes and takeaway containers. Barry examines the frame of the window; it's small, and the wood is still in good condition.

The next window catches his eye and he shines the torch over it. Carolyn almost screams and tugs at Barry's arm as she sees her own reflection in the window, mistaking it for a person watching them from the inside. Her heart begins to slow. She'll probably laugh about it later. Barry picks his screwdriver at the wood, and splinters fall to the ground. She hears him grunt a little as he slides the metal ruler into the gap. The next noise is the window sliding up.

"You made that look easy. Have you done it before?" she whispers.

"These old cottage windows are ridiculous. The wood is so rotten with damp that it literally flakes off in your hand." Barry hands Carolyn the screwdrivers and the keys to his van. "I'm taking one look around for that laptop. If I can't find it, we're leaving, okay?"

Carolyn nods and looks at the rotted window frame. "Um… I don't think you're going to fit."

"What?"

"I'm not trying to insult you, but I can't see you fitting through that gap."

He shines the torch and looks back. He looks her up and down before stopping at her shoulders. She's little more than half his height and definitely half his weight.

"I think you're right. You'll have to climb through and open the back door for me."

Carolyn swallows and thinks for a moment. If the party shop owner wakes and somehow blocks her escape route, she'll have no chance of protecting herself against him. Whereas Barry is huge; the fat man will probably tell him the combination to his safe if he raises his voice a little. Barry can make intimidating look easy.

"Okay, I'll go in," she says, not believing the words leaving her mouth. Where the hell has this newfound confidence come from? She wonders if it's here to stay.

Handing the tools and van keys back to Barry, she grabs the torch and places her foot into his huge palms as he lifts her up on to the frame. Her heart is beating worse than when she played tennis with Simon. She pushes the thoughts of being captured by the man to the back of her mind, focussing only on the image of holding the laptop in her hands.

The thought of something going wrong preys on her mind. She prays that Barry won't leave her; that he won't take off down the path and dive into his van, leaving her to fend for herself. She also can't blame him if he does; she understands it was a big ask. After all, she was the one who wanted to act brave and reckless and break the law.

Up on the window ledge, Carolyn shines the torch around the room. It's a thin hallway with three doors leading off. Below is a messy wooden table with paperwork stacked high, and letters and envelopes scattered across the desk. Carolyn places half of her body weight on top, waiting for the table to

145

give and alert the sleeping beast upstairs. It creaks a little, but it feels sturdy. She rests on it fully, feeling Barry remove his clutch from her arm – and with it the safety and security of him being there ready to pull her back out if anything goes wrong. She swallows again, this time much harder.

"There's a door to your right," Barry says, keeping his voice to a whisper. "It looks like it leads out to the garden. Go open it and let me in. You can wait by the van. Keep it running in case something goes tits-up."

Carolyn steps off the table and turns to face him. "I'm going to go look for the laptop myself, Barry," she says, her voice trembling with nerves.

Barry opens his mouth to protest, but she cuts him off.

"If anything happens, please go back to the van and take off, ok? I don't want you to have to hurt somebody to protect me; it's not right. But please... please alert the police! I'll keep you out of it, don't worry. Just ring up anonymously and let them know where I am, please." Carolyn steps forward.

"Open the door and get back out here," he whispers, reaching through the window to try to grab her.

She's too far in and doesn't respond.

Of course she's hating every second of what she's doing. But to ask him to break into somebody's home on a hunch she has was just wrong. She knew it was wrong the second the idea came to mind. If she's caught, *she'll* accept the responsibility.

Carolyn takes a deep breath and heads through the narrow hallway.

Chapter Twenty-Five

"Carolyn?" Barry tries again. Now she really is too far in to call her name again. He examines the frame. There's no chance he's fitting through without getting stuck.

What a crazy woman, he thinks, rubbing a hand over his head. He feels the small bristles of hair before holding onto the back of his neck. It's a thing he does a lot whenever he's nervous, especially while watching the football.

He heads for the back door and prays she'll come to her senses and decide to let him in.

***

In the hallway, Carolyn keeps the torch pointing down, concealing most of the light against the sleeve of her jumper. The carpet is old and tatty. It looks as if it had been laid sometime in the seventies. The pattern has rubbed away from years of repeated walking.

She comes to the first door on her left and turns the handle. It's nothing more than a small coat cupboard. It's actually a similar size to the one in the party shop, only this cupboard has no corkboard with clippings of young girls pinned to it.

She closes it slowly and tries the next one, which is slightly ajar. Carolyn shines the torch around and pops her head through the gap. The kitchen. The digital time on the microwave shines back from the corner. There's a low rattling hum coming from the fridge. Pizza boxes are stacked high alongside the cabinets, and dishes sit next to the sink, arranged from large plates to small bowls and pans. It looks as though there has been some attempt to keep the place tidy.

Carolyn heads through the third door, giving it a quick flick of the torch to make sure she's alone. Her heart is beating so fast with every step she takes. She comes to a set of stairs. The banister is cluttered with shirts, trousers and towels hanging loosely over one another. The space on the steps is taken up with shoes for different occasions: trainers, sandals, boots and lace-ups.

Carolyn studies the clothes. There is no women's clothing, just large lounge trousers and even larger shirts. She steps closer to the stairs and stands perfectly still, holding her breath for utter silence and listening for snoring or footsteps before venturing any further.

Nothing. The place is quiet.

The furniture in the front room, like the wallpaper and carpets, is dated. Clothes have taken over the entire couch, again in a tidy fashion. Piles are arranged in garment choice: trousers, t-shirts and underwear. She shines the torch to the armchair facing the television. The fabric looks to have torn throughout the years and is now exposing the cushions inside which have yellowed with age and sweat. To the left of the chair, balancing on its wheels, is a dusty wheelchair. She heads over and examines the pictures on the fireplace, showing the party shop owner smiling next to an elderly woman. He looks at least ten years younger and with more hair than now. In the next one he is with an elderly man. Carolyn assumes they must be his parents. She scans the rest of the pictures before seeing two small wooden boxes, each with a silver plate attached to the front. The first says *MUM*, the second, *DAD*.

Against the back wall stands a bed. It isn't a regular one though. This one is more of a heavy-duty care bed that hospitals issue for bed-bound patients, and it's covered in blankets and a thick layer of dust. Behind it, on the wall, are more pictures of the fat man with his arms around the elderly couple. There are no other people in the frames.

Something brushes against the top of Carolyn's thigh and she spins around, expecting to come face to face with the growling snout of a guard dog, or with the man himself. She points the torch down. Nothing.

She lifts it back up and encounters a face smiling back at her. It's a good job her throat is too dry and stops her from screaming. She holds the torch up to the figure standing tall and still against the back wall, waiting for it to gather its thoughts and rugby-tackle her to the ground.

Maybe she can make a run for it. The fat man wouldn't be able to keep up with her. She's seen how he struggles to walk. She could push things out behind her to block his path as she runs for the back door. But what if the key isn't in it? No, she'd have to head back to the window. But could she make it through in time before he can grab her leg?

The torchlight beams on the handsome face of David Beckham. The cardboard cut-out is holding a white placard with the text *Happy Birthday,* and a small blank space to write in a name of your choice.

She'd laugh if this wasn't breaking and entering.

Carolyn feels her phone vibrate in her pocket. She reaches in her jeans and pulls it out, in case it's Barry warning her that a light has come on upstairs. The half of the screen that's still working shows that it's a message from her mother. She decides to read it later and puts the phone back in her pocket.

Carolyn heads back to the armchair. A small table sits directly in front, a dirty plate on top with opened envelopes held underneath. She pulls one out and reads the name, *Mr Patrick Sawhill.* She makes a mental note of the name, then sees a black leather case on the other side of the chair, next to the wall. The laptop.

She unzips the case and pulls out the laptop, then heads back through the house and makes it outside, unheard and unapproached.

"What the hell, Carolyn?" Barry whispers as he helps her off the ledge. He closes the window silently and they walk back to the van. "Why wouldn't you let me in?"

"I didn't want to involve you any more than I have already. If he caught you in there... I'd never forgive myself."

"I can handle myself," Barry sneers.

"That's what I was afraid of. You shouldn't have to attack a man who would only be protecting his home."

Barry grunts and mumbles something under his breath that Carolyn doesn't hear.

In the van, Carolyn starts up the laptop with trembling hands and places it on the dashboard between them. Her heartbeat is slowly beginning to return to normal.

"Are you ok?" he asks.

She nods, though her palms are clammy and she's still running on adrenaline. It's not every day that she breaks into a cottage and steals a laptop. Usually at this time of night she'd be at home, flicking through invoices with a calculator at her side.

The laptop starts up quickly and then prompts them for a password.

Barry looks at Carolyn and frowns.

"I thought that it might come to this. I just didn't want to say it before and burst your bubble… or jinx us. So I didn't mention it." He leans over the keyboard and punches in *1234*. The box clears his attempt and shakes, asking them for the password again. Next, he types *Password*, then tries it in capital letters. Again, it clears the box, shakes and doesn't open.

"Try *Mum and Dad*," Carolyn suggests. "They're dead. I saw two boxes on the mantelpiece which look as though they contained their ashes. It's just an idea."

Again, wrong password.

"Shit!" Carolyn taps the side of her leg.

"Well I think that's all we can do. I'm not sure how many attempts it gives you before it completely locks up. Do computers do that? Anyway, let's return it." Barry reaches for the door handle.

"Wait," Carolyn says, thinking for a moment. She pulls her phone from her pocket and again sees the message from Jeanette on the home screen, but ignores it as she unlocks the phone. The dividing line across the middle has now grown since the incident with Owen, and makes it hard to search the internet properly.

150

"Can I use your phone?" Carolyn asks. He releases the door handle and pulls out his mobile, handing it over.

"Why do you need it?"

Carolyn doesn't answer. She is too busy typing at the screen. She does a quick internet search and places the phone against her ear.

She frowns when no one answers, and presses *Redial*. The second call is answered, and Carolyn explains the meaning of her call and hangs up. She turns to Barry. "Do you know Stratton Road?"

He thinks for a moment, stroking at the stubble on his face. "Yeah, it's not far from that function hall I saw you at the other day." He turns on the engine and pulls out on to the road. "It won't take us too long to get there."

***

"I think we're pushing our luck here," Barry says, holding a hand to the back of his neck. "What if he comes down and notices his laptop is missing and calls the police?"

They're sitting outside 82 Stratton Road. The road is dead. There are two houses further down, with lights showing in both windows, but no one else seems to be awake, apart from the person they have come to visit.

"He won't come downstairs at almost eleven looking for his laptop. Stop worrying," Carolyn says. "We'll have it back in no time. We're just borrowing it anyway."

"Right. *Borrowing* it. I don't think the police will accept that."

"Terry said he can help us, and I think he can. Oh, do you have twenty quid on you until tomorrow?" Carolyn hopes she sounds more confident than she feels.

She would be lying if she says she hasn't pictured being caught, sentenced and locked away in some shit-hole of a prison. She imagines that she'll look like an easy target to the other women in there: the petty thieves, armed robbers and murderers.

Barry checks his pockets and pulls out a crumpled note.

"Only a tenner, sorry," he says, handing it over. "So, who is this person you think can help us?" Before Carolyn can answer, Terry creeps out of his front door wearing a dressing gown, and holding a small blue laptop.

He approaches Carolyn's window.

"I know we agreed on fifty, but you'll have to wait for the other ten," Carolyn says, passing Terry the notes through the window. "I've only got forty on me."

Terry sighs and rolls his eyes, grabbing the money from Carolyn before pushing it into his dressing gown pocket. He moves the thick, greasy hair from his eyes and opens his own laptop, attaching a cable from his to a port in the fat man's – Patrick Sawhill's – laptop. He types away as Carolyn holds the *borrowed* laptop out of the window of the van. Barry watches, looking from Carolyn to Terry.

"Who owns this laptop anyway? Who's P?" Terry asks, typing away with superfast fingers.

"We also agreed to no questions asked, remember?" Carolyn replies, a little sternly.

Terry grunts, and a moment later he pulls out the cord attached to Patrick Sawhill's laptop, then turns and heads back inside without saying another word.

"He's a real charmer, isn't he? Has he done it?" Barry asks.

Carolyn turns the laptop around. The password screen is now replaced with the default home screen, a picture of beautiful scenery showing a lake and mountains.

Scattered across the screen are plenty of folders and apps. Carolyn nods and smiles. Barry turns on the engine, pulls away from Terry's house and parks in the next street. This one looks as quiet as Stratton Road.

The folders on the home screen have dates underneath. Carolyn clicks on the top one, and the file opens multiple pages that fill the screen.

"It's some sort of invoice system. Bookkeeping maybe?" Carolyn suggests. She opens the next and it is the same as the one before: long lists with the same amounts. She continues to open folders and notices a pattern.

She turns the laptop around to face Barry. "This folder is MOL35," she says, pointing to the top of the page. "It looks as if Patrick Sawhill, the party shop owner, is receiving all these credits – apart from this one and only outgoing." She points to another name further down. Barry leans in close for a better look, and Carolyn goes on. "It's the same as the other folders. Look, one hundred and fifty pounds paid to the code name B101 and the reference MOL35."

"So? It's just invoices from suppliers and customers. Looks pretty normal to me," Barry mutters.

Carolyn shakes her head. "These aren't accounts for a party accessories business." She closes the file and opens another. "Something's dodgy about these. I just can't see what it is."

"Doesn't look like anything illegal to me," Barry says.

She ignores his comment and opens others – more recent, dated during the last two months. Some names on the ledger have changed, but the main one, the one that the party shop owner pays out to, is at the top of every single document. B101, along with the same fee. Carolyn pulls out her damaged phone and snaps a few pictures of the laptop screen.

"What are you doing that for?" Barry asks.

Carolyn shrugs. "I honestly don't know. It might seem useful in the future. These are code names, and the product codes aren't the same as the ones I use to order flour or butter at my shop."

"It's different products than the ones you work with," Barry says.

"That's not it. They're different from any other code I've seen before. I used to work in retail a few years ago. These are…" she tails off.

"These are what?"

"I may be wrong, Barry, but I think these are people. I think these could be payments Patrick Sawhill is receiving online."

"Okay. Well, now you've seen what's on it. Are you ready to return it?" Barry rubs the back of his neck nervously.

"One more thing." Carolyn closes down the files and

clicks the shortcut for the internet. The screen opens with an error message, stating there is no internet connection. She ignores this and clicks on *Settings* and then searches for the *History* tab, which still works offline. She clicks it and tuts as the screen loads.

"Anything?" Barry asks.

She shakes her head. "Completely empty. Not a single web page showing that he's visited lately."

"He's hiding his search results? Hmm, maybe there *is* something dodgy about him."

Carolyn logs out and powers down the laptop. "Okay, let's return it."

"That's it, then?"

"I don't know what else I was hoping to find."

Outside Patrick Sawhill's cottage, Barry switches off the engine and they wait, watching for a light to show anywhere inside. The place looks just how they'd left it.

"There will be more chances," he insists.

"Will there?" she asks, disappointed.

Barry then attempts to argue that he will return the laptop if Carolyn opens the door. She tells him that she knows exactly where the laptop was, and it'll be much quicker and quieter to just let her go. Barry clearly doesn't like this, but reluctantly accepts and agrees to wait outside the window.

Carolyn places the laptop back where she found it, watching carefully not to bump into the cut-out of David Beckham again. On the way out she notices a newspaper clipping on the inside glass of one of the pictures of the elderly woman. She takes a closer look and finds it to be an obituary. Again, at a loss and no idea where to go from here, she pulls out her phone and takes a picture. The flash frightens her. She prays it didn't reach up the stairs.

Outside, Barry closes the window and they head for his van.

"I'm sorry I wasted your time. I'll give you your money back tomorrow," Carolyn promises, sighing deeply. "I was just really expecting to find more, you know." She pulls out her phone and begins reading the message Jeanette had sent earlier.

Barry shrugs, concentrating on the road. "It's fine. I don't know what you expected to find on that computer either. The main thing is that we got in and out undetected. And you can keep the tenner." He lifts his head and yawns.

"Well, if you won't let me pay you back, at least let me buy you a drink tomorrow night. My mum messaged earlier asking if I wanted to go to The Red Fox Halloween party tomorrow night. Apparently, it's a good night out."

"I was already planning on asking if you wanted to go. I figured you wouldn't want to stay in. You're probably used to taking Ryan out Trick-or-Treating."

"I won't be doing that this year," Carolyn sighs. "But yeah, I could do with a drink, after our failure this evening. I think we deserve one."

Barry smiles. "Yeah, I agree."

Chapter Twenty-Six

October 31ˢᵗ

Father Joseph insists that he won't be drinking, and offers to drive Jeanette and Carolyn to The Red Fox for 7:30 pm, as Frank Lloyd has not yet returned Jeanette's car.

Carolyn thinks back to what Father Joseph said at the fair in Fishguard, recalling that he'd said he had a drinking problem.

Father Joseph's face is a mess, with red gashes across his cheeks and throat which are painted on with fake blood. He's torn rips in the sleeves and across the chest of an old shirt. Jeanette tells Carolyn that he did the same last year too.

Carolyn isn't in the mood for dressing up. She and Simon would usually head to a friend's party after they'd taken Ryan Trick-or-Treating. Last year Simon went as the Scarecrow from *The Wizard of Oz*, and Carolyn as Dorothy. Tonight, though, she doesn't want take part in any of this. She doesn't want to have fun without Simon and Ryan.

She'd agreed to wear a simple masquerade mask that Jeanette picked up this morning while out shopping. The mask helps to hide the cut and bruising on her forehead from the incident with Owen Lloyd. At times, when sitting a certain way or walking, the bruise on her leg starts to hurt, and she needs to rest it or alter her position. Though she's tried not to draw attention to it in front of Jeanette, her mother has already asked about the incident with the 'fox' a few too many times. "*What else were you looking at? Not keeping your eyes on the road?*" and "*So it ran out in front of you, just like that? How big was it?*"

Carolyn has kept to the same story: "*Yes, the fox ran out in front of me. It wasn't much bigger than an average-size cat. Barry found me down the ditch and called a tow truck to collect the car before rushing me to the hospital."*

Father Joseph wanders off once they get through the doors of The Red Fox, and Jeanette begins chatting with a short woman who holds a constant open-mouth smile and wide eyes. Carolyn heads for the only free table left, at the back and up a couple of steps. She sits, resting her elbows on the table as she keeps an eye open for Barry, as well as watching her mother mix with the people of Llanbedr. Jeanette laughs and welcomes people at the bar, pointing and discussing their costumes. Unlike Carolyn, Jeanette has always been good at making friends easily. At the moment, she is speaking to an extremely skinny man who is trying to look convincing in an *Incredible Hulk* costume.

Carolyn is gasping for a drink, a cold wine to secretly celebrate breaking into Patrick Sawhill's home last night – and, of course, getting back out unnoticed. No one was hurt and no one is any the wiser. It also means no prison time, for which she is very grateful.

As Carolyn was lying in bed, with the night replaying over in her mind, she was sure she had missed something, something crucial. Carolyn hates the words 'breaking into'. It makes her feel like a criminal, a petty thief, or drug addict looking for ways to support their habit. She much prefers 'obtaining entry'.

Before leaving tonight, Carolyn had done a bit of digging on Facebook and other social media sites for Patrick Sawhill, but no results came back. The most she found was the address of P's Party Accessories, and some outdated amateur pictures of the shop and its inventory.

Carolyn wishes desperately that she could discuss the shop owner with her mother, and get Jeanette's opinion of him.

The internal voice would tell her to forget all about Patrick Sawhill and his laptop. But she can't. She's convinced there is something dodgy about those ledgers.

At some point last night, as she was thinking what the figures on the account could have referred to, she thought she had cracked it. It made sense to her and she was able to accept it and get some sleep. Now, though, she has come to the conclusion that it isn't drug-related. The amounts weren't high enough, and in any case what drug dealer accepts online payments and keeps a journal of his takings?

Carolyn debates going to the bar herself, but doesn't want to lose the table, as the room is filled with more crowds of witches, zombie schoolgirls and superheroes. It really is going to be a busy night.

"You look tired," Barry says.

Carolyn hadn't seen him enter and make his way over to the table through the crowds, even though he is abnormally bulky.

She looks up and smiles at him. "Hi. You know what? I am tired, Barry. I couldn't sleep last night. I must have managed two hours, maybe less. I couldn't help but think we've missed something in those files." She pulls out a stool next to her for Barry to sit on. He's wearing brown trousers, a khaki-coloured shirt underneath a dark brown leather jacket, and a brown Fedora hat that matches the jacket. Carolyn examines his costume with a confused look in her eye.

"Really?" he says, sounding disappointed.

Carolyn doesn't answer. She recognises the character, but still she can't quite put her finger on it.

"I'm Indiana Jones," Barry mutters, taking the seat.

Carolyn nods. "Ah, I get it now." Not that she's ever been a fan of the *Indiana Jones* films. They were more to Simon's taste.

"Anyway… I was thinking about it too," Barry says, taking off his Fedora and placing it on the table. "But we're not going back there. What would happen if we'd got caught? Lisa would have made sure that I never see Amy again. I'm sorry, but I can't risk tha—"

He is interrupted by Jeanette placing two glasses of wine down on the wobbly table, along with a Coke for Father Joseph.

"Hello, I'm Jeanette, Carolyn's mother. I love the *Indiana Jones* films." Jeanette holds out her hand for Barry to shake.

A smile grows on his face and he reaches for her hand. "Thank you. I thought it was an easy one myself, but Carolyn didn't seem to know who I was."

After arguing, he allows Jeanette to buy him a beer.

Carolyn can smell the aftershave he's wearing. It's sweet, and with a hint of ginger. It isn't the same one he was wearing the other day, the one Simon used to have. This is more potent.

Father Joseph joins them and greets Barry before taking a seat next to Jeanette.

Carolyn finishes her wine before anyone else and heads for the bar, ignoring Father Joseph's niggling eyes and humourless comments about her being thirsty, or to slow down.

On a shelf at the back of the bar Carolyn notices a bottle of *Catena Malbec*. It's the same brand Simon would pick up on a Friday night, on his way home from work. They'd usually have a takeaway too, and when Ryan had gone to bed they'd open the bottle and watch a film.

Carolyn orders herself a glass, along with what Jeanette had been drinking, and another beer for Barry. Father Joseph doesn't want another drink.

The place grows busier as Michael Jackson's *Thriller* is playing for the third time since they arrived. It doesn't stop people chanting and proceeding to the dance floor with their cringey dance moves. Carolyn makes it back to the table before the rush of people can sweep her away. A group of zombie cheerleaders sit to the left of them. Carolyn's eyes meet Inspector Richard Williams' gaze and they exchange half-hearted smiles. Williams downs the last of his pint and makes his way over to their table, almost stumbling on the step and falling into their drinks.

"Hi everyone. Hav... having a good night?" he asks, mumbling his words and burping. He has beer stains down the front of his beige shirt.

Everyone says hello back.

"Barry Cookson. I didn't know you knew Jeanette," Williams says.

"I do now, I guess. I'm here with Carolyn."

Williams places his empty glass on the table and rests a sweaty palm on Father Joseph's shoulder as if to stop himself from falling, then looks back to Barry.

"I hope she's not filling your head with crazy things and that she's keeping you out of trouble," Williams says, looking from Barry to Carolyn, a smirk appearing at the corners of his mouth.

"I think she knows it was down to stress, Rich." Father Joseph speaks for her, as if she is some mental patient unable to give an accurate reply without screaming nonsense and throwing shit at them. Carolyn's fists tighten, and she can feel the immense urge to give Father Joseph and the drunken, red-faced Richard Williams, who knows nothing about what she saw down in that well, a good piece of her mind. Barry kicks her feet under the table. When she doesn't take her stare away from the two men, he stands and grabs her hand.

"Let's dance," Barry says, pulling her over to the dance floor.

"I'm not in the mood for dancing, Barry," she shouts as they make their way through a group of people on the dance floor and take a place next to a couple who are passionately kissing. The girl has her arms slumped around the boy's neck.

"Neither am I. I hate dancing, if I'm being honest with you. But I could see how this was going to end." Carolyn looks at him and raises her eyebrows, urging Barry to continue. "You would have taken a swing for either Richard Williams or for the priest, and neither is a good idea," Barry admits, chuckling. "I can see how much this means to you... to find out what happened to those boys, but making more enemies... You don't want that, Carolyn." Barry holds onto Carolyn's hands and forces her to lift them up in the air. The faces of the judging men begin to fade.

Back at the table, Barry and Carolyn take their seats. Richard Williams straightens, taking his weight from Father Joseph's shoulder and asks if anyone wants a drink.

Nobody answers, as they obviously don't want to give

Williams a reason to sit with them.

"I think it's my round, Rich. I'll get them in," Father Joseph says, standing and pushing his thick glasses up his nose. "Same again?"

Barry and Jeanette both nod to say yes.

"I'll have a double vodka and Coke, please," Carolyn says. She wonders if she is making a mistake; she has never been a fan of spirits, but she wants to make Father Joseph pay a little more than what her favourite wine costs. He acknowledges her order and walks away with his hand on Richard Williams' back.

Two hours have passed, and the Halloween trivia quiz – mainly questions on horror movies and their soundtracks – has just finished. Carolyn is back to drinking wine; the one vodka and Coke Father Joseph had bought her was enough. She'd drunk it without grimacing, and had pretended to be enjoying it whenever his watchful eyes met hers.

Barry is at the bar, and Father Joseph is speaking to the quizmaster, while Jeanette has headed to the toilet. A man dressed as a zombie has been limping and dragging his foot behind him all night, groaning and staying in character. Carolyn watches as he struggles past her table, then her attention is caught by something she sees at the end of the bar.

A werewolf is sitting alone, looking in her direction. The mask – with a long snout, rubber teeth and big yellow eyes – covers the whole of the person's face. Carolyn can't say for sure that whoever is wearing the costume is in fact watching her. But the position of the body on the bar stool shows a direct line of sight towards where she is sitting. She looks away, bringing her attention instead to the group of zombie cheerleaders. One of them says something that must have been hilarious, as the whole table bursts out laughing.

Carolyn looks around at the other drinkers before glancing back towards the bar. The werewolf is sitting alone, not moving or chatting with anyone, not using a mobile, not bopping his or her head to the music.

161

All of a sudden she feels anxious, wary even. She tries to get Barry's attention to see if he might know who it could be, but he's standing at the front of the queue, and the bar is too noisy. There's only one way to put her mind at ease, and that's to strike up a conversation with the werewolf, and to confirm that she's just being childish and paranoid. Surely it's just an ordinary person in a costume.

The person wearing the costume looks down to their wrist before looking back up towards Carolyn. A large wristwatch with a thick red strap is poking out from their sleeve.

Carolyn stands and walks around the table. The werewolf also stands and swiftly exits through the side door. *Thriller* starts again, and the DJ announces it will be the last song of the night. The dance floor begins to flood with ghouls, vampires and inappropriately-dressed nurses.

Carolyn fights her way through the crowds.

"BARRY!" she shouts, pushing people out of her way. Pointy elbows and thick shoulders slap at her face and ribs. Legs knock at the tender side of her thigh. She pushes through. Reaching the side door is a struggle; getting outside seems almost impossible. People are rushing in to make the last song of the night, filling the narrow corridor. Carolyn bumps shoulders with a larger woman dressed as a biker; the woman has short hair and piercings on various parts of her face. The biker-looking woman frowns at her and stops dead. Carolyn turns away and heads on. Finally, she finds a gap and squeezes outside, trips off the small step and lands on her knees. The biker woman laughs from behind and heads indoors.

The werewolf is gone.

All that's left in the cold October night is a group of non-dancing, poorly-dressed demons. They chuckle quietly and watch as Carolyn gets back to her feet, wiping the dirt from her knees. The luminance from the beer garden lights ends just shy of the wooden fence that surrounds the perimeter. Beyond the fence is fog and darkness.

Barry catches up outside, followed by Jeanette, who is swaying slightly.

"What's going on?" Jeanette asks.

Carolyn looks at Barry before answering her mother. "I thought I was going to throw up."

Jeanette laughs. "Well, I'm ready to go home whenever you are. It'll be closing soon anyway. They've already called Last Orders." Jeanette turns and heads back inside in search of Father Joseph.

"So what really happened?" Barry asks.

"Somebody was watching me. Someone wearing a werewolf costume."

"Are you sure?" Barry said, looking around the beer garden and stopping at the chuckling demons to his right. They stop laughing instantly.

"Yes, I'm sure. I was watching for a few minutes, and when I got up to head over to speak to the person, he or she ran out of the side door before all the people came pushing through."

They go back inside. A glass of water rests on the bar where the werewolf had been sitting.

Who comes to a Halloween party alone and drinks water at the bar? Carolyn thinks.

Barry books himself a taxi and sees Jeanette, Father Joseph and Carolyn off outside to Father Joseph's car as he waits.

At home, Carolyn, the less drunk of the two, walks Jeanette to her room after saying goodnight to Father Joseph. She walks back to lock the front door and spots an envelope on the mat with her boot print smeared across the front.

She picks it up and turns the envelope over.

The envelope has no address or stamp, and only a single name across the centre: *Carolyn*.

Chapter Twenty-Seven

Carolyn wakes to the clanging of pans coming from the kitchen. Jeanette is preparing breakfast, loudly.

Carolyn's head throbs and her throat feels as dry as dust.

She flips the pillow and turns to face the wall, closing her eyes. She's desperate for another hour of sleep, but as she feels herself slipping off, a memory from last night enters her mind and her eyes snap open. She remembers the person in the werewolf costume who had been watching her, and how they had coincidentally left in a hurry as she approached. Then she remembers the envelope that she had found on the doormat.

The envelope is sitting on the bedside table, next to her mobile. She reaches for it and pulls out the note inside.

Meet me at the car park of the old steelworks factory at 5:30 pm.

I have information that can help you.

COME ALONE!

Carolyn had completely forgotten about it. Last night, after changing from her mud-scraped jeans, she must have read the note and fallen into bed. The party is a blur. She holds a hand to her head. Did she argue with Richard Williams about how to do his job? She really can't remember. Maybe that's why her mother is banging pans about. As far as Carolyn can remember, last night was fine. The only thing out of the ordinary was the werewolf. The person who had been wearing that costume was definitely watching her, but why, and for how long, and why take off in a hurry like that?

164

She reaches for her phone and unlocks it. The recent call list shows that she hasn't been in touch with Barry since yesterday afternoon, when he'd confirmed he was still up for a drink.

"Hello?" Barry answers. She can hear the TV volume in the background being lowered. Barry's voice, however, sounds fresh and awake. Is she the only one feeling the aftermath of alcohol?

"Hi, how are you feeling?" she asks, clearing her throat. She wishes she had a glass of water on her bedside table.

"I'm fine. I've been up since seven. What about you?"

"Yeah, me too," she lies. "Listen, after I got home last night and walked my mum to her room, I found an envelope on the mat by the front door. It had been posted through the letterbox."

Barry stays silent, waiting for Carolyn to continue with her story. When she doesn't, he says, "So?"

Carolyn tuts and rubs at her forehead. "It's not just a letter. It has no stamp, and no proper address. It's addressed to me, with my name across the middle of the envelope. Anyway, inside there's a note asking me to meet someone at the old steelworks. Do you know it?"

"The old steelworks? That's strange. There's nothing there any more; the place closed down about fifteen years ago. It's just a pile of concrete now. The construction firm working on it went bust. Why would they want to meet there?" Carolyn can hear him sip at his coffee over the low mumble of the applause on the TV.

"Whoever posted it wrote that they have information that could help me... us. What do you think it means?"

Barry blows out his cheeks; the noise is loud down the phone. *You do that a lot*, Carolyn thinks.

"I don't know," Barry says. "But I don't like the sound of it. It's weird. Kids use it now to hang out, light fires, throw parties and get drunk. The police are always there, chasing them off." He slurps more coffee before continuing. "It's probably somebody trying to waste your time. Forget about it."

"But what if it's not a waste of time?" Carolyn says. "Suppose whoever it is does have information, and for

165

whatever reason they are either too scared to come forward, or they can't speak to the police? Or they've tried and the police have shown no interest? I know how that feels."

She decides not to mention the part of the note telling her to come alone. She knows how nervous Barry gets. He'd want to take it straight to the police, and they would laugh in their faces before tossing it into the bin.

They hang up after Barry agrees to go with her. Carolyn reluctantly kicks the duvet off and heads for the kitchen. She swallows two ibuprofen, and Jeanette apologises for the noise, saying she hadn't realised how noisy she was being. Carolyn heads back to bed for another hour.

By the time the two of them are in the van on their way to the steelworks, Carolyn's headache has eased.

Barry is wearing paint-stained overalls after finishing a job before collecting Carolyn. She is wearing a pullover hoodie, jeans and her comfortable boots. The rain had stopped a couple of hours ago and now the sky is thick with fog.

Carolyn's nerves are beginning to kick in. She wishes she could forget about the missing boys and let someone else deal with it. She has enough on her plate as it is.

What she wishes for most right now is that the note hadn't told her to come alone.

"What the matter?" Barry asks.

She shakes her head and pulls out Simon's stress ball. "The..." she begins. *This is stupid*, she thinks. *Nothing good ever happens when you're prompted to come alone.* "The note had said to come alone."

"What!?" Barry shouts, slowing the van down. "We need to take it to the police. That isn't right."

"Don't stop. I went to the police before. I told them about the body I saw, remember? They're not interested in helping me."

Barry's hand is up and rubbing at the back of his neck. "Carolyn, this is different. Something is wrong if they're telling you to come alone."

Carolyn shakes her head and squeezes the stress ball again.

"Maybe this person does have information that could help and they don't feel comfortable talking to the police. The police didn't take me seriously about what I saw in the well. I know they think I'm crazy. They didn't take Sophie the shop girl seriously either, did they?"

"Yeah, and with good cause. That story she gave you was bollocks... Sorry for the language, but it was."

"I'd still like to go," Carolyn says. "I need this to be over."

"Well then, it's a good job I'm here, isn't it? If this person doesn't mean to cause you any harm, then there shouldn't be a problem with you bringing a friend." He steps on the accelerator, bringing the van back up to speed.

Carolyn feels less anxious that it's off her chest, now that she's not keeping anything from Barry. And, of course, Barry is right. If this person doesn't mean her any harm, then it shouldn't be a problem who she brings.

But why the creepy place out in the middle of nowhere, Carolyn? the internal voice asks.

"What is that thing?" Barry asks, looking towards the stress ball in Carolyn's hand.

"Oh, it was Simon's. He was going through a stressful time at work once. The company he worked for thought they might have been going into liquidation. I saw it when I was out shopping and picked it up for him." Carolyn looks at the stress ball and smiles, remembering the day. "He told me months later that he still used it when speaking with some arrogant clients. It lived on his desk for years." She hands it over. Barry squeezes it and hands it back.

"I think you need it now yourself. You know, with everything that's going on."

Barry is right about the steelworks. It is nothing more than a pile of concrete and a hangout for kids to party. A huge metal sign above the car park entrance, now faded and weather-worn, reads *MYERS STEEL*. They drive under and pull into the car park. The van bounces from side to side as they hit cracks and holes on the tarmac, causing Barry's work tools to jolt about.

He pulls to the corner of the car park, the tyres crunching

167

over the broken glass of empty bottles. The skeletal remains of a burned-out sofa, a few bin bags and a dismantled wooden bed lie around the small car park, but there are no other vehicles.

"You see, I told you it'll be people wasting your time," he says, and slips the gear into reverse, ready to back out.

"Wait, what's that entrance over there?" Carolyn says, pointing to an opening between some bushes.

"I've been here a few years back. If I remember correctly, it should be a path that used to lead up to the factory."

Carolyn climbs out of the van and walks over. He quickly follows, and they both peer down a winding path. There's a huge rock at the bottom, closing off the entrance.

Carolyn takes a step forward.

Barry grabs hold of her arm. "What are you doing?" he asks nervously.

"I'm going down there. I'm not coming all this way to turn back now," she replies, trying her best to keep a stern face and not show fear. She can feel her stomach twist with nerves.

"I think we should go."

"Look, whoever posted that note knows who I am. They know where I'm living and that I'm looking into those missing boys. If they have information, I want it." She looks down the fog-filled path and back to Barry. "If they want me to come alone, I will do. I'm not having whoever it is make a run for it because I've brought a friend who happens to be at least six foot four and built like a nightclub doorman!" Carolyn smiles, and this seems to ease Barry's nerves a little. "I don't imagine it goes much further past that first bend. If I need you, I'll scream, okay?"

He's clearly reluctant to let her go alone, but accepts.

"I'm six-six, actually," Barry mutters back and releases his grip on Carolyn's arm.

She proceeds down the grassy slope.

Rusty beer cans, empty wine bottles and small black dog-poo bags are scattered throughout the bushes and hanging loosely from the tree branches. Her boots squelch on the wet grass next to some freshly-made footprints.

What am I doing? she asks herself, not expecting an answer but getting one anyway: *You're going to die, Carolyn. It's a trap.*

"Shut up," Carolyn whispers back.

The path curves, and before she enters the bend, she takes a look at Barry's face. It shows a sickening, worried expression. Carolyn walks further around, losing sight of him completely. The path does indeed end a couple yards in front of her. She can now see, sitting on a fallen log, is a figure wearing a coat with the hood up.

She approaches slowly, bracing herself and straightening. Her breathing is heavy, and she prepares to scream at the top of her lungs if anything doesn't seem right.

None of this is right, the internal voice says. *Are you really this stupid?*

***

Up the path, Barry steps from foot to foot, his own internal voice shouting at him that something is wrong. What kind of man is he to allow her to go down there alone, especially as daylight is only half hour away from ending? His father was an old-school gentleman, and he imagines what he'd have to say about this situation. *"You let a woman go alone?"*

Barry watches carefully, waiting for Carolyn to reappear and shake her head that they've been pranked. "You were right, it was a prank," she'd say with a frown, but then show a smile. Barry has become fond of Carolyn. He already knows he's going to be devastated when she heads back to Leeds.

It's been long enough, he tells himself, and takes a step down before stopping. He turns and goes back to the van for a crowbar, just in case. As he opens the van's side door and reaches for it, he stops as he hears the distinctive sound of glass breaking underneath a shoe.

Expecting to see Carolyn, he turns round.

***

She steps closer to the figure sitting on the log. Now that she's close enough and through the thick fog, she can see the coat is green.

"Hello?" she says, her voice breaking a little. She watches carefully, waiting for the head to turn, or the shoulders to rise and fall as the person breathes.

Nothing. There's no reply or movement at all.

Carolyn steps closer with legs that feel numb.

"Hello?" she says, this time raising her voice to sound more in control. She heads around the front and soon realises why there was no movement to the figure. The dirty, tacky coat, torn in places, is held up by branches which are sticking out of the fallen tree log. She turns and sighs.

Great.

She takes a seat on the log and examines the small forest, waiting to see laughing faces hidden behind trees: the pranksters recording it on their phones, ready to show Llanbedr what a fool Carolyn Hill is. Out of anger she snatches the old coat from the branch and throws it to the ground. It lands in front of her, the sleeve resting in a puddle of muddy rainwater. The ground is littered with bottle caps, cigarette butts and used condoms. She watches the coat for a moment, lost in thought, before gathering herself together. She stands and heads for the path, to tell Barry he was right: that someone has wasted their time.

Something on the coat catches her eye. She stoops to retrieve it and stands.

She uses the last of the daylight to make out the name tag on the inside, under the hood. The ink has faded, but the name can still be made out if she strains her eyes enough.

Dylan Lloyd.

Carolyn gasps. She hears a movement to her left and spins round. The bushes rattle and a raven flutters out, cawing and eyeing her warily before taking flight. She watches it fly away and breathes, bringing her attention back to the name tag on the coat.

170

Now this I can show to the police.

Carolyn rushes up the litter-filled path.

"Barry… Barry… I've found something," she shouts excitedly.

She stops dead. Barry is lying on the cold ground in a dark puddle of blood.

She rushes over to him, dropping to her knees and taking hold of his hand. His thick fingers are shaking and feel like ice. His shoulders are shivering and his teeth jitter loudly.

"C… Carolyn… I don't know what happened… I… I… heard something but I didn't turn around quick enough—"

"Shhh," Carolyn says, squeezing his hand.

"… Then… then I was on the floor…"

Carolyn presses a hand underneath his ribs in a bid to stop the bleeding. The blood looks as though it's never going to stop. For a moment, Carolyn thinks she is going to vomit or faint, or both. But she doesn't. She fights to keep it together. With a shaking hand she reaches into her pocket and grabs her phone and dials for an ambulance.

"I… didn't see them. I… I'm sorry," Barry stutters.

"Don't be silly. This is my doing. I shouldn't have brought you here. I should have listened to you. We should have gone to the police. I'm so sorry." She cries louder, pulling off her hoodie and placing it against Barry's wound. The gushing blood makes her feel nauseous. The bitter air nips at her arms, sending goose bumps along her flesh. The tears on her cheeks feel like ice.

It then crosses her mind that the attacker could still be out there, sitting in the bushes and watching as his victim fights for his life.

Carolyn searches around her, looking left to right for the attacker.

She wants to stand and turn fully, but she can't let go of the hoodie pressed against Barry's side. She can't risk letting go until the paramedics arrive.

The longer the ambulance takes, the darker the sky grows.

Chapter Twenty-Eight

The first to arrive on scene is a police patrol car driven by PC Martin, who is accompanied by his partner, PC Young. They run over to where Carolyn is waiting, shortly followed by the ambulance.

Barry is rushed to the hospital, and the two officers leave Carolyn in the waiting area.

A little later, she looks up to see DS Hughes and DC Dixon approaching.

"Mrs Hill?" DS Hughes says, taking a seat next to her. "Are you ok?"

Carolyn lifts her head without looking at them and forces a nod. She clenches the end of her vest top and twists it between her fingers.

"Let's go to the canteen. It's a little more private there," DS Hughes suggests. "You look like you could do with a coffee, if I'm being honest." Although the detective attempts a sympathetic smile, it's clear this kind of compassionate behaviour doesn't come naturally to her.

In the canteen, DS Hughes and DC Dixon walk Carolyn over to a table at the back. They pass a table to their left where two nurses, in the middle of their shift break, are sitting. To the right of them is a mother wearing a dressing gown and slippers while she bounces a toddler on her lap. The husband sits with his arm around her shoulders, speaking words of reassurance in her ear.

The only other noise comes from the staff cooking in the kitchen. The smell of cooked meats makes Carolyn's stomach growl, reminding her she hasn't eaten all day. After waking up late to Barry being outside, she'd dressed and rushed out to the van, not wanting to keep him waiting. She didn't realise she'd be out this long.

"Dixon, go get the coffee in, would you?" DS Hughes says, pulling out a chair. Carolyn sits on the bench against the back wall, her bare arms shivering in the cold.

"I understand this must be difficult for you, Mrs Hill," DS Hughes begins. "But the statement that you gave to the officers is quite confusing. DC Dixon and I are hoping to make things a little clearer." DS Hughes shows another one of those unnatural smiles.

Carolyn isn't sure if DS Hughes, this tough cage-fighter-looking woman, is genuinely sympathising with her or if this is one of the detective's tactics to get people to speak. Carolyn assumes she probably doesn't give a toss what happened to Barry. She seems to have completely changed her approach since that night at the well, when she looked as if she wanted to chew Carolyn up and spit her out.

It only took Barry being attacked, Carolyn thinks.

Carolyn places her hands on the cold table, trying to steady the shaking.

"Calm yourself... okay," DS Hughes says. "You're safe here."

Carolyn wonders whether she is safe, and looks at DS Hughes with tired and heavy eyes. She knows that they could burst with tears at any second. She gives the detective the slightest of smiles.

"In your statement, Mrs Hill, Carolyn, you mentioned that a werewolf stabbed your friend, Mr Cookson?" DS Hughes says with confusion in her eyes.

Carolyn shakes her head. Her throat is so dry that it makes her voice sound hoarse.

"Start from the beginning, Mrs Hill," DS Hughes instructs, resting her hands on the table.

"Last night... at The Red Fox, it was the Halloween party," she starts. DS Hughes nods. "I noticed this person in a werewolf costume. They were watching me."

"Watching you? How do you mean exactly?"

"I don't know. The person had a mask on. But I could tell that whoever it was, they were staring at me."

"How do you know they were watching you if a mask was covering their face?"

"I guess that I can't say for sure then. But it was starting to creep me out."

"Understandable. Please carry on."

"I started heading towards them. I was making my way over, through the pub, when this person stood up and took off."

"And you think it could have been the person in the werewolf costume who attacked Mr Cookson tonight?"

"I don't know. But why dash out of the door when I make my way over? Anyway, after I got home last night, I found a note had been posted through my mother's letterbox."

DS Hughes leans forward a little closer. "A note?"

Carolyn nods. "The note said to meet them at the old steelworks, that Myers Steel place, and that they had information which could help me."

DC Dixon returns with three mugs of coffee. He places one in front of Carolyn. She reaches for it immediately and takes a sip. She's so thirsty that she needs something, anything, to line her stomach and replace the sour taste of adrenaline in her mouth. She grimaces as the hot liquid burns her throat.

"Thanks, Mike," DS Hughes says. She stirs in a sugar before turning back to Carolyn. "What information could this person help you with?"

Carolyn hesitates to tell them. *They already believe I'm crazy. Seeing corpses that aren't there and wasting police time. But this person that attacked Barry tonight needs to be found and locked away.*

She stays quiet.

"Mrs Hill?" DS Hughes says.

"I've been asking questions about the disappearances of Elwyn Roberts and Dylan Lloyd. I don't know if that has anything to do with it, but I guess it probably does."

DS Hughes pulls an agitated expression towards her partner, who sighs and scribbles in his notebook. The gelled hair on Mike Dixon's head stands perfectly still as he writes.

His light auburn goatee matches his hair.

"Make a note of The Red Fox pub. We'll need to pull the CCTV from last night and take a look at this werewolf person," DS Hughes says, then turns back to Carolyn. "Do you still have the note?"

Carolyn doesn't answer. Her mind has been swept away, thinking of the blood spilling out of Barry earlier.

"Mrs Hill!" DS Hughes says, loudly. The nurses from the far side look over.

"Hmm?"

"Do you still have the note?"

"Yes, I think so. It should be in my room, at my mothers. The coat... I found a coat... Do you have it?" Carolyn shouts.

DS Hughes holds her hands up and tells Carolyn to calm down. The two nurses turn and glance over again before going back to chatting quietly.

"Yes, it's in Evidence," DS Hughes answers. "We'll be sending it off to Forensics once the Lloyds have seen it and can confirm it did belong to Dylan Lloyd."

DC Dixon coughs and clears his throat. "Do you have any idea who might have wanted to hurt Mr Cookson?" he asks. "Do you have anybody in mind who might have sent you the note?"

Carolyn scans her mind as she bites at her fingernails. She thinks about mentioning Owen Lloyd, the night he ran her off the road and almost broke her back. But then why would Owen Lloyd tell her to come alone, knowing that she has no means of transport? Besides, Frank Lloyd would have him under a watchful eye for quite some time.

"Oh God... Oh it must be... It must have been him!" Carolyn shrieks, not realising she's speaking out loud.

DS Hughes and DC Dixon give each other a curious look before Hughes turns back to Carolyn.

"Who do you think it might have been?"

Chapter Twenty-Nine

"Why do you think it could be this Patrick Sawhill who attacked Barry Cookson?" Mike Dixon asks as he makes a note of the name.

Carolyn stands holding her mouth.

"Mrs Hill?" DS Hughes asks.

"Sorry. I'm going to be sick!" Carolyn mumbles through her hands as she runs off to the Ladies. It's a quick-thinking excuse to get herself away. She needs to buy herself some time to think up a story believable enough not to incriminate herself or Barry. She isn't expecting the vomit to be a reality until she enters the cubicle, and a second later she's hunched over with her head in a toilet. The image of the blood leaving Barry's side is sickening, and it will stay with her for the rest of her life.

Carolyn could never look at blood and not feel queasy. Even watching those paramedic shows on TV with Simon always turned her stomach. The worry in Barry's eyes, and the paleness of his face, had shaken her; this huge man was lying on the ground after being attacked from behind.

But it's now clear that if she'd gone alone, she wouldn't have stood a chance.

Carolyn remembers the concentration on Barry's face, his expression showing her he must have been imagining this is the end, losing his life and never seeing his daughter again. More sick flows and hits the toilet water. She wipes at her mouth and washes her face before returning to the canteen.

"I followed a man called Julio Alcala to Patrick Sawhill's party accessories shop. I learned his name from a news article."

"What party shop is this?" DC Dixon asks.

"P's Party Accessories. It's a small unit in the industrial park."

"Oh yeah, I know it."

"It's a good thirty-minute drive from Julio's home," she says, taking a sip of her coffee now that it has cooled. "He visited after closing time and went into the shop... unit... whatever you want to call it. He was in there for roughly ten to fifteen minutes, then left with something that he put inside his jacket. I have no idea what it could be."

"And what, you think it could be this Julio Alcala or Patrick Sawhill that spotted you following him?" Carolyn can't help noticing the sarcasm in DS Hughes' voice. "They found out and came after you?"

DC Dixon is keeping up with the story, writing as quickly as he can.

"No... I went the party shop one day to try to find out what could be going on. I know that it must sound ridiculous to you both. I didn't know what else to do."

The two detectives don't reply.

"At first I thought it was drug-related," Carolyn continues. "There is this door which is locked, and behind it is a shelf with a laptop on. The door was open on the day I visited and the laptop was already logged in and ready to use. The owner had to leave the shop for some reason or the other, and my gut was screaming at me to search through it. I was sure that something was up."

Carolyn breathes out. Her hands are still shaking from earlier, but the coffee seems to have calmed her a little and brought back some colour to her face. She's convinced her story sounds real enough to keep Barry and her out of trouble. She just prays that Patrick Sawhill doesn't have a home security camera showing her breaking and entering his home and stealing his laptop. She's unsure if it is a crime to search through another person's belongings, but she had to get as close as possible to the truth.

"Do you usually snoop through people's things, Mrs Hill?" DC Dixon asks, stroking his goatee.

"No, never. But I—"

"So you think Patrick Sawhill got wind of you going through his computer, and knows you saw something that you shouldn't have?" DC Dixon asks, cutting her off.

Carolyn shrugs. "I don't know. But something seemed dodgy about the files I went through. Look." She pulls out her phone and shows the two detectives the pictures she took that night. Hughes and Dixon squint and look at the files on her phone. The broken screen makes it hard to see anything.

"I'm not sure if this is illegal, or of any interest..." Carolyn tails off.

"Go on," Hughes says.

"The storage room at the party shop... unit... whatever. There are cuttings from a clothing magazine of young girls modelling bikinis and summer wear. I probably wouldn't have thought much of it if the place catered for fashion and beachwear. But it doesn't."

The two detectives pause for a moment. Dixon writes something down and Hughes stays silent, thinking. She takes a sip of her coffee.

Carolyn goes on. "You do know Julio Alcala has a criminal record and is on the Sex Offenders' Register, don't you?"

DC Dixon turns to DS Hughes and taps his pen on the pad. "I knew I'd heard that name before."

DS Hughes turns back to Carolyn and stares at her. Then she leans over to her partner and whispers into his ear. He stands and heads out of the canteen with his phone at the ready.

"Do you need a lift home?" Hughes asks Carolyn.

Carolyn accepts gratefully. On their way through the hospital, they stop by the ward Barry is on and speak with a nurse, who tells them that Barry has finished in surgery and he had a two-inch stab wound. Thankfully it seemed to have missed his vital organs, but he's lost a lot of blood and is now resting and won't be able to answer any questions.

DS Hughes parks on Jeanette's drive, next to her returned Polo. Carolyn leaves the car saying goodbye to Dixon. He replies with a grunt and continues tapping at his phone. She heads for the door with DS Hughes following behind. Carolyn tries not to inspect her mother's car too obviously. They enter the bungalow and Jeanette leaves the kitchen after hearing Carolyn's key in the door. She looks at Carolyn in confusion.

"I'll explain in a moment, Mum," Carolyn says. She turns to DS Hughes and points. "My room is in there." DS Hughes heads into Carolyn's room with a plastic evidence bag in hand. DS Hughes places the note and the envelope into the bag, thanks Jeanette and sees herself out.

"What's going on now?" Jeanette asks. "What was it that DS Hughes took from your room?"

Carolyn is too distracted to answer. She is watching the detectives reversing out of the drive and heading off down the road.

"I need you to pack a bag. We have to stay in a hotel for a night, okay?" Carolyn says, her voice on the verge of breaking.

"What is going on? Why are you acting so strangely?"

"Please, will you just do this for me? I'll explain in the car. Please."

Jeanette looks at her daughter's face and agrees. She leaves the room and begins packing a bag.

Carolyn considers taking a shower. Her skin begs for the warm water, to wash away the bitter air and the speckles of Barry's blood. But she decides to leave it until she and her mother are safe. Carolyn shoves some clean underwear into a bag, along with two pairs of jeans and a few jumpers, then stands back at the curtains, watching in case the person who attacked Barry, the person who led them to the Myers Steel works, is out there.

Five minutes later, Carolyn and Jeanette are in the car and heading down the driveway. Carolyn watches all mirrors in turn, checking that they aren't being followed. The car is spotless inside. It has undergone a thorough valet which has made it look almost brand new. It even drives more smoothly.

"The keys had been posted through the letter box when I

got back from the church," Jeanette says, inspecting the new interior of the car. "It can't have been that bad."

"Huh?" Carolyn grunts, her mind occupied on Barry.

"When you went off the road, it can't have been that bad... the damage I mean. The car looks great."

"Oh right, yeah," Carolyn says. "It looks great."

"So... What the hell is going on, Carolyn?" Jeanette asks. She turns in her seat and is now facing her. "And don't lie to me!"

Carolyn thinks about telling her mother some silly lie, anything but the truth. Instead, she decides she ought to know. She has the right to know.

"Barry's been stabbed, Mum," Carolyn says, her eyes filling with the tears she'd suppressed at the hospital. She sniffs and wipes at her nose using the back of her hand.

"What? Why? Who on earth stabbed him?" Jeanette asks, pulling a tissue from her bag and handing it over.

"I don't know. DS Hughes went into my room before to bag a note that was posted last night, when we got home from the Halloween party." Carolyn wipes her eyes.

"A note? I don't understand," Jeanette says.

"The note was addressed to me, instructing me to go to the old steelworks. I was only gone five minutes, ten at the most. When I came back... I found Barry on the ground, bleeding," Carolyn says, turning a corner and keeping an eye on the rear-view mirror for any following headlights. There aren't any.

Carolyn explains the note, the coat she had found with Dylan Lloyd's name inked inside it, and the party shop owner's laptop. She leaves out the part about herself and Barry breaking into Patrick Sawhill's home to retrieve it.

After a thirty-minute drive, mainly consisting of Jeanette screaming at Carolyn as though she was back at school, they arrive at the *Traveller's Stay*, a cosy-looking B&B.

Chapter Thirty

Carolyn parks the car at the back of the B&B, next to a rusted campervan with deflated tyres. Her idea is to hide it from anyone that drives in to park, though she needn't worry; it looks as if they're going to be the only guests. Hiding the car makes her feel paranoid. She puts it down to shock.

Jeanette's upset, angry even. But at least she's also safe.

Once inside the *Traveller's Stay,* Carolyn can see there is nothing *cosy-looking* about the bed-and-breakfast. The pictures that she'd found online don't match the room they're in now; this one is small and snug, and crammed with dated furniture that's thick with dust and deep with scratches. She could swear it isn't even the same building; the architecture doesn't match. Though she's not going to complain. She desperately needs a shower and somewhere to rest – a place nobody knows where she and Jeanette are.

The owner of the B&B is a nosey elderly woman who smells of cigarettes. She's attempted, and failed, to mask the cigarette odour with a tangy perfume, one that must be as old as the furniture itself.

Carolyn tells the woman that their kitchen has flooded and that they'll need a room for the night, possibly longer. She hopes that Barry being stabbed will give the police a good enough reason to search Julio Alcala's home, along with Patrick Sawhill's shop and laptop.

Not that she knows much about police procedures.

Carolyn's paranoid mind tells her that Patrick Sawhill and Julio Alcala must be the ones involved in all of this, the ones who retrieved the decaying body from the well, the ones watching her at the Halloween party in The Red Fox, and the ones who attacked Barry. It must be them, or at least an accomplice of theirs. After all, they're the only people she can think of who'd have a reason to silence her.

Carolyn stands in the bathroom and calls the hospital at just gone midnight to check up on Barry. The nurse informs her that nothing has changed, and that Barry is still sleeping. She leaves her mobile number with the nurse and asks that she rings her if there is any news.

It's now 4:00 am, and after showering, ordering a takeaway (not that Carolyn has eaten much of it) and filling Jeanette in with the details she missed during the car ride, Carolyn is wide awake and listening to her mother snore and grunt in the bed opposite. The cheap, itchy blanket is pulled right up to Jeanette's face and she is mumbling things like *Leave her alone* and *It's our fault*. Carolyn assumes it's stress caused by what she's just told her. It must be playing on her mind.

Carolyn brings her mind back to Barry. The thought of him being paralysed and unable to work or walk properly again, due to her foolish decision of not consulting the police, rests heavily on her mind. The thought causes her to feel like fleeing to the bathroom to throw up. The thought of having to contact Barry's daughter, Amy, and tell her that her father is dead or paralysed, brings her to weep into her mouldy-smelling pillow. She agrees that, if Barry comes through this, she'll support him and make it up to him. Whatever he needs, she'll provide, even if that means selling her shop in Leeds to pay for it.

After hours of trying, Carolyn finally begins to drift off to sleep. She's hugging the spare pillow tightly between her arms, dreaming that she's sitting on the fallen tree at the bottom of the winding path. Next to her is the coat that belongs to Dylan Lloyd. The fog is thick around her, thicker than earlier on, making it almost impossible to see more than a few metres ahead. When she hears the rattling in the bushes, it isn't the hungry raven that emerges this time, it's Patrick Sawhill. He's clutching a huge butcher's knife with fresh blood along the blade and a demonic grin on his face.

Barry's screams as he's attacked and left for dead are piercingly loud, and his cries echo around her, bouncing off the trees before fading out into the wilderness.

Carolyn and Patrick Sawhill's eyes meet. He moves forward, and Carolyn doesn't give him the chance to get any closer. She runs.

Patrick Sawhill begins chasing after her. Only in this dream, Carolyn's legs refuse to work properly; they feel tired and limp. Patrick Sawhill, overweight as he is in reality, isn't having any trouble breathing or running. Here, in Carolyn's dream, he comes at her with the speed of an athlete, slashing his blood-smeared blade side to side, barely missing Carolyn's back as he chuckles loudly.

Carolyn runs through the woods; she tries screaming for help but her throat is blocked. It feels as if she's swallowed an apple whole. She can only just breathe.

She runs, jumping over tree branches and landing in puddles full of sloppy mud. Her foot becomes stuck in the mud. Patrick Sawhill is catching up; she can hear him coming through the trees. She pulls and pulls until the earth finally releases her foot, though it keeps her boot. She hasn't the time to reach for it, so she turns and runs on without it. Thorn bushes nick at her legs and tear at her clothes, and stones pierce the sole of her foot while leafless branches whip at her face. Running alongside her, in partnership with the fat man, is Julio Alcala. He too has a wide, inhuman grin reaching to the deep scar on his cheek.

Finally the trees begin to thin out. She holds her hands out in front of her and pushes through the branches until she comes to the opening.

Out in the fog, she spins around to find that Julio Alcala and Patrick Sawhill are nowhere to be seen. Their chuckling laughs echo off the trees and thin out into the air. Her chest aches and she's panting. She bends over to catch her breath, but the dense fog makes her feel as if she's sucking air through a straw.

CAW! The raven calls from behind her, followed then by a low cry.

"Help me… please," the young voice begs.

Carolyn turns slowly and is now facing the well. The raven tilts its head at her and takes flight, heading back towards the trees.

She stares at the well. The young voice calls out again. "Help me… please."

She creeps forward slowly, and the grass squelches under her bruised, bare foot.

She peers down the well.

The mangled, bloodstained body of Elwyn Roberts stares up at her. White broken bones pierce his freezing flesh, and his whole body glints with frost.

"Help me… please," he says, from dry cracked lips.

Carolyn shrieks and wakes, seconds from crying out. Her neck and chest are wet with sweat, and the mattress beneath her is damp. She must have managed just under three hours of sleep.

Jeanette is brushing her teeth in the bathroom and glances over through the open door. She shows no sympathy, and returns to the mirror, closing the door.

Carolyn skips breakfast and tells Jeanette she has to head back into town to speak to the police. She urges her mother to stay in the room and watch some television. Jeanette doesn't argue, and makes little effort to conceal her obvious annoyance.

Now, on her way to the hospital with the radio turned off, tears fill Carolyn's tired eyes. She imagines Barry's room, only to see his usual warm smile replaced with a look of pure hatred, maybe the same hatred she felt towards the lorry driver who'd slammed into the back of Simon and Ryan, killing them. She thinks of the swearing that will leave Barry's lips as he orders her to get out and that he never wants to see her again. Or worse, the doctor taking her aside before looking at her with sympathy and informing her that Barry has not made it through the night.

Her heart thumps against her chest and pounds in her ears. She puts her foot down. She has to get to the hospital. She has to face whatever is waiting for her.

Once she's parked in the hospital grounds, she takes a moment to ready herself. A few minutes later she's walking across the car park, passing three girls in their teens. Music is playing loudly from their phones. Two of them are smoking, and one is gulping an energy drink.

Carolyn passes a car to her left and spots her reflection in the window. She'll be the first to admit that she looks like crap, but at least the heavy rain will hide her tear-stained cheeks. Her unbrushed hair has been scraped up into a messy bun, and she's not applied any makeup. She's wearing a red, baggy jumper with creased blue jeans and a pair of battered white trainers. Winning a fashion contest isn't on her agenda today. She dressed in whatever she pulled from her case this morning, eager to leave the room in a hurry, unable to stand any more of the silent treatment from her mother.

She is standing outside Barry's room with her trembling hand on the door handle and looking through the glass. Barry is sitting up on a thirty-degree angle and looking out of the rain-pelted window, rolling the stress ball between two fingers. Carolyn wonders if he saw her walk across the car park. Did he grimace at the sight of her? Did his anger build up so much that he needs the stress ball?

At least he isn't dead, the voice admits, and today Carolyn has to agree with it. A porter pushing a trolley passes behind her. He looks at her warily, which forces her to act.

She opens the door.

Barry turns and looks at her with an expression Carolyn hasn't seen before. She waits in the doorway for him to begin yelling, calling for Security and for two burly guards to turn up and order her to leave. Instead, he smiles and holds out his arms. She runs over and flings herself against his chest. He groans in pain, but keeps his arms locked tightly around her back.

"I'm so sorry. I'm so sorry, Barry. This was my fault. I should have listened to you. We should have gone to the police," she manages before Barry shushes her.

His voice breaks as he speaks. "It's not your fault. I wanted to go with you. Imagine if I hadn't? Where would you be

185

today, hey? I'm just sorry I didn't get a look at the bastard that did it." They release their hug but stay close, holding hands. It doesn't feel awkward or uneasy for either of them.

Carolyn shifts a leg on to his bed to sit at his side.

"So, you're okay?" she asks, still close to tears. It's breaking her heart to see him so defenceless.

"Well, I've had better days... But I'm okay."

"You don't hate me?" Carolyn asks, the tears now running down her cheeks.

"What? No, of course not. But I'm a little disappointed you haven't brought me grapes..." Barry says with a smile.

Carolyn laughs. After last night, she wasn't sure she'd ever laugh again. "I think it could have something to do with the laptop," she says.

Barry considers it. "I don't know. The person that stabbed me sounded lean, quiet. The man who owns the party shop wouldn't have been able to creep up on me. I'd have heard him."

"I don't mean he's the one who attacked you, but I definitely think he's involved. He has something on that laptop that he doesn't want anybody to know about. I told the police about it last night."

Barry's eyes widen. He tries sitting up straighter, but pulls a pained face and stays where he is. "You told them? Carolyn... They'll arrest us."

"No, no. I told them that I went to the party shop, and that the laptop was already open in the storage room. I left you out of it completely. I think they're going to talk to the party shop owner and Julio Alcala."

Barry tuts. "Doesn't that mean you've broken the law somehow? I'm sure there's a law about privacy or something like that."

"I don't care," Carolyn swiftly replies, and she really means it. "If they find some evidence that links them to your attack, then I really don't care what law I have broken. Barry, last night after you were attacked, you were mumbling something I couldn't make out. It looked as if you were trying to tell me something. Do you remember what it was?"

Barry's eyes concentrate on the thin hospital bedsheet covering his legs. "No, I can't remember anything from last night. All I know is that I was heading back to the van to find a crowbar," he says, rubbing at his cheeks and scratching the stubble. "I was going to follow you down there, then I heard this crunch of glass. Next thing, I was on the ground and you were leaning over me. Then I woke up here today."

Carolyn sighs and wonders if Barry is too frightened to confess who did it and is keeping it to himself. But what person in their right mind would know of their attacker and not tell the police?

"Okay, it was probably nothing. I'm sorry again, I feel awful," Carolyn begins, then stops as DS Hughes and DC Dixon knock and step into the room.

"Ah Mr Cookson, you're awake. Good. We have a few questions about your attack last night," DS Hughes says. "Mind if we call you Barry?"

"Yes, I mind. You can call me Mr Cookson," Barry replies. Carolyn chuckles under her breath but keeps herself from smiling. "If you'd listened to Carolyn when she told you lot last time, maybe this wouldn't have happened. But you can't be bothered pulling your fingers out of your arses to do anything."

Carolyn can see that DS Hughes and DC Dixon look shocked. "We don't believe that this attack has anything to do with what Mrs Hill thought... with what Mrs Hill claims she saw in the well," Dixon says, with a cocky smile.

"What about the coat I found?" Carolyn asks.

Barry looks at her with confusion. Carolyn remembers that she hasn't told him about the coat.

"Yes..." DS Hughes says. "We've shown it to the Lloyds, and Mrs Lloyd says she believes it is Dylan's coat."

"What?" Barry asks, but is ignored.

"But we still don't know if the disappearance of Elwyn Roberts and Dylan Lloyd are connected in any way," Hughes continues. "We will be sending the coat off for examination."

Carolyn turns. "Did you speak to the party shop owner?"

The two detectives look at each other before DS Hughes

closes the door and steps forward. "After what you claimed you saw in his supply cupboard at the unit, we approached Mr Sawhill this morning with a warrant to search his home, business and any computers within his possession," she says, her look fixed on Carolyn. Barry and Carolyn share a look that neither of the detectives see. "Mr Sawhill panicked and tried to flee, fighting his way past our officers... He suffered a major heart attack and died before we had the chance to question him."

Barry and Carolyn look at each other and back to DS Hughes. Hughes goes on. "We've sent the laptop he had at his home address, along with any external hard drives and any USB storage devices, off to forensics."

Carolyn and Barry are silent.

"And Julio?" Carolyn asks. "The one that visited the shop... what about him?"

"Mr Alcala has been arrested for breaking his terms of not owning or being allowed to use a computer, which we found hidden in his bedroom. We're questioning him and, so far, he has never heard of you, Mr Cookson. We're waiting for confirmation that his alibi matches the time you were attacked yesterday afternoon. His computer and any other storage device have also been sent off to forensics."

"What about the werewolf?" Barry asks. "At the party?"

DC Dixon pulls a printout from his coat and holds it up, showing it to both of them. The picture quality isn't the best. It's dark and grainy, and the shape of the werewolf costume is only vaguely recognisable.

"The only thing that really stands out here is that the person is wearing white trainers," DC Dixon says.

Carolyn frowns. "How are we supposed to identify anyone from this image?"

Barry shrugs.

"We've spoken to the staff working that night," DC Dixon says, "and they've told us they didn't even notice the person sitting at the end of the bar. As you can imagine, they were rushed off their feet for most of the night. We believe the person is male, at least from their size and build. He was at the bar for roughly ninety minutes before he was seen running through the door. We're also checking Julio Alcala's whereabouts that night."

"Mrs Hill, do you mind stepping outside?" DS Hughes asks. "We'd like to speak with Mr Cookson in private... please."

"Why? I'd like her to stay, if that's all right," Barry protests.

DC Dixon takes out his notepad. "We need to make sure your statement matches Mrs Hill's from yesterday afternoon. It will only take a minute."

Carolyn stands up, telling Barry she'll go for a coffee and bring one back for him. She nods at the two detectives and leaves the room. At the coffee machine, she pulls change from her pocket, inserts it and presses the button for a latte, moving the first cup to one side. As she searches through her change for the second cup, a man approaches and inserts the correct money.

"There you go. I could see you struggling for change," he says.

Carolyn looks up at the tall, smiling Indian man clutching his own cup. He has short black hair and thick bushy eyebrows, and looks to be in his early fifties.

"Thank you so much... Here, take whatever this adds up to," Carolyn says.

"No, it's fine, honestly. I have more change than I need," he chuckles. "So, are you visiting, or do you like to hang out in hospitals?"

Carolyn glances over at Barry's room and can see the shape of the two detectives still inside. She takes a seat.

"Visiting a friend. He... he had an accident yesterday. What about you?" she asks.

The Indian man takes the seat next to her after ordering a coffee for himself.

"My wife. She hurt her back a while ago. Fell down some stairs if you can believe that. She's never been the same since. She's always in and out of this goddamn place!"

They introduce themselves, and after Carolyn watches DS Hughes and DC Dixon leave Barry's room, she thanks Thomas for the coffee and wishes his wife luck before heading back in.

189

Chapter Thirty-One

Julio Alcala is sitting in Interview Room Two with his solicitor, Mr Nelson, at his side. His hands are stretched out in front and trembling nervously on the table, his nails bitten down almost to the cuticles. Against the recommendation of Mr Nelson, Julio has decided, after learning about the death of his friend Patrick Sawhill, that he would like to come forward and discuss what he knows.

"Mr Alcala... What is it you would like to tell me?" DS Hughes asks, having returned from the hospital a couple of hours earlier.

"The... the laptop you found hidden behind my wall. Patrick... Mr Sawhill, he gave it to me," Julio says.

"So what?" DS Hughes says. "I'm sure once we get it back from forensics, we would have found that out for ourselves."

"Patrick gave it to me last year. It's in my conditions that... that I don't own anything I can use to access the internet or download pictures." Julio stops, thinks for a moment and continues. "He... he gave it to me because I help him out... *helped* him out... running a site."

"A site?" DC Dixon asks, running a finger across his auburn goatee.

Mr Nelson leans in and whispers into his client's ear. Julio shrugs him away, frowning, and looks from DS Hughes to DC Dixon.

"This will show that I've been co-operative, won't it?" he asks, nervously.

"Well, it's on the tape and I'll make sure to add a note to your file... of course."

"The site that I'm talking about is what Patrick made most

190

of his money from. He ran two sites, but he isn't very tech-savvy, so I'd visit once a week."

"And what do you do for Mr Sawhill, Julio?" DC Dixon asks.

"I do whatever maintenance is needed on the sites," Julio says, his chewed fingertips tapping nervously at the tabletop.

"What kind of sites are we speaking of here, Julio?"

He ignores the question, his mind so full of scenarios about his future.

"Julio?" Dixon prompts.

"The type of site that is illegal and that people would pay money to visit," Julio replies, as beads of sweat form on his forehead.

DS Hughes and DC Dixon look at each other.

"For the purpose of the tape, Mr Alcala, will you confirm what type of sites you were running for Mr Patrick Sawhill?" DS Hughes says.

Tears fill Julio's eyes, and again he goes silent for a moment. His fingers continue to tap at the table.

Julio's parents will certainly wash their hands of him this time. He knows his place in the family was already hanging by a thread, and this will surely be the last straw before they cut him out of their lives completely. In his last incident, he was found with indecent pictures on his computer and phone. Julio pictures his mother sitting at the table crying. His father will be in his room, pulling clothes from hangers and packing them to leave on the front doorstep.

His breathing increases and his heart thumps.

"They were... child pornography sites," Julio finally says, keeping his eyes focused on the various scratches on the table.

DC Dixon flicks through his notes and leans over, whispering into his partner's ear. Hughes nods.

"Mr Alcala, do you know of any ledgers that Mr Sawhill might have kept?" DS Hughes asks.

Julio thinks hard about it and then shakes his head. He pinches at the bridge of his nose and brings his hand down to wipe away the tears.

His next thought is that it will take roughly six bin bags to clear out his wardrobe, and a couple of boxes to clear his DVDs and XBox games. The television isn't his, so that'll stay on the chest of drawers. The neighbours will know. They're already wary of him. The walls outside his house will once again be spray-painted with lewd words and crude symbols.

"And this coat," DC Dixon begins. "Take another look at it and tell me if you recognise it." He picks up the evidence bag containing the dirty coat Carolyn had found, and pushes it towards Julio.

"I've told you... I don't know anything about that coat!"

"You're positive you've never seen that coat before?" DS Hughes asks.

"Yes," Julio snaps. "I'm absolutely positive."

***

After the interview, Hughes and Dixon discuss their progress with Inspector Williams. Once forensics open up the laptops and storage devices, they should have clear evidence that Patrick Sawhill had been running child pornography sites with the help of Julio Alcala.

Williams nods at the report lying on his desk, and agrees that with Julio Alcala's confession, it all makes sense.

"But who attacked Mr Cookson?" Williams asks.

Hughes shrugs. "I don't know. Mr Alcala seems pretty certain he has never heard of Mr Cookson. And the coat, well, he claims he's never seen that before either. I think he's told us everything he knows in a bid to help against his sentence. But I guess we'll have more to go on once the forensics come back with their findings."

Williams nods. "Have the whole area searched thoroughly. If the results come back matching the coat to Dylan Lloyd... we might have to send out another search party."

***

Carolyn and Barry are sitting talking about his future. He tells her not to be so ridiculous, and that he'll support himself.

"It's not as if I've lost my legs," he says.

They move on, discussing his daughter, Amy, and how close he had come to never seeing her again. Barry promises that once he's up and out of the hospital, he's going to start thinking of places to take her. He could even fix up the spare room in his flat – that is, if she ever feels like staying.

"I look forward to meeting her," Carolyn says, her voice still croaky. The guilt is heavy in her stomach. The conversation turns towards Simon and Ryan, and tears begin rolling down Carolyn's cheeks. She wipes them away and stands up. "I'm getting us more coffee."

"Thank God... I need a pee anyway." Barry struggles to stand and Carolyn moves in to help. He takes her hand, and with great effort she pulls him to his feet.

"Oh crap. Do you have change for the machine?" Carolyn asks, remembering she's not got enough.

"Jeez, I'm the one in hospital and you're asking me for money!" Barry jokes. "Take it from the table," he adds, heading into the bathroom.

Carolyn takes the change from his bedside table and heads to the machine. She inserts the coins and makes her selection before noticing the Indian man sitting in the corner.

"Still here?" she says, bringing the fresh cup of coffee over. "I owe you one, don't I?" He smiles and stands up, taking it from her.

"Yes, I headed home a couple of hours ago. The wife is still in the consultation room. I'm going to have a beard by the time I leave here tonight," he jokes. "How's your friend doing?"

Carolyn smiles. The thought of turning up and finding that Barry hadn't made it is long gone.

"Yeah, he's actually doing okay, consid—" she begins, then stops. The Indian man's face loses his smile as he notices Carolyn eyeing him suspiciously. She is examining his watch that has peeked out from under his sleeve.

It's large, with a bright red strap.

"You're the werewolf?" Carolyn says. It's the first thing that comes to mind.

Before she can say any more, the Indian man drops the coffee and pushes passed her, nudging Carolyn's shoulder and swinging her around. For a moment, she is motionless with shock. She thinks of shouting to Barry for help, then realises he's useless right now. Something along the lines of *Hey!* and *Stop!* leaves her mouth, and she gives chase.

The man is lean, and fast on his feet. He's almost reached the end of the ward. He pushes and dodges between nurses and patients in the corridor. Carolyn can see his footwear. White trainers.

The hospital staff stand by and watch the commotion. Carolyn reaches the double doors at the bottom and pushes through them; she's forgotten about the pain in her leg and lower back. She looks all around for the fleeing Indian man, but he's nowhere to be seen. She takes out her phone and calls DS Hughes.

DS Hughes answers on the second ring. Before she can say hello, Carolyn is shouting through her earpiece.

"The… the man in the hospital… He… he had white trainers and a… a red wristwatch!" she says, breathless.

"Calm down and speak clearly. What man are you talking about?" Hughes asks.

Calmly, Carolyn tells her she thinks it could have been the man wearing the werewolf costume.

***

DS Hughes and DC Dixon turn up at the hospital thirty minutes later and find the Head of Security. Gan Liu has worked Security at the hospital for the last nine years. He shows DS Hughes and DC Dixon to the surveillance room. He enters the code into the door and rushes in first. Empty Pepsi cans, chocolate bar wrappers and an open crossword book are scattered across the small desk. Gan Liu smiles and pushes them aside before taking a seat. He rewinds the last

194

forty minutes, and they watch from there. Thomas, the Indian man, is seen sitting in the waiting area, with a clear view of Barry's room. The CCTV at the hospital is much clearer than at *The Red Fox*.

DS Hughes asks if she can use the computer and then makes a call back to the station. She emails the CCTV picture over and they wait five minutes before it comes back to her. She prints out the clearest picture she has of Thomas, and attaches it to the police poster template before making copies. The poster states that the police would like to speak to this man.

The pictures are posted to the notice board in Reception and also to the Llanbedr Police website.

A uniformed officer is placed outside Barry's room for the night. DS Hughes convinces Carolyn that Barry will be safe and she should head back to the hotel.

Chapter Thirty-Two

The next morning, Carolyn is sitting in the waiting area of Llanbedr police station, nervously awaiting the reason for DS Hughes' phone call.

"Carolyn... come on through," DS Hughes says, holding the door open to an interview room.

"Well... What is this about? Why did you need to see me in person?" Carolyn asks, sounding a little ruder than how she intends.

"The man you were speaking to last night at the hospital is Thomas Zaman. He's a private detective from Fishguard. Mr Zaman tells us that he was hired to keep a watch on you and report back to his employer."

Carolyn is speechless. Questions are fighting in her head.

"W... What... Why was he watching me?" Carolyn stutters.

"Mr Zaman handed himself in last night after finding out that your friend was attacked. He said you'd told him Mr Cookson was in an accident. After realising you'd figured out he was the one in the werewolf costume that night and began chasing him, he panicked and made a run for it." DS Hughes finishes her sentence as DC Dixon enters the room with two mugs of steaming tea. He places them down and nods towards Carolyn before leaving.

"But that doesn't answer my question. Why was this man hired to watch me?"

"He was hired to follow you and report back to whoever it was that hired him. Mr Zaman is a private detective who hasn't had much work in the last year or so, and when a potential job came up, even given the suspicious circumstances, he took it."

"Suspicious circumstances?" asks Carolyn, cupping her

hands around the hot mug. Her fingers are cold and numb with worry.

"The person who employed Mr Zaman has stayed anonymous, not given their name and only communicated through email. The mystery person posted the asking fee through his letterbox and Mr Zaman replies with your activities through email. We're trying to find out who the email address belongs to, but we think it may have been set up and used just for this purpose," DS Hughes says, sipping at her tea before continuing. "Anyway, he found out that Mr Cookson had been stabbed and wasn't, in fact, in an accident. After seeing the pictures of himself from the CCTV, he handed himself in in the early hours of this morning. He's fully co-operating, and giving us full control over his computer and email account."

"Who attacked Barry?" Carolyn asks.

"Well, it wasn't Mr Zaman. His alibi stands up for the night of Mr Cookson's attack. He was pictured at a birthday party all day with at least thirty witnesses."

Carolyn sighs. "And his wife, in the hospital?"

"He has no wife. He's told me to tell you he was sorry for lying to you, and didn't know the sort of trouble he was getting himself mixed up in."

"Couldn't you have told me all of this over the phone? The hospital is releasing Barry today and I'm driving him home."

DS Hughes takes another sip of her tea before placing the mug down and looking Carolyn straight in the eye.

"The forensics has come back on Mr Sawhill's computer, storage devices and the note I took from your room. We couldn't find any DNA on the note, apart from your own. But the computer... Patrick Sawhill had files well-hidden deep inside other files on the hard drive. Our computer expert said that even he struggled to find them and open them."

"Okay..." Carolyn waits for DS Hughes to continue.

"The ledgers you found when browsing through his laptop that day were only the beginning. There were hundreds of pictures and videos of... children... found and saved under a code name." DS Hughes' jaw clenches, and for a moment

Carolyn thinks the detective is either going to be sick over the table or use her wide manly frame to flip it over in anger. DS Hughes goes on. "The code names match most of the files that you snapped a picture of. Mr Sawhill was buying the content from an outside source and charging sick bast —... charging other people who have a similar interest in that sort of thing, a monthly fee to access his sites."

Carolyn can't believe how much DS Hughes is sharing with her. Her own stomach drops, and after another morning of missing breakfast, the sickly sensation hits her.

"And the supplier? What about them?" she asks.

"We're working on that. Mr Alcala seems to be pretty helpful. He thinks by telling us everything he knows, it will save him from a longer prison sentence... But that's not going to happen. The person who attacked Mr Cookson could have had a personal vendetta towards you or him. It could have been a gang who sells drugs out there. We really don't know, and with no evidence to go on there isn't much I can tell you until we search the area properly. But I highly doubt it's connected with Mr Sawhill or Mr Alcala. One's dead and the other is locked up."

"Okay... And the body I saw in the well? Is this all connected?" Carolyn asks nervously.

DS Hughes takes a moment to answer. "I don't know what you saw in that well, Mrs Hill, but we've been through this. There wasn't a body when we arrived on the scene, and even though we've caught these sick bastards, I genuinely believe they don't have anything to do with the disappearances of either of the missing boys... Okay?"

Carolyn can see that DS Hughes still doesn't believe her story about the boy in the well. Reluctantly she nods and lowers her head, pushes her chair out and begins to stand up.

"There's one more thing, Mrs Hill," DS Hughes says. Carolyn lowers back into her seat. "We wouldn't have found out this side-business of Mr Sawhill's if it weren't for you. And with the help of Mr Alcala and our computer experts, we're hoping to find the members of this site and the supplier of the content and have it all shut down."

"Is that a thank-you?" Carolyn asks, this time standing up fully.

"Yes, it is. I would like to say, thank you," DS Hughes says, with a genuine smile on her face.

Carolyn is a little taken back by DS Hughes' praise. She thinks she might have also seen a glint of respect from DC Dixon's nod when he brought in the tea.

"I... um, well, thanks, I guess."

***

On the way to the hospital, Carolyn persuades herself that what DS Hughes said makes sense. *It was probably local thugs that attacked Barry*, she thinks.

But who sent the note?

Was that genuinely a person with information?

Was it the same person who planted the coat that could potentially belong to Dylan Lloyd?

Carolyn shakes the thoughts away. If any more notes are posted, she will hand them straight over to the police and let them deal with it.

In the car, on the way home from the hospital, Barry says, "So, hang on... she thanked you?"

"Yep, honest to God. She actually said *Thank You*."

"But I was the one hurt in the line of duty and you got the thanks?" Barry jokes.

"It was hardly the line of duty, was it?" Carolyn smiles. "And I think she meant it for both of us."

Blue lights come up quickly behind them and she pulls to the side of the narrow lane to allow the fire engine to pass. The car bumps up on a grass verge and Barry groans in pain.

"Sorry," she says, re-joining the road.

"Thanks for driving me home."

"It was the least I could do!"

"So what did DS Hughes say about the person who attacked me?" he asks, the laughter gone from his face.

"She said she doesn't think it's connected, and that it could have been a gang."

Barry blows out his cheeks. "Yeah, well, it's not going to happen again. I'm not going to let anyone creep up behind me like that."

Carolyn watches him as he stares out of the window. He looks lost in thought.

"The main thing is that you're okay and alive, isn't it?" Carolyn says. Barry lifts his eyebrows and attempts a smile.

They pull into a space outside the café and betting shop, which are now both closed as it's after five o'clock. Carolyn helps Barry out of the car. He can walk on his own if he takes it slowly. She walks him up the steel steps with a shopping bag of bread, milk and other bits so that he won't have to leave his flat in the next couple of days. She sits him down in his favourite spot in front of the TV and makes him a pot of tea before leaving, telling him she'll be back in the morning to check up on him.

"You don't have to do that," Barry protests.

"I want to," Carolyn replies. "See you tomorrow."

Carolyn heads for the B&B. The elderly woman greets her at reception, bringing with her the stench of cigarettes.

"Your mother has gone. She had a friend pick her up over an hour ago," the woman explains, tapping her yellowed-stained fingers on the front desk. "She told me to tell you that she's gone home, and you can find her there if you want her."

Carolyn thanks the woman, and even though she's paid up till tomorrow morning she decides to head home herself to keep Jeanette company. Carolyn drives home slowly, way under the speed limit as there's no other traffic on the road. She figures she'll give her mother more time to herself. Cruising at this speed also means Carolyn can brace herself for more of the silent treatment.

The lack of noise in the car causes Carolyn's mind to wander. She thinks about who Barry's attacker could be and who might have sent her the note.

NO! She pushes the thoughts away and turns on the radio. A song by Rod Stewart is playing, and she sings along to the parts she knows. The faces of Julio Alcala, Patrick Sawhill and Thomas Zaman begin to fade.

This is a police matter now, she thinks.

Yeah, sure, Carolyn! the internal voice sneers back.

The sky is a dull blue. Carolyn pulls into Alexandra Road and can see billows of smoke evaporate into the darkening sky. She increases her speed and heads for the blue flashing lights outside Jeanette's home.

The bungalow is engulfed in thick, furious flames.

Still a police matter, Carolyn? the internal voice asks, maliciously.

Chapter Thirty-Three

Carolyn's legs go numb as she steps from the car. She struggles to stand straight as she walks towards her mother's home, using the car as support. The heat of the raging fire instantly scorches the flesh on her face. The surrounding noises – the chatter from the passing motorists who had been stopped and held back by the roadblock, the sounds of bricks crumbling from the walls of the bungalow, and the orders from the firefighter pushing her back – are all barely audible, as if for a moment the world is whispering.

She studies the aging, grey-haired fireman who is holding her back from the front path, his hands resting on her shoulders. She's almost certain that he's the one who'd made a comment that night at the well. The one at the back of the line as they climbed through the gap in the fence. The one who'd looked back and frowned at her.

He's probably thinking that I'm the insane woman from the well, and that I started the fire too.

Carolyn wants to let go and fall into his arms to be held. But she has to know for certain if her mother is in the burning building.

This fire is her fault. The attacker had come back and set fire to her mother's home because she'd been sticking her nose in where it wasn't wanted. As if attacking and almost killing Barry wasn't enough; the psychopath needed to see her suffer even more.

If Jeanette is in there, Carolyn won't be able to ever forgive herself, especially after what's happened to Barry. This will be the thing that finishes her. She won't be able to go on living. Forget sessions with the Bereavement Counsellor; there'll be no coming back from this.

The aging fireman's words are soundless, she studies his lips and can read them shouting at her to stay back.

Then she hears the voice behind her, audible and sharp. The world becomes unmuted.

"CAROLYN... CAROLYN!" Jeanette shouts as she fights past bystanders. Father Joseph is at her side.

"Oh God, Mum. Thank goodness you're all right," she cries as they embrace each other. "I thought... that... maybe you might have been inside." She catches her breath as warm tears trickle down her cheeks and rest on Jeanette's shoulder. The muscles in her legs begin to wake up again. "Why the hell didn't you call me?" she asks. The silence between Jeanette and her, the trouble Carolyn had brought, is completely forgotten, at least for now.

"I didn't think. I've been at the church all afternoon. Father Joseph came for me after I called him from that B&B. I couldn't stand any more afternoon TV. We noticed smoke from the window, and at first I thought it might have been someone lighting a fire behind... you know... in the woods... camping, maybe. But then we..." Jeanette begins to sob.

"It'll be all right, Mum. It will be ok," Carolyn says, holding on to her mother's hands.

"But everything I own is in there – pictures of Simon and Ryan, pictures from my wedding day, pictures of your father, your father's chair." Jeanette cries and now rests her face on Carolyn's shoulder. The battered reclining chair is nothing to look at, but Carolyn knows it holds great sentimental value to her mother, even if Jeanette has never been a very sentimental person.

"I've got copies of pictures, Mum," Carolyn says, holding her arms around Jeanette's back.

Father Joseph comes closer and rests a hand on Jeanette's shoulder. Carolyn looks up at him and attempts a smile, grateful that her mother has someone to turn to, even if he can be a hypocritical dickhead.

Carolyn attempts to bring Jeanette inside Father Joseph's home – the presbytery that is built on to the side of St Peter's church – but she refuses, saying she wants to see it through to the end.

It takes the firefighters over an hour to kill the blaze. The road is reopened, and the bystanders are ushered on their way. Carolyn, Jeanette and Father Joseph are still on the steps of the church with blankets around them, and clutching cups of tea that they aren't drinking. The smell of burning wood is overwhelming in the air. After the fire dies, and the smoke clears, all that's left of Jeanette's home is a pile of rubble.

Jeanette gives her statement to the uniformed officer and turns back to Carolyn.

"Father Joseph said we can stay here until we're sorted."

Carolyn looks from her mother towards Father Joseph. She wonders if he'd hated offering his home to her.

I bet he thinks of me as a troublemaker, and that I pushed some crazy arsonist into starting the fire across the road from his church.

She's about to protest when Father Joseph speaks up.

"There's a spare room with a single bed. You can sleep on the sofa if you like, and give your mother the bed." His icy blue eyes stare at her from behind thick-framed glasses.

"Mum, it might be safer if we stay in a hotel again. Whoever started this fire might come back—"

"Started?" Jeanette cuts her off. "They don't even know how the fire was started. It might have been an electrical fault for all you know. Besides, I'm not going back to that smelly dump of a B&B. I belong here at the church, so here is where I'm staying."

Carolyn is about to protest, and tell her mother to stay here with Father Joseph and that she'll head back to the B&B, using the excuse that she doesn't want to put Father Joseph to any further inconvenience. Then she thinks for a moment and decides to stay. If anyone wants to come back and harm her mother, they'll have to go through her first.

Jeanette looks over at her smoking bungalow and turns into the presbytery. Father Joseph shows them to the spare room and leaves them to talk.

A little later, Father Joseph knocks and enters the room.

"Here's something for you to sleep in, Jeanette," he says, handing over a pair of men's loose trousers and a baggy t-shirt. "I got these from the donation bags. I've been meaning to drop them off at the charity shop."

Carolyn's bag of clothes is still in the boot of the car after packing up her things from the B&B earlier in the day. She will lend Jeanette a few clothes tomorrow until they can get to the shop and buy her some new things.

***

The killer can't believe his luck. That fire was furious! He's confident it will send Carolyn home now and stop her from digging any further. After all, she can't stay here for ever. She'll have no choice but to head home. Out of his life *and* his business.

Maybe now he can rest. No more sleepless nights worrying about what Carolyn is going to find out next.

***

The three of them sit at Father Joseph's kitchen table eating the tinned soup he has prepared. Nobody speaks for the first five minutes. Carolyn is beginning to feel uncomfortable.

"Now do you believe me that something weird is happening, Mum?" Carolyn asks.

Jeanette doesn't answer. Carolyn isn't sure if she even heard the question.

"Let's not go into that tonight, Carolyn," Father Joseph says. "I think your mother is under enough stress right now."

Carolyn keeps her gaze on him and stands up, her bowl still full of soup. "Well, I'm not going to stop looking," she says. "Even if I have to stay in that dump of a B&B for the next twelve months."

Father Joseph holds her gaze, but doesn't say anything else. Jeanette carries on with her soup and stays quiet.

"I'm going to devote my life to finding out what happened

to them missing boys before I even think of going back to Leeds!" Carolyn promises, heading towards the front door for air. On her way out, she hears them murmur quietly to each other, but she can't make out what they're saying.

Carolyn tries Father Joseph's sofa and finds it too hard, and barely long enough to lie on full-length. Its itchy fabric and hard cushions remind her of the types you would see in the reception of an office waiting area. The huge statue of Jesus on the cross pinned to the wall gives her the creeps. She feels as if the eyes of the statue are following her around the room, watching her carefully and reporting back to Father Joseph. She doesn't like the thought of Father Joseph getting up in the middle of the night and watching her sleep. A silly thought, she knows, but it's there nonetheless.

She moves to the bedroom with her mother and decides to sleep on the floor.

It takes hours for Jeanette to finally drift off to sleep. Carolyn hadn't known what else to say after "It'll all be okay" and "The insurance will fix everything." Truthfully, Carolyn was waiting for Jeanette to jump up and scream at her, to yell that none of this would have happened if Carolyn hadn't gone round causing trouble. That none of this would happened if she hadn't been telling distraught parents that she had seen their missing child down a well. But of course, Jeanette hadn't said or done any of those things. Instead, she'd ignored her daughter's attempts at comfort and turned to face the wall.

Carolyn longs for her father. He'd always stayed calm in troublesome times and could make Jeanette feel at ease in any situation. He'd have known what to do and what to say.

Carolyn remembers past times like Christmas and anniversaries that she and Simon would spend with them. Ryan wasn't yet born, and never got the chance to meet him, which crosses Carolyn's mind from time to time. She would especially think of him after his death, when she would see kids play with their grandparents in the park or even on adverts on the television.

It's now 2:00 am and Carolyn is wide awake. The worry is back again, sitting in her stomach and refusing to leave. She's waiting to hear the sound of people walking past the bedroom window, whispering to their fellow arsonist friends, who would be trying the doors and attempting to break in to get to her. She wonders how Father Joseph can sleep with the loud ticking of the clock out in the hallway.

Jeanette restlessly tosses and turns and murmurs something Carolyn can't make out.

Carolyn kicks the blanket off her legs and sits upright. She needs fresh air to clear her head. She slips on her jeans and boots and pulls on a jumper before creeping from the room, quietly closing the door behind her.

Father Joseph's room is further down at the bottom of the hall, his door slightly ajar. The lamp in the living room is still on, and it gives Carolyn enough light to make her way through quietly. She tiptoes as stealthily as she can, but still causes the odd squeak of a floorboard, though she's confident the noise will be disguised by the clock's loud ticking. Father Joseph's home is immaculate and clutter-free, with the bare minimum of furniture. She comes to two doors, both ajar. She looks through the gap into the first room, where the majority of the space is taken up with a chest freezer and washer-dryer. She peers through the second door and finds his study. She carries on, reaching the living room. The huge crucifix on the wall looks at her with added judgement. She passes without giving it another glance and opens the front door, keeping the lock off the latch and closing it to keep out the bitter night air.

Carolyn can see what remains of her mother's home across the road. She can see that the large dark building is now nothing more than a pile of bricks and wood, with all of her mother's possessions inside, burned to an ash. She rests her back against the wall next to the front door and closes her eyes.

Carolyn wishes she had never come to stay with her mother or caused any of this trouble. If she had never come, she would never have seen that body in the well. She wishes that Simon and Ryan had never been on the motorway that day. She wishes she'd never got Barry Cookson involved in helping her, and in return, getting him stabbed. She wishes she were home in bed with Simon while Ryan sleeps peacefully in his own room. She imagines that they both would be discussing what cakes she has on order for tomorrow. She'd complain about how yet another customer had tried to haggle down the price. Simon would complain about the office manager demanding more from him and his colleagues as the firm tries cutting back on expenses. They'd discuss the MOT which is due on the car, and how the boiler might need a visit from the engineer.

Carolyn would give anything to have those problems back again.

She hugs herself and opens her eyes to forget the memories before she breaks out crying. She brings her attention back to ways she can make it up to her mother, or at least try to dull the pain. She walks down the steps and across the road to the wreckage, her boots louder than normal on the damp road surface.

She doubts there'll be anything to salvage, but she hopes to find a few pictures that she doesn't have copies of, praying that they've survived the blaze.

Jeanette would be furious knowing that Carolyn had even attempted to go near the wreck, never mind tried stepping inside it, but Carolyn hopes her mother will feel a little better having something to remember her home by. Carolyn ducks under the fire tape which is ordering people to stay out, and peers through the gap that used to be a window. The roof has caved in, and the doorway is blocked by shards of roof tiles and blackened timber. She steps around the side, crossing over the burned and flattened grass and bushes. At the rear, where the back door used to be, is a large opening in the wall. Carolyn looks up and around for anything that could still collapse on top of her, and seeing nothing but stars, she steps through. She reaches into her pocket for her mobile to use as a torch and curses herself when she remembers she'd left it on the side table next to her sleeping mother. The moonlight will have to do. She steps on top of the fallen bricks and over splintered wood. Plates and cups crunch under her boots as she steps through the doorframe into the living room. The metal skeletal remains of her father's chair sit in front of a heap of melted plastic and a crumbled TV cabinet.

In the far corner, where it looks as if the fire was brought under control, is a cabinet that's only partly affected. The wallpaper behind it is dark but still shows the swirly patterns. The sponge from the sofa cushions is exposed but not completely incinerated. The contents of a collapsed wooden cabinet are spilled across the floor.

She kneels, moving blackened, splintered wood out of the way, and begins rummaging through books, photographs and papers that were once important documents. Most of the letters are unsalvageable, while others are only suffering from curled edges and discolouration. She slips the pictures into her pocket and moves broken glass ornaments to the side, then she spots a purple lump of melted candle wax.

These were purple candles?

She thinks back to the purple candle wax she'd found at the well that day. She'd showed it to the police, but they weren't interested in hearing any more about it. Why would her mother have the same-coloured candles as the lump of wax she'd found next to the well?

Could just be a coincidence. Perhaps. Candles aren't uncommon in most households, she thinks.

She stands to take it back over to the presbytery; she'll ask her mother about it in the morning. Turning to leave, she hears wood moving and footsteps approaching fast from behind.

She spins around, but not quickly enough.

Then comes a whack on the back of her head. Darkness fills her vision, and she can feel the sharp bricks dig into her shoulder as her body hits the ground.

Chapter Thirty-Four

Jeanette wakes at 7:00 am and stares at the ceiling. She starts thinking about what she can make for breakfast. A full fry-up, or scrambled egg and toast?

For a moment, she forgets where she is. Then the reality comes and lands like a ton of bricks. She sighs, looking down at the floor to see Carolyn isn't there. She assumes she's gone to Barry's, or is speaking to the police again, most likely telling them how to do their jobs. Her daughter had not stayed put lately; she's always out getting in people's way. She thinks of what Carolyn was blabbering about last night – about getting to the bottom of the truth about the missing boys.

"After all this is cleared up, you should move to Leeds with me and leave Llanbedr behind." Carolyn had said. *But why should I?* Jeanette thinks. *This is my home. This is where my friends are based, and the church that needs me. The church that I need. I know Father Joseph will allow me to stay as long as I need to. He's a good man like that. We've grown to become good friends over the years.*

Jeanette decides that she'll talk to Carolyn today. She'll tell her that she's fine to handle the insurance, and whatever else is needed, by herself. She'll tell her that she should try to forget about all this mess, before it causes any more trouble, and that Carolyn should take herself back off home. *This unfortunate house fire was nothing to do with her,* Jeanette thinks. *There isn't anybody after her or wanting to cause her any harm. She really shouldn't have to go through finding somewhere to sleep. At the end of the day, she's still grieving the loss of her family. She doesn't need to be imagining that some crazed killer is out there hunting her. What happened to her friend Barry was just a vicious, random attack. It happens all the time, all over the country. Just watch the News.*

Jeanette pulls the covers to one side and sits up, rubbing her face – then notices Carolyn's mobile on the bedside table. The blanket and pillow are still on the floor, crumpled together. *Something doesn't make sense here,* she thinks. Jeanette knows her daughter. She knows Carolyn would never leave without her mobile, and she'd always fold and tidy away any blankets she'd been using. That's how she and her husband had raised her.

Jeanette waits, sitting on the edge of the bed, for Carolyn to come back from the bathroom.

"Breakfast is ready," Father Joseph shouts through the door as he knocks lightly. Jeanette stands up and opens the door. She pops her head out and looks at the open door of the bathroom.

"Have you seen Carolyn?" she asks. "Her clothes are gone, and she's left her phone."

"No. She must have gone out," Father Joseph replies. He doesn't sound particularly worried.

They sit at the table over three English breakfasts. Father Joseph pours the coffee.

"She's probably gone into town to get you some new clothes," he says. "She did say that last night, remember? I'll wrap her breakfast up and keep it in the oven."

At the table, Jeanette moves a sausage from side to side as she watches the steam leave Carolyn's breakfast. She has a sick feeling in her stomach.

"Carolyn wouldn't have left without her phone…" she tails off, then stands up and walks over to where Carolyn's bag is on the counter. She searches through it. "And here are my car keys. So how did she get into town?" A worried look is starting to creep on her face.

Father Joseph looks at Jeanette with a puzzled expression and shrugs. "Maybe she got that friend of hers to come for her. What's his name… that Barry. Don't worry. I'm going into town soon. I'll look for her, okay?"

Jeanette nods and thanks him, before sitting back at the table and sipping her coffee. It tastes awful, not like the one that her coffee machine at home makes... used to make.

"She's probably left the car on purpose. She knows I'll need some things after the fire and didn't want to leave me without it," Jeanette says, hoping to convince herself. "I'll go through her phone after breakfast and give Barry a call, to see if she's there."

Chapter Thirty-Five

Carolyn's head is hanging on her chest, and drool is leaving her lips. She's dreaming of being in Simon's car again. The angry lorry with the evil-looking headlights is following behind them, with its huge engine growling and hissing. It doesn't want to pass them. It wants to run them off the road and squash their car, killing them.

The frantic cries from Ryan in the back seat pierce Carolyn's eardrums. Remembering the whack from behind, she holds a hand to the back of her head and feels the warm blood trickle down her fingers and wrist. When she spins around this time to hush her frightened son, he hasn't disappeared, as he had done in earlier dreams. He looks at her with wide, wet eyes, his bottom lip is trembling as he grabs for her hand. She holds his hand tightly and looks back at Simon. He has both hands off the wheel and is facing her. The lorry has now disappeared. He rests a hand on her knee as the car drives itself. She feels herself drifting off into oblivion, and is happy to spend the rest of her time here with her dearly-loved husband and son. She opens her mouth to speak, to tell them both how much she has missed them, when Simon speaks up first.

"You have to go, babe," he says softly, and takes back his hand.

Carolyn doesn't understand. Finally they're all together, they're a family again, and now he wants her to go? She knows this is the end and she's happy for it, welcomes it even. The walk towards the white light has taken its time to reach her, but is finally here. She wants them all to be a family again and to join them on their journey to wherever they may end up. *At least it'll be the three of us, together at last,* she thinks.

"You have to go, Mummy," the little voice behind her says, and she feels his warm, tiny fingers leave her palm.

"But… I don't want to go… I want to—"

Simon leans closer and kisses her. She can smell his aftershave, the one that smells slightly sweet, the one she really likes.

"It's not your time, love. We'll see you soon. I love you," Simon says, looking behind him and back to Carolyn. "We both love you."

Then darkness takes over.

Her back hurts, she's freezing cold, and the pain on the back of her skull is excruciating. She lifts a hand to assess the damage and feels restricted, unable to move her arms and legs.

It's the smell that she notices first, before she even opens her eyes: that dreadful smell from the pig farm in the distance. She raises her head, and the tinnitus noise echoes through her ears, causing the headache at the back to increase.

As her blurred vision clears, Carolyn looks around and hears the cooing from the pigeons above. She looks down at her arms to see she's sitting on the floor, bound, with her back resting against a huge slab of concrete and the rope tied tightly around her midriff and legs.

Panic rushes through her.

This is the end. I'm going to be thrown down the well and forgotten.

The room she's in looks like an old kitchen. The floorboards are dusty, and there are fresh shoeprints either side of a thick trail where the attacker had dragged Carolyn's unconscious body. In the corner is an upturned table and chairs. A fridge is lying on its side, dented and missing a door. The counters are filled with old dusty beer bottles. The space where the oven used to be is empty, exposing the copper pipes forking out of the wall. The cracked concrete walls are covered in graffiti: marijuana symbols, nicknames, and lewd spray-painted penises. Carolyn studies the walls, imagining they could crumble at any second.

Early morning sun shines through one of the cracks, burning Carolyn's eyes. She wonders if the back of her head is bleeding, as it was in the dream.

Who the hell hit me? she thinks.

The internal voice answers. *Now you're really going to die. You should have gone home.*

She shakes her head and ignores it. *Has the attacker gone after my mother and Father Joseph? Does this psychopath want me to watch as they hurt them?*

Surely whoever attacked me last night and brought me here could have easily shoved that knife into my back as they had done with Barry. Why go to all this trouble?

She screams for help, but her voice is croaky and low. The pigeons above barely notice, flying from one ceiling joist to the other. Droppings splat on the ground next to her. She looks around the old kitchen and sees a broken wooden sign in the corner along with a pile of pallets. The sign reads **SUNLIGH-** and she realises she has been taken to The Sunlight B&B, not too far from her mother's home.

She wonders if the attacker is coming back to torture her, or if the plan is to torture and then leave her here, starving to death, or to slowly go insane, tied to a concrete slab, while probably suffering from concussion. Whoever it is, they must have been sitting outside all night, watching the church, waiting to make their move. She'd walked right into their sight and made it easy for them.

She sighs and shakes her head. She would chuckle if her life – or her mother's – wasn't on the line. Tears begin, and a lump is forming in her throat.

She stops herself. She will not cry.

Carolyn looks round and a thought comes to her, one that sends uncomfortable images through her brain. *What if whoever brought me here and tied me up to this slab of concrete is sitting outside in their car, waiting for the demolition team to turn up and start their day's work?*

Carolyn knows she has to escape these restraints. She struggles side-to-side in a bid to loosen the rope, panting and twisting her body. But it's no good. The rope is tight, and all she's achieving is more pain to her arms and shoulders. There's no escape, and no Plan B.

She has no more strength to fight. All she can do is to wait until the psychopath comes back and does whatever it is they have planned for her.

If they decide to come back at all, that is.

Chapter Thirty-Six

Barry slept on the sofa in the living room, where Carolyn had left him the night before. He'd visited the toilet twice during the night, and both times were a real struggle and very time-consuming. The hard part was standing. Once up, he could lean along the walls and steady himself. A couple of times during the night he'd felt like making a cup of tea, but couldn't be bothered with the struggle of getting over to the kettle.

Sleeping on the sofa meant he could prop himself up like in the hospital bed. This way there was less pressure on his back, which meant less pain. Not that he'd slept much at all. The attack replayed over and over in his mind, and the thought of never seeing his daughter again brought him to tears. A few times he swore he'd heard someone outside on the street, but he thought it had probably just been a fox or stray cats rummaging in the bins for food. Nonetheless, he kept a large kitchen knife at his side, just in case.

Now he's awake, and after taking the drugs the hospital gave him, he's watching his morning TV show about couples from the UK who relocate abroad.

His phone rings, so he mutes the TV and rests his long-awaited mug of tea on the side before reaching for his mobile, sighing with the pain in his back.

He answers. "Hi, Carolyn. It's only been a night. Do you miss me already?" He shakes his head at how silly it sounds.

"Barry?" Jeanette says.

"Oh hi, Jeanette. Sorry I… I thought you might have been Carolyn. Erm… Why are you calling me from her phone?" Barry asks, sitting up straight. He hears Jeanette taking a deep breath.

"So Carolyn isn't there with you then?" she asks, after a moment.

"No," Barry says. "I haven't seen or heard from her since last night, after she dropped me off at home from the hospital."

"Right…"

"Jeanette, what's going on?" Barry asks. He's beginning to feel uncomfortable.

She explains how she'd woken up and found Carolyn missing, without her phone, and the car still parked outside. She tells him why they've had to spend the night at Father Joseph's, and that Carolyn had been quite upset last night.

Barry offers his condolences.

"Father Joseph has gone into town," Jeanette says. "He's going to ask around to find out whether anyone has seen her. If she gets in touch with you, please let me know."

"Yes, of course. And I'll ring around a few places where she might have gone. I'll let you know either way."

She thanks him and they say goodbye.

***

Jeanette puts Carolyn's phone down and picks up her own. She begins dialling 999, and then clears her screen. She'll give it a little longer, or at least until Father Joseph returns and lets her know if he's seen her or not. The last thing she needs is to bother the police over something this silly, especially if Carolyn has only gone for a walk. The police already dislike Carolyn. Jeanette doesn't want them to take against her as well. After all, she'll be staying here when Carolyn heads back to Leeds.

Chapter Thirty-Seven

Carolyn doesn't hear the low rumble of the car's engine approaching. She only hears the damaged door of the kitchen scrape along the bare floorboards as it's pushed open.

The pigeons flap their wings and take flight, dropping feathers that dance through the air. She braces herself for the attacker to enter, or braces as much as the rope would allow. She's had time to think about what she's going to say to him or her. First, she'll apologise like crazy for bringing the well, their dumping ground, to light. Secondly, she'll explain that nobody believes her, and that the police aren't interested in what she has to say. Thirdly, she'll beg that they should just let her go. She'll head back to Leeds and she'll even take her mother with her. They'll never have to see her face again. She'll never return to Llanbedr for as long as she lives.

Carolyn means it; she just wants to be home and to forget all about Llanbedr.

The words are resting on her tongue and she's ready to start begging for her life, waiting for the footsteps to grow closer and for this grotesque-looking monster to enter the room. But when the monster enters, the lump in her throat grows twice the size, and she can't bring herself to speak. Shock has taken over, and the person walking over to her is the last one she'd ever expect to see.

"No," she says, feeling the colour drain from her face. Her tense body falls limp. Without realising, her head is shaking side-to-side with disbelief.

The person comes closer.

"Yes, Carolyn. It's me."

Father Joseph walks over to her with a litre bottle of vodka in his hand and places it on the floor, then takes a seat on a nearby slab of concrete which has sharp metal reinforcing bars sticking out of it.

"How… how… w-why?"

"I didn't want it to come to this, Carolyn. I really didn't," Father Joseph says calmly, removing his glasses and cleaning them with a handkerchief. "Last night at the table, you said you weren't done with looking into the missing boys. I saw in your eyes that you wouldn't stop, that you'd *never* stop, never let this go. Even after your mother's home burned to the ground."

"Did you do that?" she says.

"No, no, that wasn't me. But if I'm honest, I thought you might have run straight back to Leeds after that. I was waiting for you to jump in your mother's car and go." Father Joseph replaces his glasses.

"Mum?" Carolyn says, thinking the worst.

"Your mother is fine. I haven't done anything to her. I even plated up a breakfast for you this morning, you know, to keep up appearances, as if I didn't know where you were."

Carolyn sighs. *This is probably the end, but at least Mum is safe. After all, I caused this. And the killer was hiding right under my nose.*

She looks from the vodka to Father Joseph. He nods.

"Yes, unfortunately that isn't for me… It's for you. I heard you creeping out during the night. I never sleep any more, not properly, anyway. Not since…" Father Joseph tails off. He's looking down at the dusty floor, covered in pigeon poo.

"Not since what? What happened?" she asks, her throat dry.

Father Joseph sighs and rubs at the lines on his forehead.

"Where do I begin?" he says. "I killed Elwyn Roberts. That's probably what you want to hear, right?"

Carolyn swallows. "Why?"

"It was an accident. Not that any of that matters now."

"An *accident*?" Carolyn says, her voice not sounding like her own.

"Yes, a stupid accident. He ran out in front of my car, chasing a ball. If you can believe that." Father Joseph shakes his head. "You couldn't leave it, could you? You had to keep digging deeper and deeper and deeper. Now, well, look where you are."

He stands up and towers over her. His hand trembles as he unscrews the top from the vodka bottle. He approaches Carolyn and grabs hold of her cheeks. His fingers feel moist with sweat as he squeezes her cheeks together, shouting for her to open her mouth wide. His voice echoes off the bare walls. Carolyn fights. She shakes her head from side to side in an attempt to loosen his grip so she can scream. Father Joseph's fingernails dig deep into her flesh.

"I'll bring your mother here... Carolyn... Don't make me... OPEN YOUR MOUTH!" he orders.

Carolyn stops fighting at the thought of him hurting her mother and slowly opens her mouth, allowing the clear liquid to be poured in. She keeps it up, refusing to swallow and considers spitting it out in his face, but the seriousness in his piercing blue eyes shows he isn't joking, and that he'll do whatever it takes for her to drink it.

The vodka burns as it goes down her throat and she gags, almost throwing it back up.

"Again!" he demands.

Carolyn opens her mouth again and allows the alcohol to be poured in. Tears fill her eyes as she brings up the alcohol. It runs down her chin and onto her jumper. Father Joseph pours another mouthful in and Carolyn pulls a sour face as she swallows.

A quarter of the bottle is gone. Father Joseph screws the top back on before sitting down on the slab of concrete.

"Ever wonder why I don't drink any more?" he asks. When Carolyn doesn't reply, he continues. "I had a drinking problem once, and one day I'd had too many and drove home. My driving was fine, if I'm being honest with you. I know that's what most people would say after they've been caught drink-driving, but I genuinely believed I was fine. Then... Elwyn Roberts stepped out in front of me, chasing a football. I didn't see him, and when I did... he was too close. I took him to the hospital, but it was useless. He was gone. Dead on the back seat of my Volvo."

To Carolyn, the room looks as if it's moving. The floor she is sitting on feels as if it is made of sponge. She hates straight spirits, especially the cheap ones.

"Elwyn Roberts went missing eight years ago," she says, coughing. "I... That body I saw down the well. It hadn't been decaying for eight years. I don't understand."

"That's true. I... I kept him in the chest freezer. I kept him there for eight years – as a reminder never to drink again. Then, one day, my luck changed. It was the smell that alerted me first. The freezer had packed up, and the body had been decaying for a few days before I discovered it. And when I did..." Father Joseph turns his face, as if the memory of that scent is back in his nostrils. "I had to find somewhere else to put it... to put *him*... while I sorted out the freezer and got rid of the stench."

Carolyn grimaces.

Father Joseph stands, searching his pockets before he carries on. "Then you and your mother arrived back. That night, I waited until it was going dark before heading over. I was going to retrieve him and find somewhere else to hide him. That's when I saw you standing at the well."

"Why... why not just go to the police and explain your... yourself?" Carolyn burps.

Father Joseph is now back in front of her and holding her cheeks. He forces a handful of sleeping pills into her mouth, along with more vodka. Carolyn struggles to swallow them all and coughs a couple back out. Father Joseph pokes them back in and gives her another mouthful of vodka to wash them down.

"No... Trust me, I thought about it, about going to the police and confessing the whole story. Either way they'd look at it, accident or not, I was drunk, Carolyn. I was over the legal limit, and I shouldn't have been driving. My life would have been ruined. Can you imagine?" Father Joseph shakes his head.

"Are you being serious?" Carolyn asks.

"My church would have been taken from me, the people of Llanbedr would no longer look up to me and confide in me.

My… my title would have been stripped," he hisses, examining his hands. "No, no. I couldn't have done that. I'm sorry. I asked the Lord what I should do, and he came to me in a dream and told me to carry on. *'What has happened has already happened, and we can't change that'*, he said, so I listened, and I kept it a secret. Until you arrived!" Father Joseph snarls with an angry glint in his eye.

"W-what did you…you do with his body?" Carolyn manages. Her head is spinning.

Father Joseph thinks for a moment, tuts and walks towards the window. He pushes his glasses up his nose, puts his hands in his pockets and looks out, concentrating on something only he can see.

"He's out there, Carolyn. I buried him out there, next to a huge rock. It's nice. Peaceful."

Carolyn looks at him and drops her head back towards the floor. The dizziness has increased tremendously, causing her to feel groggy and tired again. She wishes she could vomit it all out, but that would only make him angry. Who knows what he would do then?

She forces herself to stay awake and to ask more questions.

"What… what are you… what are you going to do with me?" she slurs.

"Well, I'm not a killer, Carolyn. Whatever you might think of me." He pauses. "So, it looks to me that with everything that's gone on lately – the stress of losing your family, and causing all this trouble for your poor mother – it's all got a little too much for you to handle. It looks to me like you drank yourself into a right state and walked to the second floor of this old B&B…"

Carolyn looks at him with fear in her eyes.

"… then threw yourself out of one of the windows," he says with a cold icy stare.

Carolyn wrestles at the rope, but now, after the alcohol and the sleeping tablets, all her strength has disappeared. Her head falls to her chest, and she mumbles, "Murdered b-by Dave G-Grohl," before losing consciousness.

Father Joseph unscrews the lid of the cheap vodka. The side of the bottle reads forty percent alcohol, the rest of the words are in Russian. He contemplates a mouthful, just to take the edge off this whole mess, and lifts the bottle to his lips, but stops before it touches. He sighs and screws the top back on, placing the bottle next to Carolyn before leaving.

I'll need a clear head for this to work, he thinks.

Chapter Thirty-Eight

Jeanette has washed the dishes from this morning's breakfast, keeping Carolyn's breakfast in the fridge. She's vacuumed every room and polished every cabinet and table in the place. Anything to keep her mind occupied, which is hard, because Father Joseph's place is already spotless. Still, no harm in going over it a second time. Jeanette can't shake off the thoughts running through her mind: *Carolyn has been taken by a masked man, possibly the arsonist from last night. Or the psychopath who attacked that lovely giant Barry.* What makes it worse is that when her daughter needed her help, she hadn't believed her.

What kind of mother am I?

Barry had rung back half an hour after they'd finished talking. He told Jeanette that he'd called a few places around town. He'd even tried the hospital and The Coffee Shack, but nobody had reported seeing her, or anyone answering her description.

Jeanette has just finished making another cup of tea after leaving the others to go cold. She picks her phone up and places it back on the table. She contemplates making the call to the police. She has never been this worried in all her life. The nails on her fingers have been bitten down deep and now her fingertips ache. She walks to the window, then to the table, and takes a seat. Next she counts the lines on the wallpaper, before losing count, and starting again.

She opens the message app on her phone to see if Barry might have any news, and is disappointed when the message folder is empty.

She drops her phone and rests her head in her hands, and thinks about how she wishes she'd done more. *I should have got help for her – real help from a professional – when all this trouble first began. Seeing a corpse down a well! What kind of crazy thing is that to say?*

Besides, there's no way... unless... No, no. There's no way that's possible.

The front door of Father Joseph's home opens before the tears have time to begin. Jeanette stands to attention as he comes into the kitchen, and begins thinking all sorts of horrific scenes as she waits to hear the news. *Carolyn is dead – knifed to death by the same person that got Barry. Or perhaps she's been arrested and is currently being held in a police cell after she hurled abuse and accusations at an innocent shopper, blaming them for starting the fire.*

"Well?" Jeanette asks, anticipation in her voice.

Father Joseph shrugs off his coat and places it on the back of the chair. He shakes his head. "I'm sorry, Jeanette. Nobody has seen her. I've asked everywhere. Maybe she did go out for a walk to clear her head. Give her time. I'm sure she'll turn up. She probably just needs some time on her own."

"This is our fault... You know that, don't you?" Jeanette snaps.

Father Joseph looks down at his shiny shoes with the one-inch heel, but says nothing.

"I'm calling the police now. I've waited long enough. I'm not prepared to wait any longer." Jeanette reaches for her mobile from the table and begins to dial. Father Joseph steps closer and takes it from her.

"Excuse me—" she begins.

"Wait... Just wait, will you, Jeanette?" He sighs, holding out her mobile. "You know what this is going to do."

"They don't need to know everything. But they have to know Carolyn is missing. I know she hasn't gone for a walk. I know my daughter, and I know she'd be back by now! This is our mistake, and my daughter shouldn't have to pay for it."

***

Father Joseph remains silent. His head hurts. He's thinking, *I could really do with some of that vodka now. This whole thing has been nothing but trouble.*

He rubs at his temples as the different scenarios rush through his mind. Finally, he decides what action to take.

"Why don't we sit down and have a cup of tea?" he says. *Not the most thought-out plan. But I have to buy myself time. I have to get back over to the old B&B and finish what I started. I have to get enough alcohol and sleeping tablets into Carolyn's system before I can throw her from that top window.*

"I've had enough tea! I want to find my daughter, now!" Jeanette snaps.

Father Joseph can see, from the look in Jeanette's eyes, that she's not going to let it go.

Father Joseph really doesn't want to hurt Jeanette. She's been a good friend, not just to him, but to the church and to the people of Llanbedr. She's a good woman, and he, along with the rest of the town, respects her. He also enjoys her company.

But he enjoys his freedom more.

"Okay... okay... Listen. I might have an idea where Carolyn could be." He picks his coat back up from the chair and slips it on. "Come on. Let's go and check," he says, leading Jeanette out of his home for the last time.

Chapter Thirty-Nine

"Hey, hey. Wake up," a man's voice calls as he lightly slaps Carolyn across the cheeks in a bid to wake her.

Carolyn slurs and moans, and tells him that she isn't ready to get out of bed.

The man wipes the sticky hair from Carolyn's eyes, placing it behind her ears before shaking her shoulders.

Finally she wakes and stares up at him with pink bloodshot eyes.

"Hey... Why has Father Joseph got you here?" he asks. She recognises the voice. It's one she's heard before somewhere.

The afternoon sun shines through the cracks and makes it difficult for Carolyn to focus on the figure standing in front of her. She blinks and studies him.

"Buckles...? Mark Buckles?"

"Yeah. What the fuck is going on here?" The candle shop owner stands up and looks around the room. He pulls a face as he spots the bottle of vodka on the floor. He runs a hand down his face which is now showing two-day-old stubble. His slicked-back hair is uncombed and messy, and his clothes look as if they haven't been changed for several days.

"So that's why he bought it, then," he mutters to himself.

"What... What did you say?" Carolyn asks, trying to open her eyes wide. She forces her eyes to stay open, and tries to shake off the groggy, sickly feeling brought on by having been force-fed straight vodka and sleeping pills.

"I saw Father Joseph in town, buying that vodka," Buckles says. He looks around the room and continues. "He seemed a little shaken up, and different from his usual self. He got in his car and took off before I had the chance to speak to him. I followed him, and I tried to catch him before he got home and drank himself silly. He's been sober for a few years now."

Carolyn thinks Mark Buckles seems disorientated, agitated even.

He looks back to her. "I didn't want him to throw those years away. Then I saw him park here and come inside. I parked further down the road and waited for him to come back. What's going on here?"

Carolyn burps. She feels like throwing up, but she manages to keep her focus on the figure in front of her. "He killed Elwyn Roberts. He's drugging me, and I think he's going to kill me... to... to stop me searching for the missing boys!"

"What?" Buckles asks, visibly shocked. "How do you know this?"

Carolyn can smell that he hasn't washed for days. She wonders what might have happened. *A death in the family? Debt troubles?* But whatever it is, she doesn't have time to worry about his troubles right now. She needs to concentrate on her own immediate problems.

"He admitted it," Carolyn says. "Now untie me. I need to go and tell my mother and call the police."

Mark looks towards the huge hole in the wall. Carolyn sees the worry in his face and fights at the rope, twisting to loosen it. The alcohol in her system has now been overtaken by the adrenaline rushing through her veins.

"Quick, before he gets back!" she begs.

Mark stands quietly, then examines the rope. He steps back in front of her, shaking his head.

"The knots are too tight. I'd need a knife," he whispers, then walks behind the broken door and backs up against the wall, out of sight.

"Why do you think she'll be here?" Carolyn can hear Jeanette asking, as her mother makes her way up the stairs.

"MUM... MUM, RUN!" Carolyn shouts as the two enter the room. "You said you wouldn't hurt her!" she screams.

"Oh... my God. What have you done?" Jeanette says,

holding a shaking hand up to her mouth.

"Jeanette, listen to me," Father Joseph begins, stepping in front of her.

"Why is she tied up?" Jeanette asks with fear in her voice. She turns back to Carolyn. "Are you ok?"

"No, no I'm not. He killed Elwyn Roberts. He's admitted it. Run, please. Just go!" Carolyn shouts.

Father Joseph steps to the side of Jeanette.

"I know," Jeanette says. "But it was an accident. He... *we*... had both been out drinking, and—"

"*We*?" Carolyn says, her eyes wide. "You know? What do you mean, you know? Elwyn is still missing! His family..." Carolyn stops. Her mind is jittery with Jeanette's confession. She stares at her mother, hoping this is nothing more than a hallucination brought on by the drugs and alcohol. Though Carolyn knows it *isn't* a hallucination. She's known all along, just as she knew the boy in the well wasn't her imagination.

"His family is still wondering what happened to him..." Carolyn tails off again. She's speechless.

Father Joseph steps forward, the heels of his shoes clinking on the floorboards. "I wasn't going to mention your mother's part in all this. That's why I said it was me alone."

Carolyn doesn't look at him. Her eyes are still fixed on her mother's.

Jeanette is now standing in front of Carolyn. "We never went to the police. We tried taking him to the hospital, but when we got there, he... He was already dead on the back seat... I... well, *we* both decided there was no point in Father Joseph losing his status..."

Jeanette's words, for a moment, are lost on Carolyn. She feels her stomach drop.

"... and our respect in town, over an accident. People wouldn't be able to forgive us," Jeanette finishes, her voice now broken.

Father Joseph stands to Jeanette's left, frowning.

Carolyn can't believe what she's heard. The woman she trusts more than anyone in the world has been keeping this horrific secret, all to protect a man's status. She feels sick again, and this time it's not from the cocktail of vodka and sleeping pills mixing in her system.

"But Mum, you've broken the law. You *both* have. Elwyn Roberts... he... he deserves to have a proper burial. His family... they deserve closure," Carolyn says, fighting back the vomit. Her eyes dart from her mother to Father Joseph.

"He did have a proper burial, Carolyn," Jeanette says. "Father Joseph took him somewhere and said a prayer for him. I gave him one of my candles. One of the good ones to light in my honour. I couldn't bring myself to be there."

Carolyn watches her mother begin to cry. *You expect sympathy?*

"I know you can't understand," Jeanette continues. "I don't blame you. I just wish—"

"So Father Joseph didn't tell you, then?" Carolyn interrupts.

"What are you going on about?" Jeanette asks. "Tell me what?"

Father Joseph straightens.

"He didn't bury him, Mum. He kept him in the freezer in his back room like a joint of meat. For eight years." Carolyn watches the expression on her mother's face change. "Then, when his freezer broke down, he dumped him down the well, the well right behind your home, the well where I swore to you that I'd seen a body, and you thought I was going crazy."

"What? Is that true, Father?" Jeanette asks, turning to face him with confusion on her face.

Father Joseph doesn't respond. His face is red. He keeps his icy blue eyes fixed on Carolyn's.

Jeanette steps behind Carolyn and tugs on the knot.

"Jeanette, don't!" Father Joseph orders. "She's caused enough trouble around here. People need me in this community, and they need you. If you untie her, that will be both of our lives ruined. It'll be the end of us," he adds, stepping closer.

Jeanette looks up to meet his eyes. "I don't care any more, Father. Don't you see? Carolyn shouldn't have to pay for my mistake. She's been through enough already. It's time for us to come clean. I've struggled with that guilt for far too long, and so have you. All those sleepless nights. It's time to confess and take responsibility." Jeanette digs her fingers into the knot.

"Stop what you're doing!" Father Joseph orders, this time louder and more demanding. Jeanette doesn't even look up, but Carolyn can see his mounting anger.

He's gone this far to keep his secret, Carolyn thinks. *How much further will he go?* "Carolyn's mixed up in all of this... it's not fair," Jeanette says. She continues to fiddle with the rope.

Carolyn keeps her eyes on Father Joseph. *Just loosen the rope, then we stand a chance at overpowering him. You, me and Mark Buckles, who is still standing behind the door.*

"Well, I'm not ready to confess what I've done," Father Joseph says. "The church needs me, Jeanette." He steps closer and pulls her away from Carolyn.

"GET OFF ME!" Jeanette shouts, pulling to free her arm from his tight grip.

"You don't understand. It isn't just me that you'll ruin," Father Joseph begins, sweat forming on his brow. "It's the whole community. People need me at that church, and I'm not prepared to throw it away all because your daughter couldn't let things go and keep her nose out of other people's business."

Jeanette leaps at Father Joseph and brings her nails down across his face, leaving two long scratches.

Father Joseph shrieks in pain and his face turns a dark shade of purple. He grabs Jeanette by the shoulders and throws her to the side. She trips over her foot and hits the dusty ground with a thud. Her head hits the slab of concrete on the floor and the steel reinforcing bars pierce through her skull.

Carolyn watches helplessly as the horrific scene unfolds in front of her. She stares in shock as her mother's blood trickles down the sharp steel spikes of the concrete and forms a growing puddle on the floor. She feels as if the whole world has stopped turning, for just a moment. She has completely forgotten about Simon and Ryan, the missing boys, the secret her mother has kept, and Mark Buckles – the only other witness to Jeanette's murder and Father Joseph's confession – still hiding behind the door. At this moment, all Carolyn can see and think of is the pool of her mother's blood.

"I... my God, Carolyn... I... I didn't mean that. It... it was an accident, you saw that, didn't you? I never meant for that—" Father Joseph manages before falling silent and staring at the door, as the creak of a floorboard sounds.

Carolyn doesn't notice. Her eyes are still glued to her dead mother.

"Who's there?" Father Joseph shouts with fear in his voice. Mark Buckles stays quiet for a moment and then steps out from behind the door, holding his hands up. Father Joseph's purple face drains of colour. He steps back almost fainting and searches the surrounding floor until he finds a plank of wood. He stoops to pick it up and begins swinging it out in front of him as Mark Buckles steps out further into the open.

"Father... take it easy, ok. Just take it easy," Mark says, but Father Joseph continues to swing the plank of wood from side to side with a psychotic look across his face. He lifts the plank up high and brings it down. Mark raises his arm and takes the blow, crying out in pain, then lunges at Father Joseph and tackles him to the ground. The plank of wood is thrown across the room and lands on the counter, sending the beer bottles crashing to the ground.

Carolyn can hear the scuffle taking place to the side of her. She hears the blows landing and the groans coming from both men. But she's unable to take her eyes away from her mother's corpse. Carolyn's body slumps back against the concrete, drained of its energy and its will to live. Her mother is dead because of her. If she had just forgotten about what she had seen in the well and accepted the assumption that it was her imagination (even if that wasn't the right thing, or even the most moral thing to do), Barry wouldn't have been attacked and Jeanette would still be alive.

Carolyn tells herself that she deserves to be left there, tied to a concrete slab to die from starvation as she watches her mother's body decompose.

Father Joseph shouts and groans as Mark Buckles gets the upper hand and is now on top of him. Father Joseph's hand is tapping the surrounding floor, searching for anything he can use as a weapon. He comes across the vodka and shifts his body to the side, carrying the weight of Mark on top of him. He grabs the bottle by the neck and swings it up to Mark's temple, but the bottle doesn't shatter. Mark falls off him holding a hand to his head. Father Joseph rolls over to his knees and brings the bottle down again, towards Mark's face. But Mark manages to move out of the way, and this time the bottle hits the floor, shattering, leaving Father Joseph clutching a shard of glass two inches long. Mark grabs hold of Father Joseph's wrist, clutching the shard. The two men wrestle for a moment before Mark headbutts Father Joseph. Blood runs from Father Joseph's nose. Mark, still with a tight grip on Father Joseph's wrist, brings the shard of glass up to the priest's throat, digging the glass in deep, before rolling away from him and staggering to his feet.

Father Joseph stays on his knees. He's making a horrific gagging noise. He holds a hand to the wound, but it's no use; the glass is in deep with no way of pulling it out. His blood is spurting out, like a pierced hose pipe. Carolyn looks from her mother's corpse to Father Joseph's terrified expression, his fingers fighting to grip the glass in his neck. Then he falls on his front, next to Jeanette, and the gurgling noises stop.

***

Ten minutes pass before Carolyn and Mark Buckles speak. He's spent that time catching his breath and feeling his head for any blood. Carolyn had wanted to ask him if he'll check for a pulse on her mother, but there was no point in clutching onto this hope. She knows the truth. Jeanette is dead. Carolyn cries silently, closing her eyes, and Mark leaves her alone for a few minutes until she's ready to say something.

"Are you ok?" he asks, calmly, although they both know

the answer. Of course she isn't ok. She's just witnessed two people, one of them her mother, die in front of her. She nods anyway without speaking. A sense of awkwardness about Mark Buckles sits in her stomach, and she isn't sure if it is because he's just killed a man, or whether it's something else, though he doesn't seem too upset about the fight with Father Joseph.

"Are you ok?" Carolyn asks with a croaky voice. She coughs to clear her throat.

It takes Mark a moment before he answers. He just stands there, watching Carolyn with a strange look in his eye. Why isn't he shaken up? Why isn't he in a state of sorrow or guilt or panic about what had just happened?

"So what was his plan with the vodka?" he asks, calmly, as if the last ten minutes hadn't just happened – as if he hadn't just killed a man, or witnessed the death of Jeanette.

Carolyn can't understand why he wants to know now, and why he's asking questions instead of cutting her free.

"Um... he wanted to get me drunk... then throw me from the top window, make it look as if I'd taken my own life." Carolyn replies, studying his expression. She's trying desperately to keep her eyes off her mother's dead body, but she can't. Her gaze keeps creeping over at Jeanette's lifeless eyes and the pool of her mother's blood around her own boots.

"Not a bad plan," Mark says.

"Not a bad plan... Wha—" She stops herself. *Something is wrong about this situation.*

Mark stands in front of her, a small smile beginning at the corners of his mouth.

"Yeah... listen, we need to call the police," Carolyn says, trying to keep her voice from sounding shaky.

"Yeah, I suppose we *should* call the police... But we're not going to do that," Mark snarls, still smirking.

"Why?" Carolyn asks. She already knows the answer.

"I should have just stayed quiet behind that door. Let him kill you for me. At first I actually thought he was going to. I even had my fingers crossed." He laughs.

"What?" she asks, not knowing what else to say.

"You heard me. I didn't want to kill him, a priest of all things. He seemed like a nice man. But, you see, you've cost me a lot of money, and it'll only be a matter of time before they link those payments back to me."

"Payments… what are you going on about?"

"B101 sound familiar?"

Carolyn watches as he paces back and forth across the room, as though thinking hard about his next move.

"What do you mean?" Carolyn asks, but again, she already knows the answer. Of course she does. "Patrick Sawhill?"

"That's right. The pervert used to buy a lot of content from me, and now he's dead, because of you," Mark Buckles says, his forehead gleaming with sweat. "Yeah, I know exactly what you've been doing. It was me, if you haven't figured that out by now. It was me who hired that private investigator to follow you around and report back."

"You… you're the supplier?" Carolyn says, fear warming her belly again.

"Yeah, I'm the one that sold him the stuff. It doesn't do it for me, but sick creeps like that will pay a hefty fee for one of those videos, and I'm a businessman." Mark laughs and wipes the dust from his trouser leg. "Did you honestly think a little candle shop in the middle of fucking nowhere bought that Mercedes, or my house?"

Carolyn goes to speak, but struggles to find the words.

"Supply and demand." Mark holds out his palms. "I have a friend who works in that type of business, and he would drop me a flash drive now and then. I wouldn't want to watch what was on it, but once I knew what I was dealing with, I'd sell the content on to that fat pervert."

Carolyn doesn't answer. She just stares at him with a face of disgust.

"You see, they're going to trace those payments back to me. I know what they can do these days with computers. I've seen forensic detectives on the Discovery Channel. You couldn't give it up about those boys, could you?"

"Those boys? One was your son!" Carolyn shouts.

A couple of pigeons coo above.

Mark smiles. "Yes, Dylan *is* my son. But that has nothing to do with you. You even brought a man of God to breaking point," Mark says, pointing to Father Joseph's corpse. "Just because you couldn't let it go. And now me. You've ruined everything for me!"

"What, like your sick child porn business?" Carolyn asks, a confident smirk on her lips. The last thirty minutes has sent her past the point of caring. She now understands: it wasn't fear she'd felt in her gut earlier. It was guilt and grief and anger.

"No, not just my business. You've ruined other things you wouldn't understand. You bitch!" Mark hisses and heads for her, he picks up a piece of concrete about the size of a rugby ball. Standing in front of her with the heavy concrete held above his head, he stares down at her.

Carolyn looks up.

"Do it then, you sick bastard. Do it!" she barks, holding his gaze.

Mark stands still, thinking. Finally he lowers the concrete and allows it to drop to the ground. It thuds on the floorboards.

"You want me to kill you, don't you?" he says, chuckling. "No... No, I have a better idea for you."

Chapter Forty

5th November, 19:30

"I'm not filing a missing person for two grown adults, Mr Cookson," Inspector Williams tells Barry abruptly, chewing as he speaks. Williams is clearly finding it difficult to hide his irritation. Barry can tell he's annoyed and doesn't want to speak about Carolyn, but he doesn't care. Something bad has happened; he can feel it.

"I'm not asking you to file a missing persons, Inspector. But have a look... please. Carolyn went missing this morning and now I... I can't get through to Jeanette. Something seems wrong."

"I said—"

"You know about the fire last night, at Jeanette's bungalow?" Barry interrupts.

"Yeah, of course I know about it," Williams snaps. "What does that have to do with anything?"

"Maybe it isn't connected, but what if it was started deliberately, and now they're both missing? Come on, Richard!"

"We still don't know how the fire was started," Williams says. "All right, listen. I'll go the church on my way home and see what's going on."

Barry thanks him, though the tone in Williams' voice implies he would have said anything in order to get him off the phone and back to his supper.

It's 7:30 pm, and Barry has been trying Jeanette's phone for the last three hours. He's ringing her to check if Carolyn has been in touch.

Maybe they're talking, Barry tells himself, and waits. After a little while, and no reply, he tries again and again.

Now he's worried.

First the attack, then the fire, and now neither of them are answering my calls or texts.

He Googles the number for the church and gets Father Joseph's answering machine. He decides not to leave a message, and hangs up before the beep.

An anxious feeling rushes over him and he knows he has to do something other than sit here feeling sorry for himself. Against the doctor's orders, he stands, groaning with pain as he heads over to the window, and moves the blinds aside. The rain is coming down fast and heavy, and he can hear it bouncing off the tin roof of the café. But Barry isn't checking the weather, he's checking for any strange cars he doesn't recognise that could be watching his flat. Nothing, of course.

The main road outside is dead. The *Sleepy Nights* mattress factory across the way closed half an hour ago, and the workers are long gone. He really doesn't fancy going out in this weather, but when he has gut feelings, they're usually right.

Last night, after Carolyn had left him and headed home, he couldn't settle. It wasn't because he had to stick to sleeping and resting on one side for most of the night. No, it was the flashbacks leading up to what had happened right before the actual attack. He was having vivid thoughts and thinking whoever had attacked him would come back to finish the job. At one point he convinced himself that his ex-wife, Lisa, might have sent the attacker. Lisa might be a drug addict, but surely, she isn't a psychopath.

Barry had even opened his phone a couple of times during the night to message Carolyn, but decided not to. He wouldn't want her to worry about him any more than she was doing already. Now he wishes he had messaged her, to act as a shoulder to cry on and even offer his own home to her and Jeanette.

"Come on, Carolyn," Barry says into the phone as he tries calling her again. It rings before taking him to voicemail. "Shit."

He heads over to the sofa. The pain comes shooting up his side and all he wants to do is to fall onto the puffy cushions and not move. Instead, he slips his feet into a battered pair of trainers – they're easier to put on than tying the laces on his boots – and pulls on his coat.

Outside, he holds on to the metal railing and takes each step one at a time, searching all around for anyone who might be hiding in the shadows, waiting for him. There is nobody.

The rain soaks him in seconds. It takes Barry seven minutes of grunting and catching his breath before he reaches the bottom step. He climbs into the cold van, starts the ignition, and heads for the church in search of his friend.

***

Carolyn didn't feel any movement after Mark Buckles stood behind her and held her in a headlock, cutting off her air supply. With no way of fighting him off, it was rather easy for him, and she passed out quickly.

Now awake with a harrowing migraine and a sickly feeling in her gut, she can feel the hard ground underneath her. But this place is different. This place isn't the nearly-demolished B&B. The smell from the pig farm is no longer in the air. It's also colder – much colder – and the ground is wet and harder than before. Carolyn can feel the breeze nipping at her cheeks, bringing her to shiver and hug herself.

Yes, her arms are now free, her legs too. She can hear the wind howl and the rain pelt against a roof. She opens her eyes, but it's too dark to see anything other than a small gap. The gap is a little wider than a front door letterbox. She gets to her feet and wobbles, almost losing her balance. No food has passed her lips since the soup she had last night. The soup made by that murdering bastard Father Joseph.

As she gets close enough to feel around, it becomes clear she's touching a steel door. She puts her face to it, and looks through the small letterbox. The night sky is black. Trees and bushes blow side to side in the strong wind. There's no artificial light outside, only the glow from the moon. There's no form of life, and she begins to imagine that she's miles away from civilisation.

How long was I out? she asks herself. The internal voice doesn't reply.

So this was Mark Buckles' plan, to leave her here alone in this steel prison cell.

Carolyn tries the door, bashing her shoulder into it and kicking furiously. It doesn't budge. She shouts out through the letterbox, but her words are swept away by the howling wind. She pushes and bashes against the metal door with all her energy, but the door is securely locked and her efforts only cause her pain.

Behind her, she hears the sound of metal chains scraping along the steel floor.

"AHHHH," she screams and backs herself against the cold door. She has no idea how big the cell is, or what the hell she is locked in here with. A dog on a leash that has been set in place to eat her when it's starving to death? A sick and evil plan, but it wouldn't surprise her. She remembers the hatred in Mark Buckles' eyes.

"WHO'S THERE?" Carolyn demands. The taste of vodka is still strong on her tongue. She holds out her arms into the blackness, in a bid to fight off anyone or anything that comes towards her.

"It's ok," a soft voice says from the back, it sounds as if the person is cowering in the corner.

"Who are you?" she asks, her voice echoing around the metal hut and sounding loud in her ears.

The wind outside is thunderous, and it's doing a great job of overpowering the low voice, but Carolyn hears it clearly enough.

"My name is Dylan Lloyd."

Chapter Forty-One

5th November, 19:40

DS Hughes walks into Williams' office with a pleased smile on her broad face and holding a piece of paper. Williams stands and is ready to finish for the day. He plans to check out the firework display at Harrow Park, then head home with a case of beer.

The office smells of vinegar from Williams' recently-finished fish & chip dinner.

"Sir, the results from Sawhill's computer," DS Hughes says.

"Ah, okay," Williams replies, sitting back down and gesturing for her to take a seat. He rests his hands across his bloated stomach.

"The computer forensics went back years. We have the names of most the people who are signed up to Patrick Sawhill's two sites. We're trying to track them using their banking information. But there's one here you need to see."

"Go on," Williams urges, unfolding his hands and resting his elbows on his desk.

"The supplier, he's logged on a couple of times and I've cross referenced it to the same IP address as the emails that were sent to Thomas Zaman, the private investigator that was hired to follow Carolyn Hill. It's registered to the candle shop owner in town. Mark Buckles' shop, sir."

"Really?" Williams says, more to himself than to DS Hughes. She nods anyway.

Williams stands back up and grabs his coat. He leaves the office in a hurry, pushing past Riley on Reception.

"Dixon, get your coat," Williams orders. "Get the nearest

patrol car over to Mark Buckles' home immediately."

In the car, Williams' phone rings. It's Riley at the station. He tells him he has a Barry Cookson on the line asking to speak with him, and that he says it's important. Williams agrees for him to connect the call.

"Barry, I can't speak right now. So unless you've heard from Mrs Hill, I don't want to know!" Williams barks.

"I'm at the church across from the ruins of Jeanette's home. Father Joseph's car is gone, but Jeanette's red Polo is still here. The place is in darkness, and nobody is home. I think something's happened," Barry says over the sound of rain bouncing off the roof of his van.

"I'll give you a call back soon," Williams promises and hangs up.

PC Martin's and PC Young's patrol car is already at Mark Buckles' property as Williams' car pulls into the driveway, followed by Hughes and Dixon. The two uniformed officers head over to Williams' car.

"We've knocked and surveyed the property, sir," PC Young says. "It looks like Mark Buckles isn't home. His car is missing."

Williams curses and tells the officers to stay put and arrest Buckles immediately if he returns home. Williams, Hughes and Dixon head back into town, in case Mark is still at the candle shop.

The shop shutters are down, so they head around the back, but the back door is locked. Williams peers through the barred windows and can see into the office where the desk lamp has been left on. The desk drawers have been pulled out and the contents are spilling across the floor. Bella the cat is sleeping peacefully in the corner on a comfortable-looking armchair. The safe is empty with the door left open. A trail of muddy shoeprints, thick with chunks of earth, can be seen on the floor in various spots around the office.

"That's strange," Williams says.

"What's that, sir?" Hughes asks.

"I know Mark Buckles as a man who prides himself on

looking smart. He's always in a nice suit. There are mud trails right through, not to mention it looks like he's left in a hurry."

DS Hughes steps closer and takes a look. "What are you thinking, sir?"

"Get another patrol car over here," Williams says, and takes out his mobile. He gets the number from Riley and calls Barry Cookson back.

Barry answers on the first ring.

"Barry?"

"Yeah, go on, Rich."

"Do you know a Mark Buckles? He owns the candle shop in town. He speaks with a London accent."

"I know of him, yeah. Carolyn spoke to him once. Apparently he's Dylan Lloyd's real father. Why?"

"We think Mark Buckles might be connected in some way. I'm telling you because we can't find him. If you see him—"

"I remember the night I was attacked from behind," Barry interrupts. "When we were at the Myers Steel place. When I was on the ground, I heard a voice whisper into my ear."

Williams looks at Hughes and Dixon, both holding up the hoods of their coats.

"Well? What did the voice say, Barry?" Williams asks.

"He told me to tell Carolyn to stop digging. I thought he had a Birmingham accent, but it could have been London."

"Are you sure, Barry?"

"Yes, yes I am. It came to me the other day, I thought maybe it was a dream, that I was in shock... I don't know... I was trying to piece something together, I guess. I'm sorry I didn't mention it before. I just wanted to be certain."

"It's okay, Barry. As long as you're certain now."

"I am. So you think this Mark Buckles has Carolyn?" Barry asks.

"We don't know. It's too early to assume Carolyn is even missing. But Buckles' office has been emptied out and there are mud stains throughout. So just keep your eyes peeled," Williams says and hangs up.

Barry has an idea. He puts his foot down to get to Llanbedr Convenience before it closes, praying the girl he needs to speak to is still on shift.

Chapter Forty-Two

5th November 20:00

"Are you alone, Dylan?" Carolyn asks.

"Yes, I'm alone," he replies, his voice is soft. "I've been alone for years."

"My name is Carolyn Hill. I guess you could say I've been looking for you."

"You have?" Dylan's voice becomes excited. "People haven't forgotten about me?"

"No, no of course not, love," Carolyn replies, walking closer to Dylan. She bumps into him and takes a seat next to him, on the cold ground. She can feel his bare arms next to hers, his muscles shivering as the wind blows in from the small opening in the door, circling around the steel hut and pinching at their flesh.

She pulls her knees into her chest and wraps her arms around them. Her hand falls to the toe of her boots and her fingers touch something sticky. She quickly moves her hand away, realising it's her mother's blood. She desperately wants to cry, to break out in hysterical tears, and to scream at the top of her lungs in anger, frustration and sorrow. But Dylan is next to her, no older than seventeen, so she tries to keep in mind that if it was her son in this situation, held captive by a lunatic, she'd expect the adult to be calm and reassuring. She takes in a large breath, counts to three and wipes her tears before exhaling slowly. She'll mourn later when this is over.

If there is a later, the internal voice sneers, but she ignores it.

"Do you know how long you've been missing?" she asks the boy next to her.

"I think it's about two years. He's told me it's my birthday twice. I'm not always here, in this old bunker place. I'm usually at his house... I think it's his house, anyway. It's a house and I'm locked in a bedroom. He brought me to this bunker when he first took me. I didn't know who he was at first."

"Did he tell you why he's taken you?" Carolyn asks.

"He told me he's got to keep me here until the police stop searching for me." He coughs. Carolyn can hear that it sounds dry and painful. "Then he came back a couple of days later with food and water and I saw his face."

"Do you know him?" Carolyn asks.

"I recognised him from around town, yeah. He keeps saying we'll be a family again. Him, me and Mum. I think he's crazy."

Carolyn wonders what Dylan looks like now. His arms and legs feel skeletal next to hers.

"I think he's crazy too. How did he take you?" Carolyn asks.

"I was out on my bike. I was arguing with my brother, Owen. I just wanted to get away," Dylan says. He coughs again. "I didn't hear him behind me. His car hit my back tyre and I came off my bike. He pulled something over my head and tied my hands behind my back."

"I'm sorry. Try to stay calm, ok?" Carolyn says, resting a hand on the boy's skinny knee.

"Do my family miss me?" Dylan asks. Carolyn can hear the pain in his voice.

"Of course, they miss you. They miss you very much. Your brother, Owen, he really misses you."

"You've spoken to Owen?" Dylan asks, more excitement in his voice.

"Yes, not so long ago." She won't tell him the circumstances of their latest encounter.

"I miss them. I miss them so much, and my friends. He tells me that he's waiting for the right time."

"What do you mean, the right time?" Carolyn asks, intrigued.

247

"I don't know. He keeps promising me that Mum will eventually see that Dad, my real Dad at home, is scum... a loser, and when she eventually realises it, he'll have enough money saved to take us somewhere far away. But I don't want to go."

"Go where?"

"I don't know. I told him once that I don't want to go away from here with him, and that I think he's crazy. He beat me really bad."

"I'm sorry."

"He didn't feed me for days. I thought I was going to die."

Carolyn can hear the fear as he speaks. She wonders if she's the first person that this poor boy has been in contact with in the last two years, other than that crazy bastard Mark Buckles.

"Has Dad still got that grey moustache? He was trying to grow it before... before I was taken," Dylan says.

Carolyn thinks of the last time she saw Frank Lloyd, probably when he came to rescue her mother's car from the ditch after the mess Owen had made, almost killing her.

"Yes... Yes, he has," Carolyn replies. She can now sense he's smiling, or at least trying to. "Try to stay calm, okay? I'm sure we'll be out of here soon..." She tails off, thinking that somebody out there will be looking for her, or at least for Jeanette and Father Joseph. They'll see Father Joseph's Volvo at the B&B and investigate, finding their bodies.

Her trail of thought is interrupted; a beam of light from a torch bounces off the east side wall. Carolyn feels Dylan stiffen and his cold bony fingers grab onto her wrist, digging in.

"It'll be okay, Dylan," Carolyn says, standing and heading over to the door. Outside, the silhouette of a man is approaching, keeping a hand up to the hood of his coat to shield his face from the heavy rain. She knows there is no point in screaming for help. There wouldn't be anybody else around, not in this weather. No sane person, anyway.

Of course it's him, Mark Buckles, the deluded kidnapping murderer. Carolyn backs away from the door, trying to steady her breathing, waiting for a key to be inserted and the door to swing open. Then she can take her shot, scratch at his eyes, and kick him in the balls with everything she's got. Her boots are heavy, and he'd made a mistake not taking them away from her. The image of Mark Buckles approaching, the events of the last twenty-four hours, and the thought of her beloved mother's corpse lying on the floor of that old B&B, causes the anger to build up inside her. Carolyn's ready to use all that anger to get her and Dylan out of here. After attacking Buckles, she'll then fight him for the key to the chains that are keeping Dylan locked up like an animal.

Not that Carolyn's a fighter. The only fight she had been in was with Carly Anderson during the first year of uni. Carly had made a mum joke about Jeanette being overweight, something silly like that. Carolyn knew there was malice behind it; girls don't do banter like boys do. Boys joke and give it back, and then all is forgotten. Carolyn had lost the fight and come away with a swollen lip, but at least she'd stood her ground and defended her mother's honour. And that's what will happen now. Only this is different; lives are at stake. Mark Buckles just has to open the door.

His face appears at the hole, but no key is inserted.

Carolyn runs for it and sticks her hand out to grab at his hair, to hurt him, maybe take out an eye if she can reach. Mark moves away too quickly and then manoeuvres back in and takes hold of Carolyn's arm at the elbow, twisting it backwards. She cries out in pain.

"Get off her... Leave her alone," Dylan pleads from the corner, his voice filled with fear.

"Now you know what I meant when I said you've ruined everything for me," Mark says. "You just couldn't leave it, could you? You had to keep digging, playing detective. Now your mother is dead and so is Father Joseph... killer or not. They're both dead and it's because of you!" Mark's breath is warm in her ear as he holds her against the freezing steel door, and the stale scent of whisky reaches her nostrils.

"Please... please let go... please," Carolyn begs. He pushes her arm through and away. She falls back against the

249

wall and cradles herself alongside Dylan. Mark shines the torch through the gap, studying Dylan's face and then Carolyn's. The bright light burns their eyes. He then puts the torch under his chin, as if preparing to tell a ghost story to a group of children around a campfire.

"How do you like this little bunker?" Mark asks. Carolyn doesn't answer. "You know, Gwen and I used to come up here, now and then, anyway. We couldn't risk going to my place in case Frank had caught on. We used to meet at the car park down below and we'd wander up here. We'd even hold hands… on occasion… like we were free. A free happy couple without a care in the world."

"I don't care, Mark. Now let us go!" Carolyn shouts.

"I had a plan for us, for me, for him," Mark says, shining the torch at Dylan's face again. "And for his mother. It wasn't just a one-night stand we had. Our affair went on for years, even after Dylan was born. Gwen loved me. Then one day she came to me and told me it was over... just like that." Mark Buckles expression turns to sadness. "But I know it was him; that bastard Frank talking about me and telling Gwen lies and forcing her to hate me." His eyes are fixated on something in front of him, and he appears unconcerned by the rain beating against his face. Now Carolyn can see him clearly. He looks as if he's had more than just a glass or two of Scotch.

"Mark, let us go. This has gone on for long enough," Carolyn says.

But he doesn't seem to hear, or chooses not to listen.

"She loved being with me, you know. I loved being with her. We completed each other. That's what she'd tell me," Mark chuckles, smiling. The smile has no evil in it; it's a smile fuelled by happy memories. "And she used to tell me how unhappy she was with him. That man pretending to be my son's real father." Mark stares at Dylan. Carolyn holds a hand over Dylan's. "Bringing up my kid because she was too afraid to come out and tell him the truth. I guess I can't blame her, though; he's a drunk, and he'd get abusive and argue with her over the littlest of things."

250

"That's no reason to kidnap Dylan. This isn't right, what you're doing." Carolyn tries again, but Mark carries on as though he hasn't heard her.

"Even after I stabbed your friend, you still couldn't leave it. I brought Dylan's coat with me. He's grown out of it anyway, and I thought it'd be fun to see your face as you read the name tag. That was a mistake, I admit. I did tell you to come alone, but you didn't. You brought somebody else into this mess you've caused," Mark snarls, wiping the rain from his eyes. "I don't know how you did it. But you got the police interested in Patrick and Julio. Well done you."

"Please, just let us go!" Dylan says. At this, Mark snaps out of his delusional daydream. He looks from Dylan to Carolyn, then back to Dylan, his cheeks twitching as he frowns.

"No. She isn't here to keep you company, my son. Oh no, no, no. It isn't to keep you warm at night. She isn't a bunk-buddy for you to share your secrets with. This is the bitch's punishment for poking her nose in other people's business!" Mark looks towards Carolyn, and although she can't see his face properly after he lowers the torch, she can see the creases at the side of his eyes, indicating that he's smiling.

This smile is different from before. This smile is evil. "She's here so that when you're dying of hypothermia, or starving to death chained to that wall, when you're at your last breath, you can ask her why. You can blame her for doing this to you!"

Carolyn squeezes Dylan's trembling hand, and they both stare at Mark Buckles as he bursts into laughter.

251

Chapter Forty-Three

5th November 20:30

Barry races to Llanbedr Convenience as Sophie, the cashier, is heading out of the side door towards her car and taking long drags of a cigarette. Sophie almost screams and swallows the cigarette whole as Barry steps out in front of her.

He welcomes her with his kindest smile; he's got it perfected. A man of his size needs to know when to put on a warm and trusting smile in certain situations. This was definitely one of them.

Sophie laughs. She tells Barry that she hears all of these stories about people being taken, or attacked or raped as they walk to their car after work and how a friend of hers almost fell victim to a rapist. Barry has to interrupt her mid-sentence as she has a tendency to ramble on.

"I'm sorry, love. But listen, this is very important," he says, and the girl goes quiet. "You remember my friend Carolyn coming here? A brunette woman asking you about that time you went camping?" Sophie nods. "Where exactly was that place? Could you explain to me how I'd get there?"

"Do you know where Sandle Moor is?" Sophie asks.

"Yes."

"You head up towards the top, and by the car park there's a section of that path that isn't used. There should be a metal fence blocking off the access with a sign warning of the crumbling rocks. We'd camp up there."

Barry thinks about asking her to come with him, to show him the way. But he decides not to as it would sound way too creepy, and he doesn't need any more trouble going off a hunch. He thanks her, and with the map drawn in his mind, heads for the lookout point.

Barry's van races across town as amateur fireworks explode in the distance. The strong wind rocks his van side to side as Barry dodges rogue bin bags and other debris that has found its way on to the road. The drive over to Sandle Moor takes him fifteen minutes. Nobody wants to be out in this weather unless they have to be. He calls Williams back and explains why he thinks it might be worth checking out. Williams agrees to meet him at the entrance.

The entrance has a wooden barrier across the road saying **CLOSED, DANGER OF FLOODING**, which is usually put out in severe weather like this. Barry's tempted to drive through it and send splinters flying out from the front of his bonnet like in the action films, though he knows Williams would have something to say to that, plus he needs all the power from the old engine as he can get. The gravel ramp at the bottom of Sandle Moor is steep, and it'll be even trickier wet. Barry climbs from his van and lifts the barrier out of the way. His lower side sends a bolt of pain as he strains under the weight. Back in the van, he reverses twenty feet, slides the gear into first and builds up the revs before lifting up the clutch. He moves into second just before the van reaches the start of the slope. It bounces up upon impact. Tools, ladders and tubs of paint dance in the back. The engine screams as the speed drops.

"COME ON… COME ON, PLEASE!" he yells, rocking back and forth in his seat as if riding a racehorse. Slowly, the old van carries on up the slope, sending mud and stones flicking behind before finally reaching the top. He spins the van into the car park. Here, amid the many empty spaces, is the only other vehicle.

The black Mercedes is covered in loose tree branches from the wild wind. Mark Buckles must have had to walk back up the ramp after replacing the barrier.

Barry parks his van next to the Mercedes and checks both wing mirrors carefully before stepping out. He doesn't want a repeat of the attack.

He runs his hand over the bonnet of the Mercedes. The engine has cooled a little, but it's still warm.

He watches around him before opening the side door of his van and reaching for the crowbar from the back, before pushing his scattered tools to the side. The crowbar is for his protection and he hopes he won't need to use it.

He pulls his phone from his pocket to call Williams. Headlights appear up the steep ramp and he hears the roar of the engines. Placing his phone back inside his pocket, he walks over to them.

"I told you to meet us at the entrance!" Williams shouts, leaving his car. The whipping wind takes the volume from his voice.

"Black Mercedes over there," Barry says "Is it the candle shop owner's?"

Williams pulls up the hood of his police waterproof. DS Hughes and DC Dixon get out of their car and join them, turning on their torches.

"Yeah, it is. It's Mark Buckles' car," DS Hughes confirms.

"All right then. Barry, where did you say he could be heading?" Williams asks.

"I didn't say he was heading anywhere. But Sophie, the girl who works in Llanbedr Convenience, said she was out here one night and saw someone up here. She and her boyfriend were apparently camping and she said it was early, like really early in the morning. Sophie thought it was strange…" Barry begins looking around the dark trees, then asks DC Dixon for his torch and walks to the top of the ramp. He shines the torch around the woodland until he finds the footpath Sophie had described. Further up, he finds a break in the bushes. Then he sees the rusted, metal sign ordering people to stay out due to danger of falling rocks. Barry shines the torch towards the metal fencing, and Williams, Hughes and DC Dixon head over. The rusted gate is open, and the padlock has been left hanging on the side.

"Okay, stick together you hear me?" Williams says, catching his breath and wheezing loudly. "I don't want us getting lost out here and falling to our death… Oh and wait for us two, okay?"

"Sir," Hughes says with a nod. Dixon copies.

Williams steps aside, allowing Hughes and Dixon to take the lead.

Just past the metal gate are concrete steps, now overgrown with weeds. The dark sky and heavy rain makes it hard to see how many steps there are. This causes Barry and Inspector Williams to feel uneasy. Barry hesitates for a second, then thinks of Carolyn, and her braveness to find out the truth of the missing boys. With that he decides to grin and bear the pain in his lower back a little longer.

DS Hughes and DC Dixon are staying ahead by two steps and shining their torches to lead the way. Barry shares Inspector Williams' torch as they follow behind, panting as they hold onto the handrail.

Chapter Forty-Four

5th November, 20:40

"You would have enjoyed your life with us, you know, Dylan," Mark says. "Away from that fraudster, the loser you call a father."

Dylan protests, but Mark ignores him and goes on. "Away from that weird brother of yours, and away from this shithole of a town."

Mark's hair is now drenched after the wind blew down his hood and he gave up trying to fix it. His face shines in the moonlight as the rain trickles down his forehead. He pulls a miniature of Scotch from his coat pocket and swallows it in two gulps.

Carolyn watches him. "It was you who burned down my mother's home, wasn't it?"

Mark nods.

"She didn't do anything to you, it was all me. Why burn down her bungalow?"

Mark pulls out another miniature and unscrews the top before answering. "To hurt you, to destroy your home like you've destroyed mine," he says, pouring the whisky into his mouth. "Now I have to leave my home behind. Yes, this town is a shithole, but Gwen, my Gwen, is still here, and now I have to leave, because of you. So, it seemed fair," he says, with a smirk that Carolyn wishes she could punch until he's no longer breathing.

"Gwen… She doesn't want you, Mark. This is silly. At least let Dylan go. He's done nothing in all of this," Carolyn pleads. Her plan is for him to release Dylan, unlock him from his chains and send him home to his mother. *But he's never going to let Dylan go, not after all this time,* she thinks.

Mark chuckles at her comment.

New plan: if Mark opens the door, she'll fight like she has never fought before, dig her fingers into his eye sockets, even bite at his throat if that's what it comes down to.

"Shur… shurrup… stupid bitch," Mark mumbles. "You don't… get to ask ques—" He stops, turns and looks behind him. Carolyn can see he's straining his ears. She stands and walks slowly over to the gap in the door. Mark's attentively watching the woods behind him. Then a flicker of light shines between the trees.

Carolyn almost faints with hope. *They've found us.*

"HELLO… HEY, OVER HERE!" she screams. "WE'RE OVER HERE!"

"SSHH!" Mark orders her with a look of panic on his face.

"WE'RE OVER HERE…" Carolyn turns to Dylan. "Get up and shout as loud as you can."

Dylan stands, and the chains scrape along the floor as he comes as close to the steel door as they'll allow. Both of them begin to shout together, though it feels as if their words are lifted out of the bunker and taken by the wind. Mark Buckles scans the area, waiting for whoever it is holding the torch to hopefully stay on the path and keep walking. The lights approach closer and closer, and he's clearly not prepared to risk sticking around any longer. He turns to Carolyn and gives her one last look that says *If I come back and you're still here, I'm going to kill you!*

He runs off into the trees, in the opposite direction to the torches and up towards the cliff top of Sandle Moor.

Carolyn and Dylan continue to shout at the top of their lungs. Their voices echo round the inside of the bunker, hurting their ears. But they don't care; their freedom is more important. Carolyn kicks and punches at the steel door. The cold has turned her hands fragile. She carries on anyway.

***

"Wait, can you hear that?" DC Dixon asks, and they all stand silently still, apart from Williams, who is sweating and panting uncontrollably as he struggles to breathe.

"That way!" Barry shouts, and they follow him as he pushes, limping, past the two detectives. His battered trainers are soaked and his feet inside are drenched.

The bunker comes into view further up and DS Hughes and DC Dixon rush past Barry, reaching the bunker first.

"Mrs Hill?" Hughes shouts. Carolyn couldn't be happier to see DS Hughes' broad, masculine face. She almost forgets to tell them what way Mark Buckles is heading.

"That way... over there," she shouts and points into the trees. Hughes and Dixon give chase as Richard Williams and Barry arrive at the bunker.

"CAROLYN!" Barry shouts, tears streaming down his huge face.

"BARRY! H-How... How did you know I was here?" Carolyn asks, clutching Barry's wide hand through the gap in the door.

"It was just a hunch. I spoke to Sophie, the shop girl. I remembered you saying that she was here, camping. She gave me directions," Barry replies, fighting back tears. "I'm so happy you're ok. I thought something might have happened to you, something terrible."

"Mrs Hill, are you ok?" Williams asks, his face looking as though it could explode any second.

"I'm okay, Inspector. Thank you," Carolyn replies.

"Your mother, Father Joseph, where are they?" Williams asks.

Carolyn gives him a look and shakes her head. "My mother is dead. Father Joseph... He... he killed her."

Williams looks at her, puzzled, as though he's misheard her. He opens his mouth to ask more, but Carolyn speaks first.

"I'm okay, Inspector. Can I have your coat?" she asks, standing aside. Williams shines his torch through at Dylan's face.

"I don't believe it," Williams says, taking off his coat and handing it through the gap. Carolyn passes it behind for Dylan to slide on. It's at least four sizes too big, but it's warm and eases his shivering.

***

Dixon and Hughes come out of the trees and find themselves at the cliff top. Mark Buckles is hunched over, close to the cliff edge, catching his breath. They shine their torches at his face, and he steps back further.

"Mr Buckles, you are under arrest. Stay calm and slowly back away from the edge," DS Hughes says. The height of the cliff top is finally registering to her as nausea sets in. She's never been good with heights.

"Mr Buckles... come to us," Dixon says, but Mark Buckles shakes his head and steps back even further, closer to the edge. The rain has died off, but the wind is still furious, blowing his coat out behind him like a superhero's cape.

"Why... why the fuck should I?" Mark says, waving his arms out in front.

"Mark... listen to us. We can talk when you're away from the edge. Just come closer."

Mark shakes his head. "We're not going to talk about anything," he shouts. "That bitch doesn't want me. She's chosen HIM!"

Dixon looks to Hughes and shrugs. They walk slowly towards him.

Mark Buckles takes another step back. Soil starts to crumble away.

"Okay... Okay," DS Hughes says, holding her hands out in front and pointing the torch up to the night sky.

"Mr Buckles, don't step back any further. You're getting pretty close to the edge," DC Dixon says.

Buckles waves a hand in the air. "S-she told me she wanted me. She told me she wanted for us to be a family," he slurs. He looks back as fireworks burst in the sky, then turns back towards the detectives. "I would have been a great dad, you know."

DS Hughes has gone as close to the edge as she can manage. She already feels sickeningly dizzy. Dixon goes to speak and takes another step closer. If he can keep Mark talking and get close enough to grab his coat, he should be able to pull him back and force him to the ground.

But it's no good.

Mark Buckles stands at the very edge of the cliff top and more soil breaks off under his shoes. He gives the two detectives a smile, then takes his last step backwards.

He falls two hundred feet to his death as a firework display at Harrow Park sounds in the distance. The sky lights up purple, orange, red, yellow and blue, accompanied by a low cheer from the spectators on the ground.

DS Hughes stays where she is standing, and Dixon lies on his front creeping closer to the edge. More soil breaks off and crumbles away. He sticks his head over the edge and DS Hughes holds onto his ankles. With the help of the moonlight and the firework display lighting up the sky, DC Dixon can see the mangled remains of Mark Buckles' body lying on the jagged rocks below.

Epilogue

Four months later

The morning sun is shining through the small window of the bakery's kitchen, and Carolyn is fixing a fondant balloon to the side of a retirement cake.

The shop had lost a lot of customers due to being closed for months. Carolyn had posted the reason on her social media pages and, with the story of the two missing boys hitting the papers, customers are slowly returning.

In her statement about what had happened that day in the B&B, Carolyn had said nothing about her mother's involvement in the death of Elwyn Roberts. She'd decided that Barry and the people of Llanbedr didn't need to know about that. She doesn't want them to remember her mother as a liar or an accomplice to a murder. Instead, they should think of her as the caring, loving woman she'd always been.

She believes her mother had lied, and kept Father Joseph's crime a secret, in order to protect him. She thinks that he had told Jeanette that the Lord had insisted they must keep the truth to themselves. This would allow Father Joseph to remain free and to continue with his work. Carolyn believes Jeanette thought she was doing the right thing.

At least, that's what she keeps telling herself. One day she might even come to believe it.

Barry is sitting patiently on a stool in the corner. He's reading a magazine while waiting for the cake to be finished so he can make the last delivery run of the day. His daughter, Amy, is sitting outside on reception, manning the phone orders and playing with Bella the cat. Carolyn adopted Bella after Mark Buckles' death.

Amy is happy with her new part-time job as receptionist, and with her new feline friend. Most importantly, she's happy to have her father back in her life.

Barry had decided two months ago to move to Leeds and leave Llanbedr behind, after getting his affairs in order. There wasn't anything keeping him there. The idea to leave Llanbedr had been on his mind for some time, even before he ever met Carolyn and got involved with helping her dig up the truth. He scrapped his beloved van and sold off most of his work tools. He now has a two-bedroomed flat not far from the bakery, and Carolyn is happy to have him as a delivery driver. The last one had quit, not knowing if the bakery was ever going to reopen.

Barry has recovered well from the attack, though he occasionally feels a little pang of pain in his lower back.

Julio Alcala had confessed to everything, and had sworn he had no idea who had been supplying Patrick Sawhill with the material. The forensics had found he was telling the truth; that Mark Buckles never physically showed himself, and all the transactions were done online using an alias. Julio Alcala was sentenced to four years in prison for breaking the terms of his parole and for his role in helping Patrick Sawhill run child pornography sites. Other members of the sites were tracked down using their payment methods and have also been charged.

Kelvin and Heather Roberts had read Carolyn's statement of what Father Joseph had confessed to her: how he had drunkenly hit Elwyn with his car, had kept his body in the freezer for eight years, and recently buried him next to a large rock behind The Sunlight B&B. They too decided to move from Llanbedr and settle down somewhere else, after retrieving their son's body and giving him a proper burial. They had thanked Carolyn for her persistent searching and finally uncovering the truth.

Gwen Lloyd admitted that Mark Buckles had sent her numerous love letters over the years. She'd also admitted that their affair wasn't just a one-night fling; it had had lasted for years after Dylan was born. She'd confirmed that Mark

Buckles would talk about them running away together to start a new life, and that he'd promised she'd understand why it was a good idea when they were far away from Llanbedr. But Gwen never knew he was holding their son captive, nor that was he capable of such an evil act.

Gwen and Frank are working through things, for Dylan's sake. Owen had cried and run over to hug his missing brother when he eventually returned home. The Lloyds are overwhelmed to have Dylan back. Dylan is doing well after undergoing numerous medical examinations. He is currently seeing a psychiatrist, though he seems to be recovering well from the trauma.

The thought of Dylan keeping faith and staying hopeful during the time he was held captive by Mark Buckles has forced Carolyn to see her own problems in a new light. Of course, she's still mourning, but the courage she saw in Dylan has encouraged her to stay strong.

Carolyn gives the cake a final spin. It's perfect.

"All done, Barry. Now get up and do some work," Carolyn says, stepping away from the cake to wash up.

"About time," Barry says, standing to box up the cake. "Amy, come on. The cake is *finally* finished." Barry smirks, and Carolyn replies with a roll of her eyes.

She heads to the back door and holds it open as Barry carries out the cake. Amy follows him to the van and waves goodbye to Carolyn before climbing in the front. Barry places the cake in the back.

"So, twelve o'clock at Ashwood Forest?" Barry says.

Carolyn nods. "Yes, twelve o'clock. Remember to use the entrance on Barn Hey Road. It's always quiet."

Yesterday Barry had asked if Carolyn knew any nice walking spots he and Amy could take a stroll. He's realised shedding a few pounds would do him good. Carolyn had immediately told him about Ashwood Forest, explaining how she, Simon and Ryan used to love it there. Barry suggested they take a picnic, and Carolyn enthusiastically agreed.

As Barry's new van pulls out of the car park, Carolyn

heads for the changing room. She undresses from her buttercream-stained baker's uniform, and slips on something more casual. Before leaving, she kisses the picture of Simon and Ryan that sits on the shelf next to the door, along with the papier-mâché spaceship that Ryan had made last year in school. Bella purrs as Carolyn coaxes her into the cat-carrier to drop off at home.

After the deaths of Simon and Ryan, stumbling upon the corpse of Elwyn Roberts down the well, and witnessing the deaths of her mother and Father Joseph, not to mention being trapped in a steel bunker with Dylan Lloyd, Carolyn no longer welcomes death. She's witnessed enough loss, heartache and misery to last her a lifetime.

Carolyn wants to continue making customers happy with her dazzling cakes, and to love and care for Bella the cat. She wants to be the friend Barry needs in his life, and she wants to continue to think she is making Simon and Ryan proud.

Author's Note

Thank you for reading my debut, I hope you enjoyed it. I like writing thrillers and the idea of creating fictional characters who are, sometimes, crazy, cruel or psychotic is very enjoyable to me.

The idea of the story started with a whole lot of different characters, settings and plot before I decided to change it into something else, and slowly the story took on a life of its own and became The Boy in the Well.

I have always appreciated the quote: "Write the Story You Want to Read" and it's exactly what I did with my own story. I like to dabble a lot with "what if" and see where it takes me.

I love hearing from readers so if you would like to leave me a review, ask a question or stay updated on any future book releases, you can find me at:

Facebook: www.facebook.com/DanClarkbooks
Twitter: www.twitter.com/DanielRClark3

Fantastic Books
Great Authors

darkstroke is
an imprint of
Crooked Cat Books

- Gripping Thrillers
- Cosy Mysteries
- Romantic Chick-Lit
- Fascinating Historicals
- Exciting Fantasy
- Young Adult
- Non-Fiction

Discover us online
www.darkstroke.com

Find us on instagram:
www.instagram.com/darkstrokebooks

Printed in Great Britain
by Amazon

58028269R00154